"You and I mix like oil and water. If I hired you as my bodyguard, we'd drive each other crazy."

Dane made a leisurely inspection of Annie from head to toe, then focused his gaze on her face. "The reason we'd drive each other crazy is because we're attracted to each other. You're afraid of me, of the way I make you feel. And to be honest, I'm a little bit afraid of you, too."

Annie stared at him, her eyes wide, her mouth slightly agape. Warmth spread through her body like daybreak across the sky. "All right, so I'm afraid of this attraction thing going on between us," she admitted. "And being the smart woman that I am, I know better than to keep temptation within arm's reach twenty-four hours a day."

Dane leaned toward her. "Just how much of a temptation am I, Brown Eyes?"

Dear Reader,

It's summertime. The mercury's rising, and so is the excitement level here at Silhouette Intimate Moments. Whatever you're looking for—a family story, suspense and intrigue, or love with a ranchin' man—we've got it for you in our lineup this month.

Beverly Barton starts things off with another installment in her fabulous miniseries THE PROTECTORS. *Keeping Annie Safe* will *not* cool you off, I'm afraid! Merline Lovelace is back with *A Man of His Word,* part of her MEN OF THE BAR H miniseries, while award winner Ingrid Weaver checks in with *What the Baby Knew.* If it's edge-of-your-seat suspense you're looking for, pick up the latest from Sally Tyler Hayes, *Spies, Lies and Lovers.* *The Rancher's Surrender* is the latest from fresh new talent Jill Shalvis, while Shelley Cooper makes her second appearance with *Guardian Groom.*

You won't want to miss a single one of these fabulous novels, or any of the books we'll be bringing you in months to come. For guaranteed great reading, come to Silhouette Intimate Moments, where passion and excitement go hand in hand.

Enjoy!

Yours,

Leslie J. Wainger

Leslie J. Wainger
Executive Senior Editor

Please address questions and book requests to:
Silhouette Reader Service
U.S.: 3010 Walden Ave., P.O. Box 1325, Buffalo, NY 14269
Canadian: P.O. Box 609, Fort Erie, Ont. L2A 5X3

BEVERLY BARTON

KEEPING ANNIE SAFE

Published by Silhouette Books

America's Publisher of Contemporary Romance

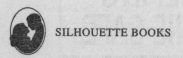

SILHOUETTE BOOKS

ISBN 0-373-07937-0

KEEPING ANNIE SAFE

Visit us at www.romance.net

Printed in U.S.A.

BEVERLY BARTON

has been in love with romance since her grandfather gave her an illustrated book of *Beauty and the Beast*. An avid reader since childhood, she began writing at the age of nine and wrote short stories, poetry, plays and novels through high school and college. After marriage to her own "hero" and the births of her daughter and son, she chose to be a full-time homemaker, aka wife, mother, friend and volunteer.

When she returned to writing, she joined Romance Writers of America and helped found the Heart of Dixie chapter in Alabama. Since the release of her first Silhouette book in 1990, she has won the GRW Maggie Award and the National Readers' Choice Award and has been a RITA Award finalist. Beverly considers writing romance books a real labor of love. Her stories come straight from the heart, and she hopes that all the strong and varied emotions she invests in her books will be felt by everyone who reads them.

In loving memory of my stepbrother,
Daniel Eugene Ramsey,
who was a very special and truly unique person.

Prologue

He dumped the body into Mobile Bay. It could take days, maybe even weeks or months, before anyone found her. Or she just might wash out to sea and no one would ever know what had happened to her. The boss had told him that if it hadn't taken them so long to discover that she'd gone off to some damn convention, they could have gotten rid of her before she'd shared her secret with anyone else. Luckily, he'd caught up with her in time to end her telephone conversation with her editor. But he had no idea how much information she'd shared with Annie Harden.

He hated having to call his boss. But before he took any further action, he needed an okay from the person who was paying him big bucks for this job. In his opinion, they had no choice but to take care of Ms. Harden before she had a chance to cause any trouble.

He closed the trunk lid, opened the driver's side door and slid behind the wheel. Within minutes he entered the main highway and headed back toward Point Clear.

Using his cellular phone, he placed the call.

"Hello?"

"I disposed of our little problem," he said.

"Good."

"But I'm afraid we have another problem."

"What went wrong?"

"She called her editor. I don't know how much she told her, but I think it was enough to make the lady suspicious," he explained. "And I didn't find the package."

"This complicates matters. We need that package. And my superior isn't going to like knowing that Annie is now involved."

"I wiped out the computer files and checked her suitcase, so there's no evidence of any kind," he said. "But if she shared enough information with—"

"I hate that this has happened. I wanted this stopped before… We have no choice now. I'm afraid we'll have to take care of the new problem in a similar manner." Pause. Deep breath. "Stay where you are until I find out exactly where the lady is. If she's still in town, I'll get someone here to take care of it. If she's on her way there, then I'll let you know and you can handle the situation."

"I'll lay low until I hear from you."

The guy who'd hired him had explained that they'd wanted to eliminate Halley Robinson before she involved this Annie dame. So he figured Annie meant something to either the boss or his superior. And if that was the case, then issuing an order to kill her might not be so easy for them.

Chapter 1

Relaxation washed over Dane Carmichael like the Gulf waters over the sandy beach beneath his feet. Maybe his co-workers had been right, after all. Maybe he did need this vacation more than he realized. He certainly had enjoyed having dinner with old friends tonight. He hadn't seen Norma Jane and Jay in years, even though he and Lorna had once been very close to the couple. Docking the *Sweet Savannah* here at Point Clear had brought back a lot of memories—memories of the life he had lost ten years ago when Lorna died. How many summers had they vacationed at the Grand Hotel, as Southern aristocracy had done since pre-Civil War days?

Dane slowed his steps, took a deep breath and gazed up at the starry sky. Clear and bright. A balmy springtime breeze drifted ashore from Mobile Bay. Sweet serenity. Only the ocean's heartbeat and his own, beating in unison.

A few years ago he'd left the Bureau and a grueling schedule that had helped keep him sane during the difficult

years following Lorna's death. He'd thought that the
change would be good for him, maybe allow him time for
a personal life. During the first few months as head of one
of the most prestigious private security and investigation
firms in the country, he had slowed his pace and actually
started dating. But as time had passed, he hadn't found
anyone who could measure up to Lorna. After that disap-
pointing revelation, he had once again buried himself in
his work, not realizing what a workaholic he'd become or
to what extent he had allowed the Dundee agency to become his whole life. Not until his co-workers had suggested he take a few weeks off.

Dane chuckled. Yeah, *suggested*. "Threatened" was
more like it. He thought back to two days ago when Murdock and Ellen Denby had cornered him in his office.

"You've become a real pain in the ass," Murdock said
in his typically brutally honest style. "If you don't get your
act together, there's going to be a mutiny and you're going
to lose some top agents."

Before he could open his mouth to protest, Ellen piped
in, "What Dane needs is to get some. How long has it
been, anyway, big man, since you had a woman?"

Dane narrowed his gaze on Ellen, Dundee's only female
agent, and grinned at her. "You volunteering for the job,
Denby?"

Murdock burst out laughing. Ellen eased her curvaceous
hip down on the side of Dane's desk and smiled coyly.

"Only if hazardous duty pay comes with it," she said.

"If you take on our Ellen, you'd be the one needing
hazardous duty pay," Murdock said.

"Murdock could be right about that." Ellen crossed her
long, shapely legs as she settled on the edge of the desk.
"Besides, I'm not your type, am I, Dane? You like your

women soft and sweet and adoring. The old-fashioned type is what turns you on."

"For your information, I don't need a woman and I don't need a vacation. I need employees who will—"

"Ask how high when you say jump," Ellen said.

"Have I gotten that bad?"

"Worse," Murdock confirmed. "You've pushed yourself to the limit for way too long, buddy boy. It's past time for you to take off to the Caribbean for a couple of weeks. Stop by and see Sam and Jeannie."

"Have you talked to Sam about this?" Dane realized that if they'd spoken to Sam Dundee, he really must have been acting like a real SOB lately.

"Sam agrees with us," Ellen said. "It's vacation time for you. Right now. Effective tomorrow."

Dane headed toward the marina, where he'd docked the *Sweet Savannah* this afternoon. He hadn't set foot on her in a couple of years. He'd almost forgotten how good it felt to be at the helm, to stand on the flying bridge and head out to sea. The yacht had been a part of his past— part of his life with Lorna. He had taken a lot of ribbing at the Bureau about being a millionaire playboy, but the people who knew him well knew that a playboy was the last thing on earth he'd ever been.

Sure, he'd been raised in the lap of luxury in Savannah, the only son in one of the wealthiest and most revered Old Southern families. But he had also been raised with a sense of responsibility and the knowledge that he was expected to become a productive member of society. His grandfather had been a federal judge, his father a prominent criminal lawyer, so his joining the FBI directly out of college had carried on a family tradition in law enforcement.

The evening breeze cooled as it came in off the Gulf

waters. He took a deep breath and closed his eyes. The face that appeared in the darkness was Lorna's. After all these years, he still couldn't forget how peaceful she had seemed lying there in her bed, looking like a sleeping angel. Only she hadn't been sleeping. She'd been dead.

Opening his eyes, he cursed under his breath. Damn! That's what came from having leisure time, from idle hours without something to occupy his mind. He couldn't spend his entire vacation thinking about Lorna. If he did, he'd go mad.

Suddenly Dane heard a whimper, then a loud gasp. He had thought he was alone on the beach.

"Help me! Please, help me!"

Dane tensed at the sound of the pleading voice. Female. Close by. And frightened.

Although his vision had adjusted to the darkness during his stroll along the beach, he found it difficult to make out anything other than a small, dark silhouette heading in his direction. He took several steps toward the shadowy figure before confirming that it was, indeed, a woman.

She reached out for him. "Oh, thank God!" She grabbed the front of his shirt and bunched the soft cloth in her tight fists. "Someone just tried to kill me. I need help. Please—"

The woman fainted dead away. Dane grabbed her up in his arms. He glanced around for any sign of an attacker, but saw no one and sensed they were alone on the beach. He had two choices—either take her aboard his yacht or carry her over to the Grand Hotel. Instantly he chose the closer and safer location. He knew the woman's attacker wouldn't be aboard his cruiser.

She was small and light in his arms, probably close to a foot shorter than his six-two. Within minutes he had carried her aboard the *Sweet Savannah* and belowdecks to the saloon. Just as he deposited her on the L-shaped settee, situated aft to port, the woman's eyelids fluttered and she groaned.

Rising to his feet, Dane stood and visually surveyed the petite lady from head to toe. About five-three, he surmised. Trim, bosomy, and pretty. Expertly styled, chin-length black hair spread out across the gray settee cushion.

She opened her eyes—big, brown, expressive eyes. Glaring up at Dane, her fear and uncertainty showed plainly in the look she gave him. "Where am I? What happened?" Her voice clearly proclaimed her as a Southerner.

Dane crouched down on his haunches beside her. "You're aboard my yacht at the Point Clear Marina," he told her. "You came running up to me on the beach a few minutes ago and told me someone had tried to kill you."

"I know that!" She glared at him in a way that told him she thought he was an idiot. "I meant, what happened after that?"

"You fainted."

"I didn't! I've never fainted in my life!" She tried to sit up, but groaned and fell back on the sofa. "Oh, God! Do something, will you?"

"What would you like me to do, Ms....Ms....?"

"Annie Harden."

"I'm Dane Carmichael."

"Nice to meet you," she said sardonically. She ran her hand over her side, then lifted the hand and moaned when she inspected it. "Do you suppose we could forget good manners and cordial chitchat for the time being, Mr. Carmichael? I think I may be bleeding to death."

Dane noticed her palm was covered in blood. Immediately he examined the left side of her burgundy suit jacket. A wet, sticky stain had formed around a wide cut in the fabric. "Tell me what happened." He began unbuttoning her jacket, intent upon examining her wound.

She slapped at his hands. "What do you think you're doing?"

"I'm trying to take a look at your wound to see how badly you're hurt." He grabbed her wrists and brought her hands over her head. Holding her arms steady with one hand, he used the other to lift her jacket. The white blouse underneath was drenched in bright red blood.

"I'd appreciate it if you didn't manhandle me." She twisted and turned her arms in an effort to free herself from his hold, but suddenly cried out in pain and quit squirming. "He had a knife. I don't think he stabbed me, although it felt like it. I think he just slashed my side."

Dane gently pulled the damp fabric out of the skirt waistband, then up and over the five-inch tear in her skin. Probing with the utmost caution, he examined the wound. Long and gaping, but not deep. "You'll need a few stitches, but I think you'll live. You probably fainted from a combination of pain and shock."

Dane stood, walked across the saloon into the galley and rummaged in the overhead teakwood cabinets. He removed a small, white towel, went back over to the woman and covered her wound with the soft, clean cloth. Then he took her hand and laid it over the towel.

"Makeshift bandage," he told her. "Keep the towel firmly over the wound. I'll take you to a hospital, right after I call the police."

"I doubt the local authorities will be of any help," she said. "I spoke to them a few hours ago and they practically laughed in my face."

Dane stared at her, puzzled by her statement. "How about filling me in on what you're talking about?"

Annie Harden took a good, long look at the man with

the baritone Southern drawl. He was big, tall, and leanly muscled. Sleek and agile. And dressed casually, in tan cotton slacks and a navy knit shirt. His short, thick brown hair looked windblown. And even though he didn't smile and there was no warmth in his rugged, tanned face, she noted something in the depth of his blue eyes. Sadness. Loneliness. And kindness.

"Would you mind helping me sit up?" She held out her hand.

He noted how small her hand was, how slender her fingers. Her nails were neatly manicured and glistened with clear polish. No rings. But a slender gold bracelet circled her wrist.

He took her hand, then leaned toward her and draped her shoulders with his arm. When he lifted her, she moaned quietly. It bothered him that she was in pain. She seemed so small and helpless cradled there in his arms.

"Thanks." She shrugged off his embrace.

"Sure."

Their eyes met and held for a brief moment. Annie's breath caught in her throat. Her rescuer was a handsome man, just the kind most women dreamed would come to their rescue if they ever needed help. She tried to dismiss the queasy feeling in her stomach, telling herself it was due to the trauma she had experienced. But in her gut, she knew that her tummy doing somersaults had nothing to do with the slash in her side nor the pain and everything to do with sexual awareness. She wasn't some naive kid who'd never experienced the effects of a powerful physical attraction. She was a thirty-four-year-old divorcée, who had learned the hard way not to give charming, good-looking men any power over her.

Sizing up this guy, she instinctively knew he was a heartbreaker. No telling how many women had lost their hearts to him and gotten nothing but misery in return. Even though Preston had been younger and smaller built, there was something about this man that reminded her of her ex-husband. Something in his manner, in the tone of his voice and his take-charge attitude.

"Want to tell me what happened to you tonight?" Dane asked as he flipped open his cellular phone. "Before I call the police."

"Go ahead and telephone them. I'll tell you whatever you want to know, after you call."

Dane nodded. "You can fill me in on the way to the hospital."

Clutching the blood-soaked towel covering her side, Annie said a quick prayer of thanks that her attacker hadn't killed her. If she hadn't taken self-defense classes and known how to handle the situation, she might be dead right now. As it was, she had a nasty wound, but she wasn't going to die from it.

While Dane made the call, Annie's mind wandered back two days to the evening when Halley had telephoned her from her room at the Grand Hotel, here in Point Clear. The moment the phone line had gone dead, Annie's instincts had warned her that Halley was in trouble—big trouble.

If anything had happened to the girl, Annie felt that it was her fault. After all, she'd been the one who had encouraged Halley to break free and become independent of the same life-style that had once smothered her.

"They'll meet us at the hospital," Dane said. "Guess I'd better call a cab. I don't have a car with me."

"We can take my car," Annie said. "I picked up a rental when I arrived this afternoon."

"Where is your car?" he asked.

"Over at the hotel."

"Why don't you tell me exactly where it's parked, give

me a description and the keys, and I'll bring it over here. You can wait belowdecks, safe and sound.''

A momentary sense of alarm tightened every muscle in her body. She didn't want him to leave her alone. ''That sounds like a good plan.'' She stuck her hand into her jacket pocket and pulled out a key ring. ''It's a blue Chevy Impala, parked on the ground level of the Marina House.''

''I'll find it.''

''Mr. Carmichael?''

He paused on the first step up to the deck. ''Yes?''

''Thank you.''

When he nodded, his lips curved upward in an almost smile. ''Are you afraid to stay here alone until I get back with the car?''

''I'm not afraid,'' she said. ''Just nervous. But I'll be okay. You go get the car.''

Dane hesitated momentarily, then turned and headed toward the steps leading to the lower deck where his stateroom was located.

''Where are you going?'' she called after him.

''Be back in a minute.''

True to his word, within a minute, he emerged from the stateroom below and came back up into the saloon. He held a gun in his hand. Annie shivered.

''Here.'' He laid the weapon on the sofa beside her. ''Do you know anything about guns?''

''Not much,'' she admitted. ''Mother keeps my father's old Smith & Wesson revolver in a desk in the den. It's not loaded and neither of us has ever used it.''

''Well, this one is loaded and ready to fire. All you have to do is release the safety.'' With a quick flick of his finger he showed her how to accomplish the simple feat. ''Just be sure you don't shoot me when I come back.''

''How about a password, so I'll know it's you?'' she

suggested, half joking but partly sincere. She didn't want to be afraid, was trying very hard not to be. But she was. Not that she'd admit it to this man—to any man—but knowing that someone wanted her dead scared the hell out of her.

"A password, huh?" Dane's lips quivered as he tried not to smile. Who the hell was this woman—this Annie Harden—and why had fate thrown her into his arms? he wondered.

Little Miss Annie sat there, a nasty knife wound in her side, and stared up at him with defiant dark eyes that dared him to even suggest she might be afraid. No doubt, she was one of the new breed of independent women.

"How about driftwood," he suggested.

"Driftwood?"

"Yes, driftwood." *Because I found you on the beach,* he almost added, but didn't.

There was no reason for him to feel so protective of this woman, even if she was injured. Hadn't he learned by now that helpless creatures were his weakness? He had spent a lifetime taking care of wounded creatures. Birds with broken wings. Stray cats and dogs, hungry for nourishment and love. And people. Misfits seemed drawn to him. *Because you have an understanding heart,* his mother had said. Was that why he'd been so drawn to Lorna? Sweet, beautiful, perfect Lorna. So fragile and helpless. So in need of his constant love and approval.

"What are you waiting for?" Annie asked when she realized he'd made no move to leave.

"Nothing," he said. "I'm gone."

When he disappeared from her view, she glanced down at the handgun lying on the sofa. She really didn't know much about guns. Although she'd taken self-defense classes and carried pepper spray in her handbag, neither had prevented the attack on her tonight. She had left her bag in her room when she had walked over to the Bay View Restaurant for dinner. Upon her return to the Marina House, she'd opted to take a stroll on the beach and enjoy the beautiful June evening, while she tried to decide what to do next in her search for Halley. Walking always helped her clear the cobwebs from her mind and put things in the proper perspective. It had never occurred to her that she might be in danger, that someone knew Halley's last phone call had been to her—about what Halley had called *the story of a lifetime.*

The man had come from out of nowhere, brandishing a knife. A well-aimed knee-thrust into the man's groin had probably saved her life. She shuddered as she remembered the sheer panic that had raced through her when he'd jumped her.

Annie held the damp towel to her side and wished Dane Carmichael would hurry. She'd tried not to let on that she was in a lot of pain. She prided herself on not being the weak, weepy type.

Then you shouldn't have fainted right into his arms, she reminded herself. That was a great show of strength!

No big deal, her conscience chided. *The guy will drive you to the hospital and you'll never see him again. You don't have to prove anything to him. He's a stranger who just happened to be there when you needed him.*

She cringed at the thought of needing anyone, especially some big, macho guy who seemed quite comfortable in the role of her protector.

It seemed as if only a few minutes had passed when she heard footsteps above, on the deck. Her heartbeat accelerated. A tremor racked her body. Oh, God, what if the knife-wielding attacker had found her?

She undid the safety on Dane Carmichael's gun and aimed it directly at the steps leading to the deck. Whoever was up there, she was ready for him.

Chapter 2

"Driftwood," a baritone voice called from above.

Annie heaved a sigh of relief. Her whole body shivered
as the fear clutching her heart released and allowed her to
breathe again. "That was quick."

Dane descended into the saloon. "I ran. Come on, let's
get you to the hospital."

He lifted Annie up into his arms before she knew what
was happening. She opened her mouth to protest, but
didn't when she reluctantly admitted to herself that, in her
present state, she was better off letting Mr. Macho carry
her. After all, it wasn't every day that she lived through
an attempted murder.

"So, Ms. Harden, want to tell me about the attack?"
Dane asked as he carried her off his fifty-foot cruiser.

"You sound like a policeman." The pain in her side
intensified with each step he took, but she gritted her teeth
and didn't complain.

"I used to be a federal agent," he said.

"Which agency?"

"FBI." He leaned down, opened the passenger door of her rental car and slid her into the front seat. He closed the door, rounded the hood and got in, then glanced over at Annie. "Now I'm the CEO of Dundee Private Security and Investigation in Atlanta."

Annie laughed. Leave it to her to run right into the arms of a trained bodyguard. No wonder the man acted protectively toward her. That's how he made his living. "Boy, was I lucky. Just think, you could have been a shoe salesman from Memphis."

Dane chuckled, then started the car and drove away from the marina. "It shouldn't take us long to get there. The policeman I spoke to told me to take you to Thomas Hospital, on Murphy Avenue."

She nodded. "I suppose you know where that is."

"Yeah, I've been to Fairhope and Daphne and Spanish Fort before. I even have a general idea of where the hospital is." What he didn't say was that the last time he'd visited this area, he'd been with Lorna on one of her antique-hunting expeditions in Fairhope.

"I haven't had stitches since I was a kid and fell out of a tree in the backyard." Annie curled up on the seat, the darkness surrounding her like a comforting blanket. "They took ten stitches in the back of my head. Boy, was my father upset."

"You can't blame him for being worried about you. Head injuries can be serious."

"He wasn't upset about my injury. He was angry with me for being such a tomboy." She'd been a disappointment to her father for as long as she could remember. He had wanted a daughter as genteel and dignified as his perfect wife. Unfortunately, Annie had inherited very little of her mother's sweet, docile nature and a great deal of her grandmother Harden's stubborn, independent, adventurous characteristics. According to family members, Grandmother Harden, the Italian war bride who had died in childbirth at the age of twenty-four, had been a fiery, temperamental, headstrong woman who hadn't fit into her husband's genteel Southern family. "My father told me that if I acted more like a little lady the accident never would have happened."

Dane glanced at Annie and caught a glimpse of some long-ago pain as it flashed across her face. "So, tell me, this guy tonight, did he try to steal your purse or was he trying to rape you or—"

"Neither."

"Did you know him?" Dane wondered if the attacker might have been a boyfriend or an ex-husband.

"No, I didn't know him. I didn't even get a good look at his face. It was dark and he came out of nowhere. It happened so quickly that all I remember is he wasn't very tall. Not nearly as tall as you. And he was wiry."

"Did he say anything?"

"Not a word."

"So you don't have a clue as to why this guy tried to kill you?"

"I didn't say that." She shifted uneasily in the seat. The pain in her side was getting progressively worse and the wound hadn't stopped oozing blood. "I have a good idea why he came after me. I just don't know who he was or who sent him."

"Why don't you start at the beginning? Maybe your explanation will make more sense that way."

"What difference does it make to you? You can drop me at the hospital and be on your way. There's no need for you to become involved in any of this."

Dane knew she was right. Any sensible man would do

just that—drop her at the emergency room and leave her and her problems to the police. "You mentioned earlier that you'd already been to the police today and they hadn't been of any help to you. Want to explain that to me?"

Annie huffed loudly, letting out a long, exaggerated breath. "The investigator in you just has to know, doesn't he?"

She glanced at the big man, who didn't take his eyes off the road. Why was it that she instinctively trusted this man—this stranger? For all she knew, he might be lying to her about his credentials, might even be involved in Halley's disappearance. Okay, enough of that, she told herself. That kind of thinking is paranoid.

"To make a long story short, a friend of mine, a staff reporter on my magazine, came down here to the Grand Hotel for a Society of Professional Journalists workshop a couple of days ago. She called me the evening after she arrived and told me that she had some information on the story of a lifetime, something I wasn't going to believe. It seems she had received a package in the mail right before she'd left home, but she just stuck it in her suitcase and didn't open it until the next day."

"Your magazine? Does that mean you're a reporter or—"

"It means I'm the Publisher and the Editor-in-Chief. *Today's Alabama* is my brainchild."

"So what does your magazine and your reporter's story have to do with your being attacked tonight?" Dane asked.

"I'm not sure, but my guess is that Halley had come across something really big. Believe me, she isn't the type to exaggerate."

"So, what was the big story?"

"I don't know."

"What do you mean you—"

"If you'll stop playing Twenty Questions, I'll explain!" Annie took another deep breath. "When Halley called me, the phone line went dead before she could give me any details. I called her back, but there was no answer. I called the hotel and had them check her room. She wasn't there, but she hadn't checked out. She's been missing for two days. She just disappeared."

"You contacted the local authorities about her disappearance, didn't you? That's what you meant about talking to the police earlier today."

"There was no sign of foul play in her room and it seems that several hotel guests saw a woman fitting Halley's description leave the hotel with a man that afternoon. They claim the two were laughing and acting very chummy, so the police think she just took off that night with some guy for a wild fling. Can you believe it?"

"But you don't think she'd do something like that."

"Halley Robinson would never go off with some man. She's practically engaged to a great guy back home. If he hadn't been in Pittsburgh on a business trip, I'm sure Clay would have come with me to look for her. I haven't told him or her parents that Halley is missing."

"Maybe the guy who attacked you had nothing to do with your friend's disappearance," Dane said.

"Maybe, maybe not. I don't know. I'm going strictly on instinct. I believe Halley uncovered something terrible, something that put her life in danger."

"You think your friend has been murdered?"

Annie clenched her teeth tightly. Dane Carmichael had just put her greatest fear into words. Yes, she was afraid that Halley was dead and that whatever "story of a lifetime" her friend had unearthed had not only cost her her own life, but had put Annie's life in danger, as well.

"If that's true, if Halley is dead, then it's all my fault," Annie said.

"Why is it your fault?" he asked.

"Because I'm the one who encouraged her to follow her dream and become a reporter instead of playing it safe and settling into the life her parents chose for her. I'm the one who took her under my wing and advised her to be her own woman—to break free from tradition."

Dane didn't respond. Annie couldn't even hear him breathing. She glanced over at him and noticed how tightly he gripped the steering wheel. What was wrong with him? He looked as if he was in pain. A mental agony brought on by unhappy memories, Annie surmised. She knew only too well how memories could wreak havoc on a person's present contentment.

Revising his earlier opinion, Dane decided that coming to Point Clear had been a major mistake. Ever since he'd docked at the marina this afternoon, he hadn't been able to get Lorna off his mind. And now, Annie's comment about her encouraging her friend to break free from tradition made him wonder if Lorna had wanted to break free? Had she longed for a different life, far removed from the one her father had chosen for her? Had she regretted marrying him instead of pursuing some personal dream buried deep in her heart? He didn't know. Had never asked her. Had never questioned the idyllic life he had thought they shared. And now it was too late. He would never know.

Dane drove up to Thomas Hospital's ER, parked the car and carried Annie inside. A boyish-looking policeman met them as they entered. Dane wondered how long the guy had been out of the academy. Six months? A year at the most, would be his guess.

"I'm Kyle Yarborough," the young officer said. "Is this the victim?"

"Ms. Annie Harden," Dane told him. "She's got a nasty knife wound that should be taken care of immediately."

"Go right on back." The policeman stepped out of the way. "Dr. Meeks will check her over and then I'll take her statement."

Once Dane deposited Annie on the examination table, a nurse asked him to please step outside. He hesitated, wondering if Annie would be all right without him. Fool, he chided himself. Of course she'd be all right. There was no need for him to take a possessive attitude where she was concerned. He could leave right now and she wouldn't care. So why didn't he just go on back to the *Sweet Savannah* and get a good night's sleep?

"Dane," she called to him when he turned to go.

"Yeah?"

"Will you hang around for a while?" Dammit, why had she asked him to stay? She didn't need him, even if for some reason she couldn't fathom, his presence was reassuring.

"Sure. I'll be waiting right outside." Why hadn't he told her that he didn't want to get involved? He was supposed to be on vacation. There was no rule that said he had to step in and play bodyguard for some woman he'd just met.

Thirty minutes later Dr. Meeks, a bespectacled, balding physician in his late fifties, came out and spoke to Dane and the police officer.

"Ms. Harden will be just fine. She's been given a tetanus shot and a couple of prescriptions. She's free to leave as soon as she gets dressed."

"You aren't keeping her here overnight?" Dane asked.

"I see no reason to keep her," Dr. Meeks said. "And Ms. Harden seems eager to go home."

"Is she physically able to drive?" Dane narrowed his gaze on the doctor's face.

Dr. Meeks cleared his throat. "Well, I'd suggest she get a good night's rest before trying to drive all the way back to North Alabama from here, but the lady seems quite determined."

"I'll need to question Ms. Harden before she leaves," Yarborough said.

"She's getting dressed now," the doctor told him. "She should be with you in a few minutes."

"I'll hurry her along," Dane said, then made his way down the hallway and to Annie's ER cubicle.

Dane knocked on the partition and waited. Annie pulled aside the curtain and stepped out into the hallway.

"Are you all right?" he asked

She nodded. "The doctor says I'll be fine." She pointed to her side, covered by her bloody white blouse, which hung loosely about her hips. "Twenty little stitches. He said to see my doctor back home in a couple of days." She held up two small pieces of paper. "One antibiotic prescription and one for pain, if I need it."

Dane grasped Annie by the elbow and pulled her to his side. "Officer Yarborough is waiting to ask you about the attack."

"Fine, let's get this over with."

Dane escorted her out into the waiting area, where the young policeman met them. He led her over to the far end of the room and eased her down onto a vinyl sofa.

Annie sat, nervously tapping her foot on the floor. Dane hovered over her. Strangely enough, his presence was comforting and not at all intimidating or threatening. He didn't make her feel the way her father had when he'd scrutinized her actions, nor did he affect her the way Preston had when he'd watched her every move and voiced his disapproval.

Don't let Dane Carmichael's Southern gentleman facade fool you, she reminded herself. He's the old-fashioned macho type, Annie, old girl, and don't you forget it!

Dane remained silent while she told the officer how a man had grabbed her and tried to kill her. And then she told him about her suspicions that her attack and Halley Robinson's disappearance were somehow connected.

"I talked to a Lieutenant McCullough over the phone yesterday and explained about Halley's disappearance, and he told me he'd check into it. Then I stopped by the police station and saw him when I first arrived this afternoon," Annie said. "The news story Halley told me about must be the reason she's missing and the reason I was attacked."

"What did Lieutenant McCullough say, ma'am?"

"Oh, he has a couple of eyewitnesses who think they saw my friend leave the hotel with some man earlier that day. So, your lieutenant thinks she's gone off with that man of her own free will."

Officer Yarborough cleared his throat several times. "I'll file this report and we'll take a look around where you say the incident occurred, but I have to warn you, Ms. Harden, there's not much chance we'll catch this guy." Officer Yarborough closed his notebook. "You can't ID him and there were no other witnesses. I'd say the best thing you can do is count yourself lucky and go home."

"What about Halley Robinson?" Annie asked.

"Ma'am, I don't know anything about that case, but if Lieutenant McCullough thinks your friend is just off somewhere with a guy, then she'll probably show up. If she doesn't, then her family can file a missing person's report and—''

''I told your Lieutenant McCullough this afternoon that Halley isn't the type to run off with some man!''

''I'm sorry, ma'am.'' Pink splotches stained the policeman's cheeks. ''Are you going to see Ms. Harden back to the hotel?'' he asked Dane.

''Yeah, sure.'' Dane felt a bit sorry for the young officer. Dealing with Annie's barely controlled ire seemed to unnerve the boy.

The minute Officer Yarborough left, Annie gritted her teeth, groaned, and knotted her right hand into a fist. ''It's obvious that the police aren't going to do a damn thing to find Halley. I'll have to go home and tell her parents and Clay that she's missing. I suppose the next step is for her parents to file a report with the police. Amelia and Dennis are going to blame me for what's happened and they have every right to.''

''You truly believe something bad has happened to her, don't you? You don't think she just ran off with some guy for a romantic fling and she'll show up in a few days.''

''How many times do I have to say it—Halley isn't the type!'' Annie rose to her feet, then groaned when pain sliced through her side.

Dane lifted her off her feet. Annie gasped. Responding instinctively, she placed her arm around his neck and gazed into his sky-blue eyes.

''I'll take you back to the hotel. On the way we can stop at a drugstore and get both your prescriptions filled. Then you're going straight to bed.'' Dane carried her out of the ER waiting room and into the parking area. ''You need somebody to look after you tonight, Ms. Harden, so it seems you're stuck with me.''

Oh, God! He was definitely one of *them.* The protective

male. The take-charge man. The Southern gentleman, who assumes it is his right and his privilege to play white knight to any and all damsels in distress. She knew his type— knew it firsthand. She'd been fathered by just such a person and she'd also been married to one.

Well, if Mr. Dane Carmichael thought she needed him, he was wrong. And if he thought she would be grateful for his macho chivalry, then he was wrong again. The last thing she wanted in her life now or ever was some big, strong man telling her what she could and could not do.

Dane eased Annie into the car, then got in and started the engine. He supposed it wouldn't hurt to postpone his vacation for a day or two, just long enough to get Annie Harden back home safe and sound. After all, the woman obviously needed him.

Yeah, sure. Aren't you being noble, he told himself. Admit it, you need something—anything—to put your mind on, something to occupy your time. Cruising off to the Caribbean for a couple of weeks wasn't a good idea, nor was stopping in Point Clear, a placed filled with so many memories of Lorna.

"Sit back and relax, Annie," Dane said. "Just leave everything to me."

Annie cringed. Leave everything to him. Not likely. Once he took her back to the hotel, she'd tell him *adios*. She was perfectly capable of packing her bags and driving to Florence in the morning without any help from him. She supposed she could fly home, but the drive would take much longer and allow her more time to prepare herself to give Clay and the Robinsons the news about Halley's disappearance. After all, she could be wrong about the situation and Halley could show up alive and well in the morning.

"Give me the prescriptions." Dane held out his hand.

Annie rummaged around in her pocket, pulled out the two sheets of wrinkled paper and glanced down at the doctor's barely legible handwriting. She stuffed one of the prescriptions back into her pocket.

"Here." She handed the other over to Dane. "If you'll go in and get it filled, I'll repay you when we get to the hotel. Thank goodness my insurance company has a twenty-four-hour hotline, so the hospital was able to get the information they needed without my insurance card."

"This is only one prescription." Dane waved the paper in front of her face.

"It's for the antibiotic," she told him. "I won't need the pain medication."

"Take my word for it, honey, you'll need it before morning."

"So pick me up a bottle of aspirin while you're in the drugstore." She settled back in the seat and looked out the window, deliberately avoiding making eye contact. "And please don't call me 'honey' again. Okay? I don't like it."

"Suit yourself. About the pain medication. And I'm sorry if I offended you by calling you honey. Force of habit. I call most females honey."

"I figured you did." She cast her gaze quickly in his direction. His lips twitched slightly with that almost smile of his and she knew he was trying not to laugh. At her! "For your information, Mr. Carmichael, I'm not like most females. I dislike being lumped together with all the other Southern belles who've been taught since kindergarten that it's their duty to boost men's egos."

He shifted the gear into Reverse, backed the car out of the parking place and pulled into the street. "So who was he?"

"I beg your pardon?"

"The guy who did a number on you—who was he?"

"What makes you think—"

"Because, Ms. Harden, you've got a chip on your shoulder the size of a boulder."

"Just because I told you that I didn't like being called honey, you jump to the conclusion that some man broke my heart and turned me against men in general."

"So, tell me I'm wrong. Tell me that you don't have an ex-husband or former boyfriend who called you honey and expected you to stroke his ego."

Annie stiffened her spine. Damn know-it-all. "My ex-husband called me honey. And he had an ego that needed more than one woman's stroking."

"Just because I called you honey, don't lump me into the same group as a man who'd cheat on his wife."

Annie turned then and stared at her rescuer. There had been something in his voice, in the tone and even in the pronunciation when he'd said the word *wife*. A sweet, tender sadness. He'd been married, she realized. *He'd had a wife. Maybe he still did.*

Dane kept the speed below the limit as he cruised along searching for a drugstore that was still open this late at night. When he spotted a small strip mall, he decided to turn off and check out the row of stores.

"Are you married?" Annie asked just as Dane stopped in front of a Super-Mart.

"I was. I'm a widower." He held out his hand. "How about giving me the other prescription? I'll get it filled and if you don't need it, you don't have to take it. Better to have it, though, just in case."

"I told you that…" Her gaze locked with his. She could tell by the unyielding look in his eyes and the stern set of his jaw that he wasn't going to back down on this issue. And she didn't have the strength for a battle. Not over something this unimportant. She jerked the prescription out of her pocket and handed it to him. "Here!"

His face softened as he snatched the paper out of her hand. "Keep the doors locked. I'll be back as quick as I can."

"Thanks. I know I haven't acted very appreciative, but I am." When he gave her a skeptical look, she smiled at him. "Really, I am."

He smiled back at her, opened the car door, then got out and went into the Super-Mart. Annie leaned her head back against the seat and closed her eyes. Dane Carmichael was a nice man. A real gentleman. She felt a twinge of remorse that she'd taken out some of her anger and frustration on him. After all, he was right. If she didn't want to be lumped together with a group of old-fashioned Southern belles, then she had no right to compare him to Preston, her Southern gentleman ex-husband who'd lived the double standard concerning extra-marital affairs. Preston actually thought she should understand that his brief affairs had nothing to do with her or their marriage. Unfortunately for other women like her, there were a lot of men who felt the same way Preston did.

When Dane returned with the filled prescriptions, he found Annie asleep. He unlocked the car, slid behind the wheel and started the engine. She didn't budge. Poor little thing, he thought, she had to be exhausted. A strand of her blue-black hair clung to her cheek and another rested across the side of her forehead. He had the overwhelming urge to brush back those loose strands of hair, to caress her pale face, to cradle her in his arms and keep her safe.

Don't go there, he told himself. Don't make the mistake of thinking this woman wants you or needs you. She's made it perfectly clear that, although she appreciates the help you've given her, she'd resent it if you did anything more for her.

Dane let her sleep until he pulled her car into the ground-level parking deck at the Marina House. As he shook her gently, he called her name.

"Annie? Annie, wake up, hon—" He stopped himself just as he started to use the endearment she disliked. "We're back at the Grand Hotel."

She opened her eyes slowly, groggily, and gazed up at Dane, whose face was only inches from hers. She smiled. "Thank you." She reached up and placed her hand on his cheek. "You're probably very good at your job. You've certainly taken good care of me tonight."

Dane wanted to kiss her, and if she'd been just about any other woman, he would have. After all, he recognized that look in her eyes, that warm, sultry invitation. But Annie Harden probably didn't realize that her expression was either provocative or inviting. She was definitely one of those women whose lips would say no, while her eyes were saying yes. He wasn't fool enough to mess around with a lady like that.

"Come on, Ms. Harden, I'll walk you to your room."

When Dane opened the door, Annie tried to get out, but the minute she turned sideways, pain ripped through her. Clutching her bandaged side, she doubled over as the pain radiated out from her wound and through her entire body. She couldn't stifle the moan that rose in her throat.

"Take it easy, honey." Dane eased one arm around her and the other under her. "Sorry about the honey. It just slipped out." He lifted her from the car and up into his arms. "I hate to say I told you so, but—"

"Please, put me down. I think I can manage to walk."

He hesitated, then gauged the determined set of her jaw and the pleading look in her eyes, and set her on her feet. Slowly. Carefully. But he did not release her completely. He kept his arm around her waist.

"You were right about the pain medication," she admitted. "I'll probably need it tonight."

He could tell that she was struggling to stay on her feet. All the way into the small, glass-enclosed lobby of the Marina House, onto the elevator and down the corridor to her room, she refused to give in to the pain. With every step she took, he had to fight the urge to lift her into his arms again. Why the hell did she have to be so contrary, so stubborn? What would it hurt if he carried her? Why was it so damn important to her to be independent, to prove to him, and maybe to herself, that she didn't need him?

He unlocked and opened the door. Annie walked just inside the room, then turned to him. "Thanks again, for all your help." She held out her hand.

He put the small plastic bag that contained the two bottles of prescription medication in her hand. "I'd feel much better if you'd let me stay with you tonight." He glanced over her shoulder. "This room has two double beds."

"That's very nice of you to offer, but I'll be fine. I'll get a good night's sleep and then I'll head for home in the morning." She sighed. "I dread telling Halley's parents and Clay that she's disappeared."

"Annie, why don't you let me stay?" Bracing his hands on either side of the door frame, Dane leaned toward her. "If you're right and the man who attacked you tonight is connected to your friend's disappearance, you're still in danger."

"I'll lock the door and if anyone tries to break in, I'll call for help."

"I could check the bathroom and under the bed and—"

Laughing, she clasped his arm, then suddenly wished

she hadn't touched him. His arm was big, muscular, and hard as a rock. Something entirely feminine in her reacted to his masculine strength. Releasing him abruptly, she stepped backward into the room.

"Please, be my guest." She ushered him inside with a magnanimous sweep of her hand. "We'll both sleep better if you make sure I'm safe."

Dane checked the bathroom, which was empty. The closet held only Annie's suitcase and several wooden clothes hangers. The beds were too low to accommodate even a small child crawling underneath. The sliding-glass doors that led to the balcony were closed, locked and secured. Unless someone had a key or burst down the door, no one was getting inside this room.

Annie followed Dane as he started to leave. He paused in the doorway. "Take care of yourself, Annie Harden. And if you decide you need a bodyguard or an agent to do some investigative work for you, let me know." He pulled his business card out of his pocket and handed it to her. "I'll be sailing around for a couple of weeks, but they know how to get in touch with me."

"I… Thank you." She walked him out into the hall. "Enjoy your vacation."

"Go back inside and lock up."

He waited. She hesitated.

"I could stay," he said.

"Go," she told him, then returned to her room, glanced over her shoulder for one last glimpse and closed the door.

Dane stood outside Annie's room for several minutes, until he finally talked himself out of hanging on her door and demanding that she let him stay to watch over her.

He grumbled to himself on the elevator ride down to the lobby. She'll be all right, he told himself. She's locked in, all safe and sound.

Dane checked his watch before he exited the building. One-twenty. He could sleep as late as he wanted to in the morning. Sam and Jeannie Dundee's island was only a short distance from Point Clear. He could leave on up in the day and still get there in time for lunch.

The nighttime possessed a still, hushed quality, as if the earth slept peacefully and the ocean breathed deeply in slumber. Dane inhaled the scents of the seashore as he headed toward the marina. With each step he took, his gait slowed until he stopped suddenly.

A sick feeling hit him square in the gut. Something was wrong. He shouldn't have left Annie. No matter what she'd said, no matter how much she would have protested, he should have stayed with her. His instinct told him that she was in big trouble.

"Damn!" The murmured curse echoed in the plush, dark stillness.

Dane ran back toward the Marina House. His heartbeat accelerated. He broke out in a sweat as pure fear pumped adrenaline through his body. He punched the elevator button and waited. Come on. Come on. Hell! Unable to wait another minute, he flung open the stairway door and raced up the concrete steps that led to the second floor where Annie's room was located.

Upon reaching the second level, he stopped momentarily to regroup and get his bearings. The stairs had brought him to a different location than the elevator would have. Right! he told himself. Go down the right corridor.

Running, his pulse wild, the sound of his pumping heart drumming in his head, he reached Annie's room. The door was closed. He stopped and took a deep breath. Maybe he was wrong about her being in danger. Maybe she was

38 *Keeping Annie Safe*

brushing her teeth or taking her medicine. Whatever she was doing, he had to see for himself that she was all right.

Dane lifted his hand to knock on the door. Before his knuckles made contact with the wood surface, a terrifying scream chilled him to the bone.

Chapter 3

Dane tried the doorknob. It wasn't locked! Resisting the urge to hurl open the door and barrel in, he twisted the knob and quietly eased the door open enough to look inside the room. Taking in several things all at once, he allowed his eyesight to adjust to the semidarkness. A lamp lay broken on the carpet, the bulb still burning, casting shadows on the walls. Annie was slumped on the floor, as if she'd been recently tossed there. Her face was etched with a combination of fear and anger. A wiry, dark-haired man, his back to Dane, stood over her.

"Your little knee-to-the-crotch trick didn't work this time, honey." The man laughed as he took a step closer. "You got away from me on the beach, but you aren't going anywhere this time."

Dane surveyed Annie from head to toe. She glanced past her attacker and made instant eye contact with Dane. He shook his head and placed an index finger over his lips, warning her to not alert the intruder to his presence. Instantly she looked away and focused her attention on the other man. Dane slipped inside the room, then pushed the door partially closed. His heart thudded against his chest, beating at breakneck speed.

"You know, you're a good-looking woman," the man said as he slipped a switchblade from his pocket and flipped it open. "A little older than the Robinson dame, but prettier, and I'll bet a lot more experienced."

Annie scooted her butt across the carpet, backing farther and farther away from the man wielding the sharp, shiny weapon. Dane's breath caught in his throat. Would he be quick enough to make his way across the room in complete silence to tackle the man before he hurt Annie? Her attacker stood less than three feet from her, while a good twelve feet separated them.

"Where is Halley?" Annie's voice possessed a note of nervous fury. "Did you hurt her? If you've done anything to—"

The man laughed again and took another step toward Annie. He held the knife up in his hand, as if it were a trophy he was showing off to impress a lady. "You talk big for such a little thing. You got guts, honey, I'll give you that. A feisty bitch always turns me on, so what do you say we have us a little fun before…"

He let the sentence trail off, but Dane knew what kind of fun the man was referring to and was sure Annie did, too. This slimeball wasn't going to touch her again! He'd rip him apart and feed him to the sharks.

Dane crept cautiously nearer and nearer to his objective. Just a couple more feet and he'd take the man out. The very thought of this bastard harming Annie brought Dane's primeval killer instincts to the surface.

"The only fun we'll have is when I scratch out your eyes," Annie said tauntingly.

Just as the man bent to grab Annie, she flayed her arms, kicked her feet and began screaming, taking him off guard. He hesitated momentarily. Obviously, he hadn't been expecting her to go berserk on him.

"Shut the hell up! I'll slit your neck and be out of here before anybody comes to help you."

The minute he reached down for her, Dane made his move. Standing, Annie slid back against the wall and watched. She itched to do something. To find a heavy object and bash the guy over the head. To kick him and claw him and knock him to his knees. Despite her violent thoughts, she made no move to interfere. She had every confidence in Dane Carmichael's ability to defend her.

Dane grabbed the man around the neck, choking him with the force of his muscular arm. The guy gasped for air. Dane tightened his hold.

"Drop the knife," Dane ordered. "Drop it or I'll break your freaking neck."

The knife slipped from the man's fingers and hit the carpet with a dull thud. He kept gasping for air.

Dane loosened his hold just enough to allow the man to breathe, then looked over at Annie and inclined his head toward the nightstand. "Call the police."

She nodded agreement. Avoiding getting anywhere near her attacker, Annie slid along the wall, making her way toward the telephone. Before she reached her objective, the outer door burst open and two men came rushing inside, then stopped abruptly. One of the men held a small handgun.

"It's all right, lady," the middle-aged man, wearing nothing but his boxer shorts said. "Don't you worry." His hand trembled, shaking the Smith & Wesson 9 mm he held.

The other man, who sported a silk robe and leather slippers, assessed the situation. From past experience Dane realized these two good Samaritans had no idea what they'd interrupted and might not know the good guys from the bad guys.

"She doesn't need any help," Annie's attacker said. "This woman is a hooker. She and her boyfriend set me up and were trying to rob me."

"He's lying!" Annie's dark eyes flashed a warning at her attacker. "He tried to kill me."

The two partially dressed men glanced from Annie to the two men, looks of confusion on their faces. Hell, just what he needed, Dane thought, a couple of good citizens wanting to do the right thing, but uncertain just what the right thing was. And one of the men was holding a gun, aimed right at him. He knew how dangerous a weapon was in the hands of a frightened, uncertain man with no training in matters such as this.

"Don't listen to anything they tell you," Annie's attacker pleaded. "They're a couple of con artists who tried to take advantage of me. Help me, please, before this man—"

Dane tightened his hold on the guy's neck, putting a stop to his lies. Too late, he realized his actions had given the good Samaritans the wrong message.

"Let him go," Boxer Shorts said. When Dane didn't obey instantly, he waved the gun around and repeated his order. "I mean it. Let him go."

"You don't realize what you're doing," Annie said. "This man—"

"Hush!" Silk Robe pointed his finger at Annie. "I don't want anyone else to say a word. Mister," he said to Boxer Shorts, "you hold that gun on those two men and I'll call the police. We'll let them sort this out. But for now, you two guys separate. Nobody's going to hurt anybody."

Reluctantly, Dane eased his hold on Annie's attacker, then when Boxer Shorts used his gun to indicate for Dane to release his captive, he took his arm from around the guy's neck. He couldn't take a chance on what Boxer Shorts would do. A man unaccustomed to using a gun might lose his cool and start firing.

"Thanks," Annie's attacker said. "You men probably saved my life."

Boxer Shorts took several tentative steps further into the room, then edged toward the bathroom to stand with his back to the wall. With his free hand, he motioned for Silk Robe to come on in.

"Call the police," he told the other man.

The attacker eased away from Dane. When Dane made a move to grab him, Boxer Shorts issued another order.

"Leave him alone, dammit!" Fear and frustration edged Boxer Shorts's quivering voice.

Dane could tell that Boxer Shorts was trying to keep everybody under surveillance, but with four people in various areas of the room, his attention was divided. The minute Silk Robe headed toward the nightstand, Annie's attacker made his move. By the time Boxer Shorts knew what was happening, the attacker had knocked him to the ground and fled from the room. The gun Boxer Shorts gripped so fiercely went off, sending a bullet straight up into the ceiling. Dane cursed under his breath.

"Call the damn police!" he shouted as he dashed out the door in pursuit of the attacker.

Annie issued Silk Robe a deadly but silent warning, then walked over, lifted the telephone receiver and dialed 9-1-1. His eyes wide with shock, Silk Robe slumped down onto the edge of the bed. Across the room, Boxer Shorts laid his gun on the carpet, stared at it as if it were a live grenade, then picked himself up off the floor.

Annie gave the police the pertinent details and was assured a patrol car in the area would be dispatched to the scene immediately and Lieutenant McCullough would be called at home and notified about what had happened. Annie replaced the receiver, then faced the two men who had botched their well-meaning rescue attempt.

"So, have you two geniuses figured out that you helped a criminal escape?" Annie crossed her arms over her chest and tapped her foot on the floor.

"I'm sorry," Silk Robe said. "But how were we supposed to know who was telling the truth? The big guy— your boyfriend? your husband?—seemed dangerous. I thought he was going to kill the other man."

"Mr. Carmichael is a former FBI agent. He came to my rescue earlier tonight when the man you let get away tried to kill me." Annie lifted her blouse and pointed to her bandaged side.

"We heard you scream the first time and this gentleman and I both came out of our rooms," Boxer Shorts said as he approached Annie. "When we didn't hear anything else, we decided maybe it had come from a television, so we went back to our rooms. But then when you screamed the second time, we both came back out into the hall and agreed that we should investigate."

"I know y'all meant well," Annie said. "But why do you think I'd be screaming, if I was trying to rob somebody?"

Silk Robe hung his head. "I don't guess we were thinking straight. But you've got to admit that the man—Mr. Carmichael—seemed to have the upper hand. We thought he was...well, it was an honest mistake."

Annie sighed. "The police are on their way. You two just stay put right here until they arrive." Annie headed toward the door.

"Where are you going?" Boxer Shorts asked.

"I'm going to find out if Dane caught that man!"

Leaving the two remorseful do-gooders seated, one on each bed, she walked out into the hallway and down to the elevators. Just as she punched the down button, the elevator doors swung open. Instinctively, she took a step backward and held her breath. Dane Carmichael glared at her as he emerged from the elevator.

"What happened?" Annie asked, the question gushing out on her released breath.

"He got away," Dane mumbled disgustedly. "I could see him ahead of me, until we reached the parking deck. Then he just disappeared. I searched every inch of the deck, but he was long gone."

"At least now I can give the police a description of him. That should help them track him down."

"Just how the hell did he get into your room in the first place?" Dane asked.

"I let him in," she reluctantly admitted.

"What?"

"He told me he was a policeman. He even showed me his badge." Annie rubbed her forehead. "I feel like such a dope."

Dane slipped his arm around her shoulders and pulled her to his side. "Don't beat yourself up about it, hon— Annie. My guess is the guy's a local hood. A hired gun. I doubt he'll be caught. Being so near the Gulf, he's got too many ways to escape."

"If he's just a hired gun, then he's not important, is he?" Annie allowed herself the luxury of leaning on Dane, of absorbing his strength. As much as she usually hated relying on a man—any man—she couldn't resist accepting the comfort and support Dane offered. "I mean, if the man who tried to kill me is just an employee, that means someone hired him. That's the person I have to unearth—the person who thinks I know what Halley knew.''

"Come on, let's go back to your room and wait for the police.'' Dane led her down the hall.

"I'm not expecting much from the local authorities,'' Annie said. "After all, they've got a very limited force and I'm sure they aren't accustomed to attempted murder cases or kidnapping or—''

"Don't go writing these guys off before you give them a chance. I have a feeling your lieutenant McCullough is going to pay attention to your suspicions now.''

Dane had been right. Lieutenant McCullough did pay attention to her suspicions and promised a full-fledged investigation into Halley Robinson's disappearance and an all-out manhunt for Annie's attacker. But she surmised that the lieutenant's sudden about-face had as much to do with his discovery that Dane Carmichael was a former FBI agent as to the actual events surrounding Halley's disappearance and the two attacks on her.

Annie checked the time on her wristwatch. Four thirty-eight. She'd had quite a night. One she hoped to never repeat. She kicked off her shoes and lay on the bed. Exhaustion claimed her body the moment she relaxed atop the quilted floral comforter.

Dane locked the door and secured the safety latch, then dropped his duffel bag on the floor. He paused by the bed, removed his hip holster and laid it on the nightstand. On their drive back from the police station, they'd stopped by the *Sweet Savannah* to pick up his things.

"I hated having to call Halley's parents from the police station. Her father didn't say so, but I know he blames me.'' Annie closed her eyes and let her body go limp. God, she was tired! Tired and angry and frightened. And her side ached unbearably. "I blame myself. If I hadn't given her a job on *Today's Alabama,* she'd be married to Jonathan Lyles Wilkerson IV, be a member of the Junior League and probably secretary of her mother's study club. And she'd be alive."

Dane remembered that Lorna had belonged to the Junior League and been the treasurer of her aunt's study club. And she had married Beauregard Dane Carmichael III.

"You don't know for sure that Halley's dead," Dane said.

"Yes, I do. You know it, too."

Dane flipped on the bathroom light switch. "Where's your medicine?"

"Over here in the nightstand drawer." When she turned and reached toward the drawer pull, excruciating pain took her breath away.

"Just lie still," Dane told her. "I'll get it." He turned on the sink faucet, filled a glass with water, brought it over and set it on the bedside table.

"I'm not used to someone waiting on me, taking care of me."

"Make an exception this time, Brown Eyes," Dane said. "I promise I won't think of you as a weak, helpless female."

While he jerked both pillows out from underneath the comforter and braced them against the headboard, he slipped his other arm around Annie and lifted her. He placed her in a semi upright position, then handed her the glass of water.

"You're very astute, Mr. Carmichael." Holding the glass in both hands, she tilted her chin and stared into Dane's bright blue eyes.

He grinned. "It wouldn't take a rocket scientist to figure out you're no helpless Southern belle or that once upon a time some guy made the mistake of trying to turn you into one."

Dane opened the nightstand drawer, pulled out the paper sack and dumped two small plastic bottles into his hand. After crumpling the sack, he tossed it across the room. It landed in the wastebasket by the dresser. Then he read the prescribed dosages, snapped open the lids, one at a time, and removed the medication.

He put the capsules in her hand. "One of each."

"I hate taking—"

He laid his index finger across her lips. "Hush up and take the medicine. It's no disgrace to admit you're in pain. Even big, tough guys like me have downed pain pills."

Without another word of protest, Annie popped the capsules into her mouth, gulped several sips of water and swallowed the medication. Dane took the glass out of her hand and set it on the table.

"Now, lie down, close your eyes and try to rest," he told her, then turned off the bedside lamp, leaving only the light from the bathroom to illuminate the room.

"What are you going to do?" she asked as she scooted down in the bed.

Dane leaned over, rearranged her pillows and slid his hand beneath her hips, lifting her just enough so that he could jerk the covers down to the foot of the bed. He helped her adjust into a more comfortable position, then pulled the sheet and blanket up to her waist.

"I'm going to try to get some shut-eye, too." When her gaze skipped past him and focused on the outer door, he gently grasped her chin. She looked up at him. "I'm a light sleeper. No one is going to get in here without my hearing them first."

She nodded, smiled weakly, and closed her eyes. Dane lay on the other bed. Lifting his arms, he placed his hands behind his head and stretched out. He glanced over at Annie. She was staring right at him.

"What's wrong?" he asked.

"Thanks for coming back to the hotel to check on me. If you hadn't come back, I might be dead now."

He didn't want to feel anything for this woman. Annie wasn't sweet and demure, as Lorna had been. Nor was she quiet-spoken and soothing to a man's nerves. But despite the fact that she was nothing like Lorna, didn't even come close to being his ideal woman, he was attracted to her on some basic, even primitive level. Something about her drew him to her, made him not only want to possess her, but to protect her, as well. He hadn't felt possessive and protective about a woman, in a personal sense, in years. Not since Lorna. But he had loved Lorna. She'd been his wife. Annie Harden was little more than a stranger. And although she begrudgingly accepted his protection, he suspected her independent nature would balk at ever being totally possessed by any man.

"I can postpone my vacation long enough to see you safely home," he said. "You might not be safe making the trip alone."

"I hadn't realized... You're right, though. Whoever hired that man to kill Halley and come after me, isn't going to give up. They have no idea that Halley didn't give me all the information about the story she'd uncovered."

"I suggest we take your rental car to the airport and fly back to... Where do you live anyway?"

"Florence. That's in the Shoals area. You know, the University of North Alabama. The Alabama Music Hall of Fame. And the birthplace of Helen Keller over in Tuscumbia."

Lorna's father lived in Florence now. At one time Dane and Richard had been as close as father and son. To this day he loved and respected the man who had served as a role model for him when he'd been younger. There was no man, other than his own father, whom he admired more.

Dane eased up, resting his jaw in his palm as he braced himself on his elbow. "One of my former father-in-law's companies is in Florence. He and his second wife have had a home there for years."

"Who is your father-in-law?"

"Richard Hughes. Do you know him?"

"Richard Hughes! I never knew he had a daughter. I know his son, of course. Dickie is CEO of Hughes Chemicals and Plastics. And Richard and my uncle Royce are business associates and golf buddies." Annie clicked her tongue against her teeth. Small world. No wonder Dane had reminded her of her father and ex-husband. If he'd once been married to Richard Hughes's daughter, then he had to be a part of *their* world. Her feminine intuition had been right on center. Dane Carmichael was a Southern gentleman, a member of the exclusive good ole boys' club. He and his kind represented what Annie hated most—men who still thought of women as possessions, and felt that those women should be grateful for their benevolent protection and submit happily to their rules and regulations.

"Richard took Lorna's death very hard." Even after ten years, Dane could barely bring himself to talk about Lorna's death. "I imagine he finds it difficult to remember and... Small world, isn't it, your knowing my father-in-law so well? If your family lives in Florence, I'm surprised that Lorna and I never met you when we visited her father there." *And I would have remembered you, Ms. Annie Harden.*

"I moved to Florence a few years ago," Annie explained. "I grew up in Chattanooga, and lived in Memphis for years. After my father died, my mother moved to Florence, her hometown, and I moved there so I could be close to her.'' So I could look after her, Annie thought. Her mother wasn't entirely helpless, but she was lost without someone to lean on, the way she'd leaned on her husband.

"I haven't seen Richard in years." Dane had kept in touch with Lorna's family for a while, but communication with them had seemed to cause them as much grief as it had him. Talking to each other, being around each other, always brought back memories of Lorna, especially memories of the way she had died. "I suppose I should drop in on him, after I see you safely home."

"Dane, I... It really won't be necessary for you to fly home with me. I was going to drive back, but now that I've told Halley's family... Well, you can just take me to the airport tomorrow and I'm sure I'll be safe enough on the flight into Muscle Shoals." Although she was grateful to Dane, perhaps even owed him her life, she knew he could be as dangerous as the man who had tried to kill her. She found Dane attractive, far too attractive. And she had one hard and fast rule: whenever she found a good ole boy Southern gentleman attractive, she ran like hell. After divorcing Preston, she had not only taken back her maiden name, but the right to live her own life—to make her own choices. Never again would any man run her life!

"And what about when you get home?" Dane asked. "You don't think you'll be out of danger then, do you?"

"What are you suggesting?"

"I'm suggesting that you need an investigator to help you find out what Halley Robinson knew and who wants you dead because of it. And I think you need a full-time bodyguard."

"Are you saying that I should hire you?" The effects of the painkiller began spreading through Annie's body, liquefying her bones and muddling her brain. "I can't have you around all the time. No way."

"I think you're confused, Brown Eyes. I'm one of the good guys. Remember?"

Dane eased up off the bed, stood and looked down at Annie. Her dark eyes challenged him. The defiant thrust of her chin dared him. Despite her attempt to warn him off, he sat on the edge of her bed, reached out and ran the back of his hand across her cheek. She shuddered.

A knot formed in the pit of his stomach. He couldn't remember the last time he'd wanted a woman so badly. And Annie wanted him. Her lips might deny it, but her small, luscious body gave her away. Dane knew the signs. Peaked nipples pressing into her bra and silk blouse. Flush spreading across her cheeks. Fire in her eyes. And her deep, labored breaths.

But, dammit all, he couldn't take advantage of her—not in her condition. She had a nasty gash in her side and the medication would put her to sleep soon.

"You can't go home with me." Annie's speech was already slightly slurred. "I can't handle you."

Dane chuckled. "You're getting loopy. The pain medicine must have already kicked in." He leaned over and kissed her on the forehead. "You're not going to have to *handle* me, Annie. Not tonight, anyway."

"That's good to know," she said. "I really like you. And I appreeze…appreshe…I'm thankful you were around to save my life. But you're bad for me, you know. Southern gentleman are always bad news."

"So *he* was a Southern gentleman, huh?"

"Mmm-hmm." Annie patted Dane's shoulder.

"Go to sleep."

She nodded her head and closed her eyes. Dane lay

down again, but it was more than an hour before he shut his eyes and another hour before he finally dozed off.

Dane lifted Annie's suitcase and his duffel bag from the floor and followed her out into the hallway. Taking short, quick steps, she headed for the elevators. They had been arguing for the past thirty minutes, ever since he'd mentioned flying to Florence with her. Annie Harden had to be, without a doubt, the most stubborn, mule-headed woman he'd ever had the misfortune to run across. He was beginning to think she really didn't know just how much danger she was in.

Annie jabbed the down button. Dane glanced up at the ceiling. She tapped her foot on the floor. He cleared his throat.

The elevator doors opened. Dane waited for her to enter, then stepped in beside her. She looked straight ahead, deliberately avoiding eye contact with him.

"I've got a good mind to buy a ticket and get on that plane with you, whether you want me to or not," Dane said.

She snapped her head around and glared up at him. "Don't you dare!"

Dane mumbled a few well-chosen obscenities under his breath. "Fine. I give up. Fly home alone. But I'm going to have Lieutenant McCullough get in touch with the Florence police department and have an officer meet your plane."

"Fine. Go right ahead. Have him notify the Alabama Highway Patrol, for all I care."

When the elevator doors opened, Annie stomped out into the mini-lobby of the Marina House, swung open the outer door and headed into the ground-level parking deck.

Dane caught up with her before she reached the blue rental car.

"Wait!" he called to her.

"Now what?" She paused, pursed her lips and narrowed her gaze.

"Leave the car here," he said. "We'll call a cab to take us to the airport."

"I have to turn this car in before I go home."

"I'll take care of it. Later."

Annie reached for the door handle.

"Don't open the door!" Dane dropped the suitcase and duffel bag to the concrete floor, then grabbed Annie and whirled her away from the car.

Chapter 4

"What's wrong with you?" Annie glared at Dane. "Have you lost your mind?"

Forcibly keeping her away from the car, Dane explained. "One of the simplest ways to kill somebody is to plant a bomb in their car."

Annie stared at him, disbelief in her eyes. "I thought...I mean, surely he didn't stick around last night, knowing the police might catch him."

"He could have come back later," Dane said. "But my guess is he sent someone else."

"God, I feel as if I've walked right into the middle of a spy novel and gotten myself involved with James Bond."

Dane released his tenacious hold on her. She relaxed against his side, her small frame just barely touching him.

"The name is Carmichael," he said with a straight face. "Dane Carmichael."

Grinning, Annie jabbed him in the arm. "So, why don't

you just check the car and see if there really is a bomb, 007?''

"A thorough inspection could take hours, but if you'd like, I could do a quick check in about fifteen minutes and eliminate the most likely places someone would have put a bomb."

"Maybe we should just call the police and—"

"We could leave the car here, call the police from the airport, and I could escort you home," Dane suggested, but could tell by the look on Annie's face that she wasn't going to agree.

"I need to know for sure, before I make any decisions," she said. "If there is a bomb, then you're right about my needing a bodyguard."

Dane sighed. Realizing there would be no use to argue with her, he reached inside his hip holster, pulled out his Ruger P95DC and handed it to her.

"I'm going to crawl underneath and take a look. You keep watch." He winked at her, then bent and slid under the car. "And remember that Ruger has an ambidextrous decocker."

Ambidextrous what? Oh, yes, she remembered now. He was talking about the safety mechanism on the gun. Why hadn't he just used plain English? Showing off, like most men!

"Dane?" Annie held her breath.

"What?"

"Are you in any danger under there?" she asked.

"Why do you ask?"

"Because if you are, I don't want you checking out anything. Do you hear me?"

"Look in my duffel bag and hand me my flashlight and mirror," he called from beneath the car.

After placing the gun on the top of the car, she followed

Dane's instructions. She retrieved the flashlight and mirror, then knelt on one knee. "I've got them."

Dane stuck out his hand for the objects. She laid the flashlight in his palm. Then he switched hands and motioned for her to give him the mirror.

Annie lifted the gun off the roof and began pacing back and forth along the side of her rental car. Although the weapon in her hand probably didn't weigh two pounds and was less than eight inches long, it suddenly felt large and heavy. She'd never owned a gun. Didn't even like guns. But she had to admit that if her life were threatened again, she didn't think she'd hesitate to use Dane's Ruger.

She couldn't believe what had happened to her in the past twenty-four hours. Her well-organized, neat little life was suddenly completely out of control. And Annie prided herself on being able to control every aspect of her life, on a daily basis. Being her own person, making her own decisions and, yes, even making her own mistakes, were of the utmost importance to her. Control had been an issue in her relationships with her father and her husband. Both had wanted her to be docile and sweet and obedient.

Minutes seemed like hours to Annie. Every sound, be it children's laughter from the nearby pool or the cry of gulls as they swooped down on the beach, was intensified by her nervousness. When a young couple entered the parking deck, she nearly jumped out of her skin. They didn't even notice her. They got into a little red sports car and zipped out of the deck and onto the circular drive.

Finally Dane emerged from beneath the car. He stood, brushed his hands off on his gray cotton slacks and tossed the flashlight and mirror into the open duffel bag Annie had left lying near the car trunk.

"So?" She handed him the gun. "Did you find anything?"

After slipping the Ruger into his hip holster, he grasped Annie by the shoulders. She stared up at him, her big brown eyes wide as saucers. "Yeah, I found something."

Closing her eyes for a split second, Annie bit down on her bottom lip and sucked in a deep breath. "A bomb?"

"Yes. And in one of the all-time favorite spots to put plastic explosives."

"Where?"

"On top of the gasoline tank, between the tank and the car body. There's hardly enough room there to even stick your finger."

"So what do we do now?" She hated having to depend on anyone, especially a man—and in particular, a man like Dane Carmichael. But she had little choice at this point. Whether she liked it or not, he was her rescuer, her protector, her only safe harbor in the storm that threatened to destroy her.

"We don't do anything." He ran his hands down the length of her arms, stopping when he gripped her wrists. "Except call the police."

Involuntarily, Annie began shaking from head to toe. Her breathing became erratic. Her heartbeat went wild.

Dane grabbed her face between his big hands. "Take some slow, deep breaths. Do you hear me? You're starting to hyperventilate."

Annie nodded that she understood and sucked in a deep breath, filling her lungs with air. Then she exhaled—a long, slow release. She repeated the procedure again and again, until a sense of calm prevailed. When her breathing and heartbeat returned to normal, she suddenly felt light-headed.

"I'm all right now. I... The reality of my situation just hit me," she said. "Someone *is* trying to kill me and they're not going to stop until they succeed."

"They're not going to succeed. I promise you." He took her hands in his. Lifting her clasped hands to his lips, he kissed first one and then the other. "We're going to find out who's behind Halley's disappearance and these attempts on your life."

"I can't believe all of this has happened because of some story Halley unearthed." Annie clung to Dane's big, strong hands, as if they were her lifeline. "*Today's Alabama* isn't the type of magazine that's ever dug up dirt or exposed scandals. We cover the human interest stories. What information could have been in that package Halley received that was so horrible she lost her life and put mine in danger? And how—"

"Let's take this one step at a time." Dane picked up her suitcase and his duffel bag in one hand, wrapped his arm around her waist and tugged her close to his side. "Come on. We'll go over to the *Sweet Savannah*. You can sit down or even lie down for a while and I'll put a call in to Lieutenant McCullough."

Annie nodded, then allowed Dane to take charge—of her and her life. She hated to admit, even to herself, how very glad she was to have Dane around at a time like this.

"Here, drink this." Dane shoved a shot glass into her hands.

She wrapped her fingers around the small crystal container and stared down at the strong-smelling bourbon. She wasn't much of a drinker. Wine occasionally. A Marguerita when she felt like celebrating. She wasn't surprised that Dane's drink of choice was bourbon. Good old Kentucky rye whiskey. A Southern gentleman's drink. It had been her father's favorite.

"You need something to settle your nerves and relax

you,'' Dane told her. "It's not going to hurt you and it just might do you some good."

"Regardless of what you think, I'm not a nervous wreck. I am not falling apart!"

Huffing in exasperation, Dane speared his fingers through his hair. "Dammit, woman, do you have to make everything a battle of wills?"

"All right, all right! I'll drink the blessed bourbon!" She downed the liquor in one swallow. The smooth whiskey burned a path from her throat to her belly, where it ignited a raging fire. She coughed uncontrollably for a couple of minutes, then blew out a hot breath. Tilting her chin haughtily, she cast a quick go-to-hell glance his way. "Now, are you satisfied?"

He nixed the first reply that came to mind. A highly inappropriate sexual response. Instead he said, "When you're ready to get off your high horse and discuss the situation reasonably, you can find me topside."

Annie turned her back on him, but she heard his heavy footsteps when he left her alone in the *Sweet Savannah*'s saloon. She crossed her arms over her chest, then winced when a twinge of pain rippled through her side.

He was treating her as if she were a child or, worse yet, a woman incapable of thinking or acting rationally, simply because she didn't want to follow his orders. From the time she'd been old enough to have an independent thought, she and her father had fought over her constant unruly behavior, her rudeness and her disobedience.

She had tried. God knows she had tried to please him, but in pleasing him, she'd had to go against her basic nature. He had loved her best when she'd agreed to marry Preston. The son he'd always wanted. A carbon copy of himself. And he had hated her the most when she had gotten a divorce. She didn't think he ever forgave her for that one major act of treason.

And Dane Carmichael was cut from the same cloth. He was a man who believed in taking care of his womenfolk and in making their decisions for them. He so obviously prided himself on his Southern chivalry.

Ever since Lieutenant McCullough had left, she and Dane had been arguing about the best course of action to take. From the time Dane had called the local authorities until the lieutenant had departed from the *Sweet Savannah,* Annie had been caught up in a whirlwind of emotions unlike anything she'd ever known. The lieutenant and Dane had agreed that Annie needed protection, that her life was in danger and another attempt on her life could come at any time. What they couldn't understand was how difficult it was for her to absorb and comprehend the nightmare proportions of the situation. In twenty-four hours, her world had made a hundred-and-eighty-degree shift—from safe, secure and sane to crazy, dangerous and unreal.

"I'm a highly trained professional," Dane had explained. "Believe me, Annie, if anyone can keep you safe and help you discover the truth, I can."

She didn't doubt for a minute that he was right. Didn't think he was exaggerating his skills as a bodyguard and an investigator, or that he was bragging when he told her about the high success rate the Dundee agency had had in similar cases. She wasn't an idiot. And she'd told him so— loudly and vehemently.

She was well aware of the fact that she needed both a bodyguard and an investigator. And she knew that if she couldn't afford the fee of a professional, her mother could. That was one thing a Southern gentleman always did—left his widow well provided for.

The problem wasn't that she disagreed with Dane's assessment of the situation or his solution. The problem was that she didn't want Dane Carmichael spending twenty-four hours a day with her, for God knew how long. But how could she make him understand, without admitting to him that she was afraid of him? Afraid of her attraction to him. Afraid of the way he made her feel. Afraid that she would succumb to the heady aphrodisiac of his protection.

Standing, Annie combed her fingers through her hair, adjusted her red blouse so that the buttons lined up in a straight row down the center of her chest and ran her hands over her hips to smooth the wrinkles in her white slacks. Taking a deep, steadying breath, she squared her shoulders and climbed the stairs up onto the deck.

She found Dane resting in the center of the wraparound seating on the flying bridge. He didn't stand when she approached, nor did he speak. In fact, he didn't acknowledge her presence in any way.

"May we talk?" she asked.

"Talk or argue?" He crossed his arms over his chest.

"Talk." She sat beside him and surveyed the hundred-square-foot deck. "This is a beautiful cruiser. My parents had one when I was growing up. My father was quite a fisherman."

"If your father were around now, he'd make sure you were safe."

Annie balled her hands into fists, then relaxed her fingers. "You're right about that," she said. "Earl Harden would have locked me in a golden cage, if he believed that was what was necessary to keep me safe."

Dane stared at her. Feeling the scrutiny in his hard gaze, she turned to face him. "But my father's dead and my ex-husband is out of my life and remarried, so I don't have a man to decide what's best for me."

"I didn't mean—"

"Yes, you did."

"I thought you said we weren't going to argue."

"We aren't," she said. "I came up here to apologize for being so bitchy and acting ungrateful. You can't help treating me the way you do. Hell, you were raised to be a gentleman."

"You say the word as if being a gentleman was a bad thing." Dane's voiced was tinged with just the slightest bit of aggravation.

"Sorry." Annie forced a smile. "I tried to apologize and wound up saying something bitchy again."

Dane stared at her. His look plainly said that the ball was in her court. The next move was hers.

"I need a bodyguard and an investigator." She paused, but when he didn't respond, she went on. "The only way to save my life is to find out what Halley discovered and who is afraid that information will become front-page news."

"Are you asking me to take the job?" Dane studied her face. Beautiful, in an exotic way. Dark. Earthy. Like a Gypsy.

The light springtime breeze blew her ebony hair across her face and into her eyes. When she brushed back the flyaway strands, their soft, natural waves fell behind her ear. Small gold hoops glistened in her earlobes.

"Yes and no," Annie said. "I'd like to hire someone from your agency."

"But not me."

"No, not you."

"I can call and have someone fly down tonight or first thing in the morning, at the latest. But until then, I'm afraid you're stuck with me."

"Thanks. I appreciate this so much, Dane. And I hope

you understand that not wanting you isn't anything personal, it's—"

He grabbed her so quickly that she cried out, startled by his actions. "Oh, it's personal, all right, and we both know it. You've got some bee in your bonnet about me being a Southern gentleman, which in your book must rank up there somewhere between being Jack the Ripper and Attila the Hun.

"Somebody...maybe your father...maybe your ex-husband...or maybe both of them did a number on you, *honey*." He emphasized the word and smiled when she flinched. "But I'll be damned if I'll take the wrap for them or apologize for being the kind of man I am."

She opened her mouth to speak, but he cut her off. "Strange thing is," he said, "until I met you, I had no idea that being a gentleman was such a terrible thing. Believe it or not, most women seem to like that about me." Dane released her as abruptly as he'd taken hold of her.

Annie closed her mouth. She could make a smart-ass comeback. She could give him her opinion of gentlemen. And she could tell him that her past relationships with her husband and her father were none of his business. Or she could try apologizing again.

As if reading her mind, Dane said, "Don't bother apologizing again. You have as much right to your opinion of Southern gentleman as I do of mule-headed feminists."

"I'm not a... What is your opinion of mule-headed feminists?"

"Let's just say they're not my type."

"What is your type?"

"A lady who enjoys being a woman and wants her man to act like a man. A lady who is gentle and caring and loving and—"

"Submissive and obedient." Annie finished his sentence.

"Now, Miss Annie, you're putting words in my mouth."

"You and I mix like oil and water," Annie told him. "If we spent a lot of time together, as we'd have to do if I hired you, we'd drive each other crazy."

Dane made a leisurely inspection of Annie, from head to toe, then focused his gaze on her face. "The reason we'd drive each other crazy is because we're attracted to each other. You're afraid of me, of the way I make you feel. And to be honest, I'm a little bit afraid of you, too."

Annie stared at him, her eyes wide, her mouth slightly agape. Warmth spread through her body like daybreak across the sky. Her nipples tightened. Her femininity clenched and unclenched, sending a tingling sensation radiating through her nerve endings. She wanted to make a vehement denial. But she couldn't. There was one thing Annie Harden didn't do—she didn't lie to herself.

"All right, so I'm afraid of this attraction thing we have going on between us," she admitted. "And being the smart woman that I am, I know better than to keep temptation within arm's reach twenty four hours a day."

Dane leaned toward her, just enough to bring them closer without actually touching. "Just how much of a temptation am I, Brown Eyes?"

Annie felt herself swaying toward him. No! Mentally, she put on the brakes and came to a screeching halt. "I'm not going to scratch your itch, Mr. Carmichael. Not now. Not ever."

Dane traced the lines of her lips with his index finger. She didn't move. Barely breathed. He circled her chin—twice—then slid his finger down her neck and into the exposed vee of her blouse. She sucked in her breath. He delved his finger deeper inside her blouse and discovered the perspiration between her full breasts. She quivered as desire sped the blood through her veins, pounding her heart and quickening her breath. Then he lifted his finger to his mouth and licked her musky sweat off the tip.

Annie moaned, the sound low and soft and just barely audible.

Dane stood. "I'll go put in a call to the office to see who's available to fly down tonight or in the morning." He turned and walked away.

Annie sat there for several minutes, completely unnerved by the intimacies Dane had taken. She could resist him, she told herself. Even if he were around all the time, she wouldn't let him bend her to his will.

But what's the point of taking any unnecessary chances? the voice of reason within her asked.

No point whatsoever, she conceded.

Annie sat on the flying bridge and waited for Dane to make his phone call in private. Besides, she needed a little time to cool off. The man was as lethal to her as poison. Taking a whiff of it might only make her a little dizzy, but consuming it would destroy her.

Dane emerged from below within five minutes. "Matt O'Brien can be here first thing in the morning. He's the only agent available, but Matt's a good man."

"Thank you for making the arrangements," Annie said, wondering if Dane was going to stay on the deck and not join her on the bridge.

"So, do we stay aboard the *Sweet Savannah* until morning, or do we see if the hotel has a vacancy?"

"Oh, that's right, you'll have to act as my temporary bodyguard, won't you?"

"I'm afraid so."

"I hate to delay your trip to visit your friends." Annie

got up, made her way down from the bridge and onto the deck.

"Another day won't matter."

"If we're stuck with each other until tomorrow, then why don't we just go ahead and sail off to—what's the name of the place where your friends live?"

"Their island is called Le Bijou Bleu," Dane said. "It's about an hour and half from here."

"They have their own island? Must be nice." Annie sighed dramatically. "If you don't think your friends would mind my staying overnight—"

"Actually, your coming with me to Le Bijou Bleu is a good idea," Dane said. "Whoever's after you won't be looking on Sam Dundee's private island. You'd be relatively safe there. I could have Matt meet us in Biloxi. It's a fairly short boat ride from the island to Biloxi."

"Then call your agent back and tell him to fly into Biloxi instead of here," Annie said.

If we go to Le Bijou Blue, we'll be in the company of other people, Annie thought. She and Dane wouldn't be spending the night alone together if they were in his friends' home. She would be safer on the island, not only from her would-be killer, but from Dane.

"Matt will have to bring you back to Point Clear," Dane said. "You'll have to start the investigation here before y'all head to Florence."

"I don't mind retracing my steps," Annie said.

Once again, as if he'd read her mind, he responded to her thoughts. "You think it's worth going a little out of your way in order not to have to spend the night alone with me."

She glared at him, her nose crinkling, her lips curving upward. "You're the one who said I'd be safer on Le Bijou Bleu."

"Safer from whoever wants to kill you." He eased his aviator sunglasses down his nose, just enough so that she could see his sky-blue eyes. "But not necessarily safer from me...or from yourself."

An hour later Annie balked when Dane insisted on familiarizing her with certain pertinent facts about the yacht. She knew the basics. What more did she need to know?

"This is the VHF radio." Dane showed her, then went on to explain how to turn on the set and dial in channels 16 and 9. "The calling sign numbers for the *Sweet Savannah* are taped right here on top of the set, along with a description of the boat."

Annie nodded. "Got it, Captain."

"Look, Miss Smarty Pants, if we're out at sea and something were to happen to me, you'll need this information in order to call for help and other information in case you need to take over for me."

Feeling duly chastised, she hung her head and looked as humble as she knew how to look. "You're right, Dane. Please continue."

"I'll write down the loran coordinates and compass headings and put them here near the VHF. Just in case."

"What are the odds that I'll have to call for help or wind up piloting this cruiser?" Annie asked. "You don't happen to have any medical problems you haven't told me about, do you?"

"As far as I know, I'm as healthy as a horse," he said.

Imagining just how healthy and strong his body was sent her mind off into the danger zone. When she felt her cheeks warm, she prayed they hadn't turned pink. She wasn't a woman who blushed easily, but her thoughts about Dane were down and dirty enough to make a sailor blush.

Annie laughed. Dane stared quizzically at her.

"Is this all?" she asked.

"I'll show you how to start the engines and—"

"I'm sure I know how to do that."

"All right. Do you know how to parallel the batteries, make sure the drive is down, and how to check that the kill switch lanyard is installed?"

"Oh, sure," Annie quipped. "Those three little items are part of my daily itinerary."

Dane smiled at her and her stomach did a silly somersault. Oh, God, she was in big trouble with this man. He was as wrong for her as Preston had been. Do you hear me? she silently asked her body. You may want him, you may even think he's good for me, but you're not going to get what you want. He's wrong for me. W-r-o-n-g.

"Did your father ever let you play skipper?" Dane asked.

"You're kidding, of course. Earl Harden would never allow a woman to pilot his yacht."

"Well, you should know that handling a boat is not like driving a car. I'll go over the basics. All you really need to know is enough to aim the boat toward shore."

"I think, with a little instruction, I could manage that."

"And I suppose you already know how to use the head properly, since you did spend time on a boat as a kid."

"Aye, aye, sir." Annie saluted him.

"You've got a smart mouth on you, Miss Annie."

She slipped her arm through his and smiled devilishly at him. "Come on, Captain, and show me where the lifejackets are stowed, and the flares, the fire extinguishers and the first-aid kit."

He did just that. And when he had completed his instructions and the tour, he led her up to the helm and asked her to start the engines.

"You want me to... Is this a test?" she asked.

"Not a test, just thought that, being the bossy, independent type, you might want to take us out to sea."

"You're going to let me take over the helm?"

"Weigh anchor and start the engines," he said.

She did. "Now what?"

He placed her hands on the wheel, positioned himself directly behind her, slipped his arms around hers and covered her hands with his. "Now we sail to Le Bijou Bleu."

Annie loved the new experience, the exhilaration of being at the helm as well as the sweet torture of being wrapped in Dane's arms. And even though it was Dane's knowledge that actually maneuvered the *Sweet Savannah* out of the harbor and into Mobile Bay, Annie didn't care. He had included her. Had instructed her in a task some thought was a man's domain. And he had respected her intelligence.

"There's something you might want to think about the next time you compare me to your father and your ex-husband," Dane said.

Cocking her head to one side to see Dane's face, Annie asked, "What's that?"

"Your father never taught you how to handle his yacht, did he? And I'll bet, if you ever sailed with your ex-husband, he never let you even touch the helm."

The truth of his statement jarred her like a sudden stop on a Ferris wheel. She felt suspended high in the air, rocking precariously back and forth, waiting for the downward spin to plunge her back to earth.

But for now she was safe. Safe in Dane's arms. Or was she?

Chapter 5

"Things didn't go as planned," he told his superior. "I'm afraid our man in Point Clear has let Ms. Harden escape, and the police are now involved."

"Is he in police custody?"

"No, he's too smart to get caught. I told him to get out of town and wait for further instructions."

"Did he find out how much she knows and just what she told the police?"

"No." He felt as if somehow this was his fault. That he shouldn't have sent a subordinate, no matter how capable, to dispose of Ms. Harden.

"Do we know where Annie is?"

"No. But we do know that she isn't alone," he said.

"What do you mean? She traveled to Point Clear alone, didn't she?"

"Yes, but it seems she's hooked up with some man. The same man who rescued her on the beach last night. He thwarted the second attempt to dispose of Ms. Harden, and it's my guess that he's the one who figured out there was an explosive device rigged to her car.''

"Find out who this man is!" Several deep breaths. Fury subsided. Calm returned. "Be discreet, as always."

"Leave everything to me," he said, trying to be as reassuring as possible. He knew how much was at stake, how much they had to lose. "From here on out, I'll take care of this matter personally."

Annie Harden was a beautiful woman, Dane thought. No doubt about it. Her spirit was as beautiful as her physical attributes, and those were numerous. Shiny, black silk hair framed a face of striking, well-proportioned features. Expressive brown eyes and thick, dark lashes. A nose perfect in shape and size. And a mouth so ripe and full and alluring that Dane's gaze lingered on the sweet temptation more often than it should have while they talked.

He enjoyed watching her, the wind in her hair, the sun on her face. He liked her laughter. Loud and throaty and genuine. She seemed totally carefree here on the *Sweet Savannah*, as if she didn't have a worry in the world. He was glad she had this chance to escape from the nightmare her life had suddenly become. He had intentionally said nothing about her situation during their cruise, wanting to give her these few stolen moments away from reality. But she had to know, as he did, the seriousness of her problems. The thought that someone was intent on killing Annie brought out the most primitive emotions in Dane. Feeling that protective, on a personal level, of a woman who was a client, albeit a temporary client, could lead to serious trouble—for Annie and for him.

Being such an independent little cuss, Annie no doubt liked to think of herself as totally self-sufficient. If he told her how possessive and protective he felt, she'd probably laugh in his face. She would assume his show of concern was some sort of macho come-on. Or even worse, just another of his Southern gentleman traits, for which she would condemn him.

It shouldn't bother him so much that she scorned him for being the kind of man he was. He'd always been rather proud of being raised with the values his father and all his predecessors had lived by. Generations of Carmichael men had set great store in honesty, loyalty and service to their country. And they had treated their women with the utmost respect, putting them on pedestals as objects to be honored and protected.

Perhaps the notion that a man should take care of his woman was a little outdated in this day and age, when many women were financially independent. But taking care of a woman meant a lot more than providing for her. It meant loving her, treasuring her, sharing with her and guarding her from all harm. And if necessary, it meant dying for her.

He'd been called a gentleman many times, by many people, and he'd always known they meant it as a compliment. Most women seemed fascinated by his good manners and protective attentiveness. Then again, Annie wasn't most women, a fact she'd made perfectly clear.

"How much farther to Le Bijou Bleu?" Annie asked.

"Are you sure you don't need anymore sunscreen?" Dane picked up the plastic bottle, doused a quarter-size blob in his hand and spread the white cream over his bare arms and face.

"No, thanks. I don't burn easily." She had inherited her deep olive complexion from her Italian paternal grandmother and from the Cherokee Indian ancestry, that, until recently, when it had become quite fashionable to have

Native American blood mixed with good Scotch-Irish, her maternal side of the family had long denied.

She wondered about Dane's ancestry. His eyes were the bluest blue she'd ever seen. His skin was as dark as hers, but she suspected that beneath his tan he was much fairer. From the sun streaks in his hair and the depth of his tan, she imagined he spent quite a lot of time outdoors.

"Do you spend most of your free time on the *Sweet Savannah?*" she asked.

"As a matter of fact, I haven't had this yacht out to sea in a long time."

"Then where did you get your tan?"

He hesitated momentarily, then said, "Working outside helping build houses."

She gave him a questioning look.

He cleared his throat. "Dundee employees support the Habitat for Humanity and volunteer some of their time to help build houses."

"Why did you hesitate to tell me?"

"Because I didn't want you to think I was trying to impress you."

"Hmm, modesty. An admirable trait for a gentleman."

Dane cut his eyes in her direction, trying to discern whether she was mocking him or giving him a compliment. From the expression on her face—a rather sweet, happy smile—he couldn't tell.

"We should arrive at Le Bijou Bleu in ten or fifteen minutes," he said.

"Are you sure your friends won't mind my staying overnight?"

"Sam knows that you're a client." Dane brushed some flyaway strands of hair from her face. "And Jeannie is the consummate hostess. She'll welcome you with open arms and… You'll love Jeannie. Everyone does."

"And just what does Mr. Dundee think about you and everyone else loving his wife?" Humor curled her lips into a warm smile.

"Sam's used to it by now." Dane grasped Annie's hand and pulled her toward the wheel. "Want to take us into Le Bijou Bleu?"

Grinning like a child who'd just been offered all the candy she could eat, Annie caressed the wheel, then gave Dane a gentle shove. Instead of swapping places with her, he pulled her over onto his lap. Squealing and squirming, she gave him a dirty look. He shrugged as if to say "I'm innocent." She knew she should scold him and get out of his lap immediately, but for the life of her, she could do neither. Dane could have spent the past hour reminding her of how much trouble she was in, how serious the threats on her life had been, but instead, he'd made their sail from Point Clear to the Dundee's island hideaway an adventure. He'd been funny and flirtatious and downright charming.

Annie settled onto Dane's lap, totally aware of the intimacy of her bottom nestled against his groin. The moment she stilled, she felt the bulge of his arousal. She closed her eyes, savoring the moment, then warned herself that she was a fool to give in to her feminine needs. She shouldn't be enjoying this—knowing how much Dane wanted her and well aware that he wouldn't make another move without her consent.

Dane struggled to control his traitorous body. He'd thought that the minute Annie became aware of how hard he was, she'd jump out of his lap and let him have it with both barrels. But she didn't. Instead, she settled against him and took charge of the helm.

Maybe she was trying to torment him. Maybe she was delighted by his discomfort. But maybe, just maybe, she

liked turning him on because she wanted him just as much
as he wanted her.

He longed to caress her hips, to slide his hands around
and dip them between her thighs. Just the thought of touching her in that way hardened him even more. Think about
anything except making slow, sweet love to Annie, he told
himself.

He wrapped his arms around her waist. "I hope you like
children," he said.

"What? Why?" The blood pounding in her ears obliterated every other sound. What reason did he have to ask
her if she liked children?

"Because Sam and Jeannie have two kids. A three-year-
old daughter and a two-month-old son."

"Oh, I like children just fine," Annie assured him. *As
long as they belong to other people.* One of the problems
early on in her marriage to Preston had been his insistence
that they have a child right away. She had thought she'd
made it perfectly clear to him, before their marriage, that
she didn't want to start a family for several years. She
wanted to get her career off the ground first, before she
tried to juggle a job and motherhood. Preston hadn't been
understanding. In fact, he had used her reluctance to have
a child against her every time they had an argument, thus
turning any dispute, even those caused by his philandering
habits, into a battle over parenthood.

"Do you like kids?" she asked Dane.

"Yeah, I like kids a lot."

"You don't have any, do you?"

"No, I don't have any," he said.

She wanted to ask him why not, after all, he'd been
married. But if she asked him, then he'd have every right
to ask her, and that was one discussion she'd prefer not to
have.

"What about brothers and sisters?" Annie asked, turning the subject away from why neither of them had any offspring.

"Two younger sisters," Dane said. "Both happily married, with two children each. What about you?"

"I was an only child."

Her mother had gone through five agonizing miscarriages, each one more emotionally difficult than the last. She'd never understood why her mother had put herself through the torment, time and again. Not until, after the last miscarriage, Annie had overheard her father and uncle talking. She was twelve years old when she'd learned to what lengths some men would go to have a son.

"If only she hadn't lost this one," Earl Harden said. "It was a boy, you know. My son."

Royce placed his hand on Earl's shoulder in a consoling gesture. "I'm sorry, Earl. So sorry."

"The doctors say that we shouldn't try again. Jennifer's not up to another pregnancy, either physically or emotionally."

"Be thankful that you have Annie," Royce said. "Some people, like Vera and I, aren't blessed with even one child."

"I wanted a son. Why couldn't the one child who lived have been a boy?"

Earl Harden cried. His big shoulders shaking as he mourned the loss of his most treasured dream.

That had been the one and only time Annie had ever seen her father cry. He had never known that she'd been standing just outside the partially closed door of his study the day he shared his grief with his brother-in-law.

Shaking off the painful memory, Annie turned her face

to the sun. She loved being outdoors, and suddenly realized how much she missed spending time on the water. Maybe when she got home she'd talk to her mother about bringing her father's old boat out of dry dock and—

What was she thinking? When she returned to Florence, it would be with a bodyguard in tow and a would-be killer on her trail.

"Dane?"

"Hmm?"

"Is Matt O'Brien very good at what he does?"

Dane ran his hands up and down Annie's arms. "If he wasn't, I wouldn't have hired him in the first place. We employ only the best. Dundee agents are the cream of the crop."

"That's good to know."

Releasing her arms, Dane thought; *Matt's good, honey, but I'm better. And if I had my way, I'd be the one going home with you tomorrow. I'd be the one putting myself between you and danger.*

Fifteen minutes later they docked the *Sweet Savannah* in a small, snug harbor, alongside two smaller crafts. The clouds moved across the sky, blocking the sun and creating a gray overcast.

"Wait here on the aft deck," Dane told her. "I'll go below and get our bags."

She surveyed what she could see of the island, lush and green in all its springtime glory. The beach spread out before her and the blue-gray Gulf waters met the azure sky behind and around her. Pearl-white sand covered the beach.

Dane has brought me to a tropical paradise, she thought.

As her gaze traveled across the beach, she saw a curving set of rock steps leading to the hill above. She gasped loudly. Loping downward, his huge feet pounding the sturdy steps, was a bald man the size of an eighteen-wheeler. His mahogany skin was weathered, but Annie couldn't tell how old he was. She had the oddest notion that the man was ageless.

"Ready?" Dane came up on deck, her suitcase in one hand, his duffel bag in the other. When Annie didn't respond, he followed her line of vision and laughed. "Don't let him frighten you. That's Manton. He's in charge of Le Bijou Bleu and he's one of Jeannie Dundee's adopted fathers."

"He's enormous."

"About seven feet tall." Dane gave her a gentle nudge, using the end of his duffel bag to prod her into movement.

By the time they disembarked, Manton was on the beach, waiting for them. He neither smiled nor spoke, simply nodded and took the bags from Dane.

As they followed him up the ancient curved stairway, Dane placed his hand in the small of Annie's back. She glanced over her shoulder and smiled at him.

"He's not very friendly, is he?" Annie whispered her question.

"Manton is a deaf mute," Dane explained. "You can talk to him, if you know how to sign…or if you have a telepathic link to him the way Jeannie does."

"Oh, he's deaf." As she gazed up at the giant's broad back, a shudder racked Annie's body. "What do you mean, a telepathic link?"

"That's something else you need to know before you meet the Dundees—Jeannie is an empath and a telepath."

"You're kidding?" Annie considered most empaths, telepaths and psychics to be phonies. However, during her days as a Memphis reporter, she'd met a so-called psychic who, from time to time, worked with the police department. The woman had been unerringly accurate in her visions.

When they reached the top of the hill, Manton proceeded, his heavy, pulverizing footsteps lumbering ever forward. Dane grabbed Annie's arm and pulled her to an abrupt halt. She drew in her breath when she looked out over the wide, grassy meadow and her gaze caught a glimpse of the two-story, raised French cottage that lay a quarter of a mile ahead. The old house, circled with porches that were edged with banisters, had been built on a rise, giving its owners views of the ocean from every direction.

After a trek across the spacious, verdant lawn, they reached the house. An assortment of dogs and cats greeted their approach. Manton disappeared inside as a big, blond man came out and stood on the veranda. He threw up his hand and waved. Within minutes, a woman, with a cane in her hand, emerged from the house, an infant braced against her chest and a towheaded child at her side.

"Welcome to Le Bijou Bleu," the woman said, a welcoming smile on her pretty face.

Dane shook hands with Sam Dundee and hurriedly introduced Annie to the man and his wife. "And this little lady, tugging on her mama's shirttail is Samantha."

The girl, a tiny, feminine replica of her large, rugged father, looked up and smiled. She pointed to the baby in her mother's arms. "His name is Manton Julian Dundee, but we call him M.J.," she informed them. "He's named after PaPa Manton and Grandfather Julian. He's only two months old, so all he does is cry and eat and make a mess in his diapers."

The four adults laughed in unison and Samantha Dundee beamed happily, knowing she had secured their attention.

"Won't you come inside, Ms. Harden?" Sam held open

the door. "We need to go over some particulars of your case so that we can set the wheels of our investigation in motion before Matt meets you in Biloxi tomorrow."

"Sam, can't that wait," Jeannie said. "I'm sure Annie would like to freshen up and have dinner before you and Dane interrogate her."

"I don't mind—" Annie said.

"No, Jeannie's right," Sam said. "As always."

The expression in Sam Dundee's eyes when he looked at his wife said more than words could ever express. Here was a man totally besotted with a woman and didn't care who knew it. A strange, little ache gripped Annie's heart. What would it be like, she wondered, to have a man love you like that?

When they entered the foyer, Manton emerged from the staircase that led to the ground level of the house. Jeannie offered her infant son to the silent giant.

"Please take M.J. and Samantha to the nursery," Jeannie said. "You can let Samantha help give her brother his evening bath."

Without so much as a whimper, the little girl followed her "PaPa Manton." Jeannie turned to her guests.

"Sam, I'm sure you and Dane can find something to do while I show Annie to her room." She laced her arm through Annie's and led her toward the staircase. "Our guest rooms are on the ground level. Manton has placed your bag in the Sunlight Room."

Following her hostess's lead and being careful to keep her own gait in step with Jeannie Dundee's hampered walk, Annie descended the stairs. "It's awfully nice of you to welcome me this way. I suppose I actually invited myself, but I didn't want to delay Dane's vacation and he wouldn't leave me and—"

"And you are much safer here on Le Bijou Bleu than

you will be in Point Clear or back at home." Jeannie gave Annie's arm a reassuring squeeze. "You must trust Dane, you know. Unlike other men in your life, he will never hurt you nor disappoint you."

Annie jerked away from Mrs. Dundee and stared at her with wide, suspicion-filled eyes. "How did you know... Dane told me that you are an empath and a telepath, but I have to tell you that I really don't have a great deal of faith in any of that hocus-pocus stuff."

Jeannie laughed, the sound pure and sweet. She gazed sympathetically at Annie. "I have nothing to gain by lying to you, in pretending to have abilities that I don't."

"I'm sorry. I'm being terribly rude, aren't I?"

"You're being honest, not rude."

Jeannie limped only slightly as she made her way down the hall, then stopped in front of an open door and waited for her guest. Annie squared her shoulders, walked quickly to catch up and breezed into the room. She halted the moment she entered, realizing that this wasn't just a room, but a suite, which extended the width of the ground floor. Windows on all sides, except the north side, wrapped around the sitting room and the bedroom, which lay just beyond the open French doors. Annie noticed her suitcase resting at the foot of the massive cherry four-poster bed.

"Please, make yourself at home," Jeannie said. "Dinner will be ready in about two hours, but feel free to join us upstairs whenever you like."

"Thank you." When Jeannie turned to leave, Annie took a tentative step toward her. "Wait."

Jeannie turned to face Annie, who immediately reached out and grasped Jeannie's hand. An odd sensation struck her and suddenly she felt an inexplicable sense of something releasing inside her. Fear. Guilt. Uncertainty. All melted away like winter snow at the first touch of spring-time sun.

"What did you do?" Annie asked. "I felt it, but... It's as if you... I can't explain it."

"It's as if I took away all your worries." Jeannie clasped Annie's hand tightly, then released it. "The effect isn't permanent. Just a temporary remedy." Jeannie turned and walked out into the hall, paused briefly and said, "Even a strong woman needs a man, one who is equally as strong."

Annie stood in the middle of the room, silent and un-moving, until Jeannie disappeared up the stairs. What an unusual woman, Annie thought, and for the first time since her early childhood, she felt totally carefree and at peace. No unhappiness. No fear. No pain.

After removing the soiled bandage on her side, Annie took a shower and reapplied a sterile dressing, then she blow-dried her hair and slipped into clean underwear. Re-laxed and sleepy, she turned down the covers on the four-poster. Once she'd taken a short nap, she put on a pair of black slacks and a beige silk blouse. Then she applied a light coating of makeup, neatly rearranged the rumpled bed linen, and headed out the door. Checking her watch, she noted that she'd spent nearly two hours in the suite.

When she reached the top of the staircase, she heard voices coming from the front parlor, a spacious room with soft white walls. Entering the room quietly, she found Dane and Sam, drinks in their hands, standing in front of windows facing the veranda. Jeannie sat demurely in one of the cream damask Victorian chairs on the other side of the room. As her gaze scanned the room, Annie noticed a gleaming black baby grand and wondered who played.

"Manton plays," Jeannie said as if she'd read Annie's

thoughts. "Please come and join us. We can go in to dinner whenever you're ready."

"Oh, I hope y'all haven't been waiting for me."

"You're right on time," Jeannie assured her.

Dane moved in beside Annie and draped his arm around her shoulders. "Sam and I have been discussing your case."

"I wish we didn't have to think about that now." Annie heard herself say the words, but knew the sentiment wasn't her own. She'd never been the type to pretend everything was all right when it wasn't. "But I'm sure we need to talk about it. Have you and Mr. Dundee come to any brilliant deductions?"

"I think we can postpone business until after dinner," Jeannie said. "Come this way." She gave her husband a beguiling smile.

"Business talk after dinner," Sam agreed.

The dinner postponement turned out to be a three-hour event. The meal itself took thirty minutes, then coffee and dessert were served on the veranda. Jeannie and Sam excused themselves for twenty minutes to put their little ones to bed, but returned to share Manton's speciality drink with their guests. The fruity concoction was a secret blend, Jeannie told them. Annie could taste pineapple and rum, but try as she might, she couldn't quite make out the other ingredients.

The foursome sat on the veranda in huge wicker chairs. Annie couldn't remember a time in her life when she'd been more relaxed and content. It was all Jeannie Dundee's doing—her hocus-pocus magic touch.

Piano music drifted outside, something powerful and beautiful, but completely alien to Annie. She'd never heard the piece before and asked Jeannie about it.

"Manton is a composer," Jeannie explained. "That's one of his sonatas."

"But if he's a deaf mute, then how can he... No, don't bother answering that. It's a magical, supernatural thing, isn't it? Just like your abilities."

Sam and Dane both chuckled, the sound drifting off on the night breeze. Jeannie rose from her chair to bid them good-night. Dane and Sam stood immediately, and Annie couldn't help but wonder if there wasn't a touch of Southern gentleman in Mr. Dundee. Jeannie paused at her husband's side. He leaned down so that she could whisper something in his ear.

"I'll say good-night, too." Sam shook Dane's hand and then nodded to Annie.

"What about discussing my case?" Annie asked.

"Dane is in charge of your case, until Matt takes over tomorrow. You can discuss things with him." With that said, Sam left them alone on the veranda.

"That wasn't very subtle, was it," she said. "Their leaving us alone." Annie looked up at Dane, who had braced his hip on the banister and was gazing out at the ocean.

"Did it ever occur to you that they weren't thinking about us, that they were the ones who wanted to be alone?"

Annie rose from the chair and glided down the veranda toward Dane. "I don't think I've ever seen two people so much in love. It's almost painful watching them, knowing—" She stopped herself, realizing what she'd almost said. What the hell was wrong with her? It wasn't like her to get all sentimental and romantic. She'd outgrown that girlish hogwash a long time ago.

"Knowing what?" Keeping his back to her, he glanced

over his shoulder. "That you'll never love or be loved that way."

She swallowed hard. He had known what she was going to say and finished her sentence for her. "Yes."

"This island does strange things to people," Dane said. "Makes you start thinking all sorts of odd things."

Annie moved closer, as if drawn to him by some powerful magnet. She longed to reach out and touch his broad shoulders, to lay her head on his back and wrap her arms around him. She could almost feel the loneliness in him— a loneliness so great it was palpable. He turned slowly, his gaze fixed on her eyes, and she wondered if he could sense her loneliness the way she had his. Could he read in her eyes what she felt?

Dane reached out and grasped her face with both hands. She held her breath as his head descended. When he pulled her toward him, she closed her eyes, desperately wanting what she knew he was going to do to happen. Wanting it in a way she had never wanted anything else. The air between them was so hot and heavy, neither of them could breathe properly. Tension spiraled higher and higher, like a live wire ready to ignite a spark that would set the world on fire.

His lips were warm and moist and demanding. If she had struggled, he would have released her. But she didn't struggle. She participated. Willingly. Wholeheartedly.

She had no idea exactly when she wrapped her arms around him and pressed her body into his. She only knew that as he deepened the kiss, she wanted it to last forever.

They stood under a tropical moon, with a cool, June breeze drifting in off the ocean, and devoured each other with the hunger raging inside their bodies. When Dane lifted her off her feet, she draped her arm around his neck.

"Are you sure you want to do this?" he whispered in her ear.

If only he hadn't spoken, if only he hadn't left the decision up to her, they would have become lovers. She shuddered when reality severed the sexual chain that bound them.

A fragile smile trembled on her lips. He eased her down his body, allowing her to feel his erection, then set her on her feet.

"We never got around to discussing my case," she said.

"We can do that tomorrow when I turn you over to Matt." Dane shoved his hands into the pockets of his slacks.

"Yes, of course." Annie hesitated for a split second, a part of her somehow still connected to Dane—an invisible cord that tied her to him. "Good night."

"Good night, Annie. Sleep well." He turned away from her and faced the ocean again.

She left him there on the veranda. Only when she entered the house did she realize that Manton was still at the piano, the tune he played, soft and melancholy. She paused, looked back onto the porch where Dane stood, then ran to the stairs and hurried down to the ground level. Once inside her suite, she closed and locked the door, then rushed into the bedroom and threw herself onto the bed.

Annie cried. Cried as if her heart would break. She hadn't cried over a man since the first time she discovered that Preston had been unfaithful. But this was different. She had loved Preston, had been his wife. They had shared a life together, had made plans for the future together. Dane Carmichael was little more than a stranger. They had no past and no future. What she felt for Dane wasn't love. It couldn't be love!

Chapter 6

"**D**amn!" Dane slammed the receiver down on the telephone.

"What's the problem?" Sam asked.

"Matt O'Brien was in a minor car wreck last night. He's got some cracked ribs, a broken leg and—" Dane released an exasperated breath. "And he's the only agent who isn't on a case, other than Denby, and she agreed to man the office so I could take a vacation. There's no one else free and probably won't be for another couple of weeks."

"Looks like you'll have to refer Ms. Harden to another agency."

"I could take her case myself."

Yeah, Carmichael, you do that. You take this case yourself and you know what will happen. You almost made love to Annie last night. If she hadn't come to her senses in time, you'd be in her bed right now.

"Let someone else take this case. You badly need a vacation," Sam told him.

"I need to keep Annie safe," Dane said.

Sam placed his hand on Dane's shoulder. "If I gauged the lady correctly, I'd say she'll throw a fit when you tell her that you're taking the case. That one isn't going to give in without putting up a fight."

"Did you know that she thinks being a gentleman—a Southern gentleman—is similar to being a devil with a couple of horns and a forked tail?" Dane chuckled, the sound edged with indignation.

"Just the woman for you, huh?" Sam laughed, but gave Dane's shoulder a sympathetic squeeze.

"Don't you know it," Dane said. Annie Harden had none of the qualities he usually found appealing in a woman. She was the exact opposite of Lorna. But there was something about Annie that excited him in a way no other woman ever had. Maybe it was that hint of vulnerability beneath all the I-am-woman-hear-me-roar attitude.

"When are you going to tell her?" Sam asked.

"Tell her what—oh, about Matt not being available." Dane shrugged. "No time like the present."

"I think she and Jeannie are in the nursery with the children."

Dane nodded, then headed out of Sam's study. "Why do I feel as if I'm about to go into battle."

Sam's husky laughter followed Dane down the hallway. He stopped outside the nursery door, which stood wide open. Jeannie rested in a white wicker rocking chair, her son at her breast, and Annie sat on a large oval rug in the center of the nursery, Samantha Dundee at her side. Little Samantha turned the pages in the book Annie held as Annie read to her all about farm animals.

Why was it that all nurseries had that sweet baby scent—infant purity laced with powder and lotion? Dane wondered. When he'd visited his sisters while their chil-

dren were young, their nurseries had smelled like this. And
what was it about women caring for children that gave a
man the sense that all was as it should be, that all elements
in the universe were harmoniously aligned? Annie would
certainly consider that a male chauvinist thought.

Annie probably had no idea how she looked sitting there
in Mother mode. She appeared comfortable, relaxed and
perfectly natural in the role. A sudden, unbidden image of
a pregnant Annie flashed through his mind. He vanquished
the image as quickly as it had materialized.

"You'd make a wonderful mother," Jeannie said. "Samantha has certainly taken to you."

"I like children," Annie admitted, then ruffled Samantha's blond curls. "And I especially like this young lady."

Samantha giggled and scooted closer to Annie. "I like
you, too."

"Have you ever thought of remarrying and having some
children of your own?" Jeannie asked.

"Oh, I've thought about it," Annie said. "And I've
come to the conclusion that neither husband nor children
are for me. My career is very important to me and I'm
afraid marriage and motherhood would bore me to tears."

Dane felt as if he'd been sucker punched. For a couple
of minutes he couldn't seem to find his equilibrium. Why
the hell did Annie's statement bother him so much? He
barely knew the woman. They'd met only thirty-six hours
ago. What difference did it make to him that the idea of
marriage and motherhood bored her?

Dane treaded quietly down the hall, needing to get away
before Annie and Jeannie were aware of his presence. He
had to have a few minutes alone to sort out why he'd
overreacted. No big deal, he told himself. Nothing to sort
out. It's just that he thought it unnatural for a woman not
to want marriage and motherhood. Annie's attitude went

against everything he had grown up believing in—everything he still held true.

That was all there was to it. Nothing personal. Just a gut reaction. He'd have felt the same way if he'd heard any woman make the comment.

"I'd never think of marriage and motherhood as boring." Jeannie caressed her son's head as he lay at her breast, nursing greedily. "Being married to Sam and raising a family together fulfills me as nothing else ever could, not even the most successful career. But then, that's me."

Annie understood that it was true for Jeannie Dundee and countless other women like her. But her own disastrous marriage had left her gun-shy. And having a child without having a husband wasn't something she'd ever considered.

"I need my career," Annie said. "Perhaps 'bored' was the wrong word. It's just that I wouldn't be happy and completely fulfilled without my career, no matter how many children I had."

"Or how wonderful your husband was?"

"Daddy's wonderful, isn't he?" Samantha beamed as she looked to her mother to confirm her comment.

"Yes, sweetie, your daddy is wonderful."

"I suppose, if I were honest…it's not that I don't want a child." Annie chose her words carefully, hoping anything negative she had to say about men in general wouldn't affect Samantha's hero-worship of her own father. "My father was very overbearing and so was my ex-husband. Our relationships were doomed because I wouldn't conform to their wills. I had a mind of my own and I used it."

"All men aren't like your father and husband," Jeannie said.

"I suppose not, but I'm not willing to take that chance."

"You think Dane is like that?"

"I know he is. Good Lord, Jeannie, he's a prime example of a Southern gentleman. And believe me, I won't allow anyone to drag me back into the type of life-style I hated."

Jeannie smiled sadly, her eyes filled with compassion. Annie couldn't bear the other woman's sympathy. She handed Samantha the book, stood hurriedly, and said, "Please, excuse me. I need to pack and get ready to leave."

"Of course, you go right ahead." Jeannie motioned for Samantha to come to her. "I'll see you before you leave. To say goodbye."

Annie rushed out of the room, trying to escape Jeannie's tender concern. She didn't want anyone to feel sorry for her, least of all this kind, gentle woman, who had somehow cornered the market on happiness.

Just because Jeannie is blissfully happy as a wife and mother doesn't mean you would be.

Halfway down the hall, she ran straight into Dane. The unexpected collision threw them both temporarily off balance. Dane grabbed her shoulders in an effort to steady himself and her. They stared into each other's eyes. Boldly. Hotly. The uncertainty of their feelings and of the moment itself robbed them of rational thought.

Finally, after endless moments of silence, Dane released her and said, "Are you all right?"

"Yes." She took a deep breath. "I'm fine. How about you?"

"Yeah, fine."

"I was just going downstairs to get ready to leave for Biloxi."

"Annie…" Dane paused, reluctant to tell her about

Matt's accident. "There's no need to rush. Matt O'Brien was in a car wreck last night and he's in the hospital with some cracked ribs and a broken leg."

"Oh, I'm sorry. I suppose that means a delay in sending someone down here."

"There is no one to send," Dane told her. "All the Dundee agents are on other cases."

"Oh." Annie's mind tried to assimilate the information and its ramifications. The main thing she understood was that she didn't have a bodyguard or an investigator.

Dane noticed her frown, the worry wrinkles lining her forehead and the dejected slump of her shoulders. "It's all right. I'll take the case and we can return to—"

"You can't take the case!" Annie said, near hysteria in her voice. "I don't want you!"

"I realize that, but you don't have any choice. It's me or nobody." He wasn't going to give her the option of hiring someone from another firm. Dundee Private Security and Investigation was the best and that's what he wanted for Annie—the best.

Leaning back against the wall, she closed her eyes and sighed. "Damn!"

"I'll put in a call to Lieutenant McCullough to find out if there's anything new there, then if necessary, we can dock at Point Clear, check things out and then either drive or fly to Florence."

Annie opened her eyes and faced him.

"How long will it be before there's another Dundee agent free?"

"At least a week, maybe two. Why?"

"I'll agree to your taking the case, if…and this is an important *if*…you'll turn over the case to another agent as soon as possible." She realized she could go to another agency and not wait for a Dundee employee to become available. Her common sense told her that was exactly what she should do. But she couldn't bring herself to sever ties to Dane and the agency he headed. As irrational as it seemed, even to her, she felt a bond with Dane, and thus with his agency. He had saved her life more than once and that alone made her trust his abilities.

Dane didn't flinch, didn't show any response, but she sensed his anger. He wasn't a fool, she told herself. He had to know the reason she didn't want him as her body-guard, at least not on an indefinite basis. He had to be as aware as she was that the sexual electricity between them was powerful enough to light up a whole city. If they ever acted on their desire, the end result could be lethal for both of them.

"Fine." Dane snapped the word out quickly. "I'll get our bags and we can set off for Point Clear after I call McCullough."

"Then we have a deal?" Annie asked.

Dane held out his hand. "Yes, we have a deal. I'll take the case on a temporary basis, only until another agent is free."

Annie accepted his hand, shook it and released it as quickly as possible. Touching him was something she had to avoid from now on. In the days ahead, she would have to remember not to get too close and allow temptation to lead her astray.

Once they entered the police station, Annie ran directly into the young man's arms. Tall, lanky, and wearing a pair of gold-framed glasses, the guy looked to be in his mid-twenties.

Dane hesitated before he moved inside, crossed the room and stood at Annie's side.

"Oh, Clay." Annie patted the man's back, her actions

that of a friend giving comfort. "When did you arrive? How much have they told you?"

"I flew in this morning," Clay said. "Mr. and Mrs. Robinson were too upset to come down, so I'm acting on their behalf."

"Calling Halley's parents was one of the most difficult things I've ever had to do," Annie said. "But after three attempts were made on my life, I knew I had no choice but to let them know that Halley was missing."

"Somebody tried to kill you?" Clay's eyes widened in shock.

"If it hadn't been for Mr. Carmichael—" Annie nodded toward Dane "—coming to my rescue, I might be dead now."

"Mr. Carmichael?"

"Dane Carmichael." He held out his hand. "I'm CEO of Dundee Private Security and Investigation. Ms. Harden has hired me to take this case—protecting her and investigating Ms. Robinson's disappearance."

Clay shook hands with Dane. "You don't think the police can find Halley?"

"Even if they can find her, they don't have the manpower to investigate the story she was working on," Annie said. "And unearthing the details of that story may be the only way to find her killer."

Clay's face paled. "She can't be dead."

"I'd give anything if—" Annie said.

Lieutenant McCullough came through the open door, a coffee mug in his hand. He nodded to Dane, then said, "Won't you have a seat, Ms. Harden?" He gestured toward a chair across from his desk. "I'll fill y'all in on what we know at this point."

Annie sat. Clay stood. Dane eased into position behind

Annie's chair. McCullough perched on the edge of his desk.

"The last anyone saw of Ms. Robinson, she left the Grand Hotel with a man and they seemed to be on friendly terms," the lieutenant said. "We found the man. He's still at the resort. It seems he was a college friend she hadn't seen in years. Jarrod Fines." McCullough checked his notes. "The two went over to Foley for lunch that day and Mr. Fines says that Ms. Robinson stopped by the post office and mailed a package."

"To whom?" Annie asked.

"Mr. Fines told us that she said she wanted to send her boss a little gift."

"A gift for me?" Annie asked.

"You didn't receive anything in the mail from Ms. Robinson before you left home, did you?" McCullough asked.

"No, nothing, but maybe something came after I left."

"Mr. Boyd got in touch with your mother this morning and she told him that no packages came for you yesterday or today." McCullough eased off his desk. "I want to apologize for not taking your concerns more seriously when you first came to me day before yesterday, but we don't have much crime around here and—"

"Did Ms. Robinson mention anything to Mr. Fines about a story she was working on?" Dane asked.

"He said that they just reminisced about old times and about how surprised he was that she wasn't married and raising a family. She told him that—" McCullough checked his notes again "—she loved being a reporter, that she wouldn't have her exciting career if it hadn't been for the encouragement and help of her boss, Ms. Harden."

"But nothing about a special story?" Dane prodded.

"Only that she told him he shouldn't be surprised if her name became a household word in Alabama pretty soon."

McCullough flipped his notepad closed. "We picked up Ms. Robinson's suitcase and computer from the hotel. The maid took the items to the manager once they realized Ms. Robinson had left without checking out."

"Anything in her suitcase or on her computer to give you a clue as to what happened to her?" Dane asked.

"Nothing." McCullough sat behind his desk. "There were no fingerprints on the computer or the suitcase. Somebody wiped both clean as a whistle. The computer had been erased—completely. Every program on the thing was gone and all the files. The only thing we found in the suitcase, other than clothes and toiletries, was this key." McCullough opened his desk drawer and brought out a plastic bag. "Mr. Boyd has identified it as the key to a lake cabin owned by Ms. Robinson's family."

"Halley and I went up there sometimes for a weekend, and occasionally she went up there alone when she was working on a story."

Clay Boyd swallowed, then huffed out a calming breath as moisture coated his eyes. "What the hell has happened to her? Who would want to hurt Halley?" He turned his gaze on Annie. "How could a story for the magazine have endangered her life? Lieutenant McCullough told me that you think somebody killed Halley because of a news story. How is that possible?"

Annie tensed. Clay hadn't meant for his question to sound accusatory, but that's the way she'd heard it. Her guilty conscience kicked into overdrive. Whatever happened to Halley was her fault. She should have left the girl alone, allowed her to be swallowed up by the ancestor-worshiping, male-ruled world of her parents and grandparents. Being a reporter, even on a regional magazine, wasn't really a ladylike career. Dennis and Amelia Robinson had been outraged that Annie had encouraged their daughter to wait before she rushed into marriage at the age of twenty-two. Annie had married at twenty-one, to a suitable young man she had adored, and within a year she'd known it was a mistake. Unfortunately, it had taken her nearly four years to end the farce. By walking out on her marriage to Preston and starting a new life for herself in Memphis, she had turned her back on everything her parents held dear—custom, tradition and male authority over her life.

"Why would anybody have killed Halley to keep her quiet about a story for *Today's Alabama?*" Clay's pleading stare focused on Annie. "What did you have her working on that was so dangerous?"

Dane slid his hand down to Annie's shoulder and gripped her firmly, a comforting, I'm-here gesture that Annie both appreciated and resented. "None of the stories I had assigned to Halley were dangerous. I think she came upon something else, by accident, through a package that someone sent her. She told me that it was the story of a lifetime."

"Are you certain it wasn't in connection to one of the stories she was already working on?" McCullough asked.

"I don't think so," Annie replied. "She was working on a story about the upcoming gubernatorial race, interviewing all the candidates and their families, and one on food poisoning—you know, symptoms, what foods are most likely to be affected, any outbreaks in Alabama in the past year—and the third story was on Judge Weaver's indictment for misuse of state funds. Actually about how it has and will continue to affect his career and his family."

"None of those sound potentially dangerous," Dane said. "Unless while uncovering facts in one of those stories, she stumbled across something no one was supposed to find out about, something that could cause major trouble if it became public knowledge.''

''All I can do is try to find Ms. Robinson,'' McCullough told them. ''We don't have a body—'' he glanced at Clay Boyd, then cleared his throat ''—and we have no witness to any foul play. Without some sort of proof that a crime has been committed, we can do only so much.''

Annie jumped to her feet. ''I'll find you proof! I'll find out what this story of a lifetime was. If someone killed Halley to keep her quiet, I'm going to reveal their dirty little secret to the world and—''

''Maybe she isn't dead.'' Clay's face crumbled like old plaster, leaving behind a mask of fear and uncertainty. ''Maybe they just kidnapped her and are holding her or maybe she did just run off...'' Clay stumbled across the room, leaned his arms against the wall and buried his face in his hands.

Annie went to him, laid her hand on his back and soothed him. ''I hope you're right, but we have to prepare ourselves for the very worst. Halley could be dead. And whoever tried to kill me thinks that I know something about the story, at least they think I know enough for them to want to see me dead.''

Clay turned to Annie. He stared at her with watery eyes. ''I'm going to stay here until... But y'all go ahead and check out things around here, then go back home and maybe he—'' Clay nodded to Dane ''—can find out what Halley knew that put her life in danger.''

''We're going to find out what happened and why,'' Annie said. ''I promise you.''

Clay rammed his hand into his pants' pocket and pulled out his key ring. He removed two keys and handed them to Annie. ''Here's my key to Halley's apartment and my key to the cabin on the lake. I know Mr. and Mrs. Robinson won't mind y'all taking a look. Maybe y'all can discover something that will help us find Halley or…or…her killer.''

After two days of following every lead, all of which led to dead ends, Dane told Annie it was time to go home. The post office in Foley hadn't been able to help them trace the package Halley had mailed because she'd sent it regular mail and hadn't insured it. Dane thought that, perhaps, they could find some clues in Halley's apartment or at the Robinsons's cottage. Maybe Halley kept backup files or notes. Or it was possible she'd discussed her big story with someone in Florence. When Annie called and questioned the other staff members of *Today's Alabama,* they'd been unaware that Halley was working on anything other than the three stories Annie had assigned her.

Dane made airline reservations and then rented a car. If someone was keeping tabs on Annie, he wanted to throw them off. Of course, it was only a minor maneuver, but at this point, Dane didn't know whom he could trust. Until they proved otherwise, all of Annie's family, friends, employees and business associates were under suspicion, as were the people who had known Halley Robinson. Including Clay Boyd. Although Dane thought that the man's grief was genuine, he had seen more than one guilty man give an Academy Award winning performance.

Even the employees at the Grand Hotel were suspects, but he doubted any of them knew something that they hadn't already told the police.

Dane and Annie were driving between Montgomery and Birmingham when Dane asked her about lunch. "Are you hungry? We can stop in Birmingham, if you are."

"I'm not hungry. But I am a little thirsty." Annie gazed out the side window of the beige sedan.

Dane wanted an excuse to stop soon—an excuse that wouldn't upset Annie. He'd noticed that a black car had been behind them ever since they went through Spanish Fort, hours ago. Either the two men were coincidentally taking the same route as he and Annie or they were following them. If that were the case, the driver knew how to keep a discreet distance, often allowing one or two cars to come between them. And Dane hadn't made any sudden moves to test their followers, because he didn't want to let them know he was aware of their presence.

"How about stopping for a milk shake?" Dane suggested. I think I saw a sign about a Dairy Dip a few miles up the road."

"Chocolate." Annie sighed.

"Two chocolate milk shakes. I knew we had to have something in common, other than our love for the sea."

Dane took the next exit and within minutes pulled up in front of the Dairy Dip. The black car exited, but drove past the Dairy Dip and parked at the Mini-Mart across the street.

"Do you think it's safe to get out?" Annie asked.

"What?"

"Do you suppose those two men in the black car are going to whip out an Uzi and blow us away?"

Dane chuckled. "You already knew, didn't you, that they've been behind us ever since—"

"Spanish Fort."

"Smarty-pants."

"So, do you think they're following us...following me?"

"Maybe," Dane said. "Maybe not. I thought we could pull off for something to drink or eat without arousing their suspicions that I—pardon me—that we were on to them."

"What if they hadn't exited off of I-65?"

"Then we wouldn't have anything to worry about, would we?"

"But we have something to worry about now, don't we?" Annie glanced across the street at the dark car that seemed to be waiting. But waiting for what?

Chapter 7

"So what are we going to do?" Annie asked.

"I'm going to get us a couple of chocolate milk shakes," Dane said as he opened the door. "I can keep an eye on you from the walk-up window."

"I meant, what are we going to do about the men who are following us?" Annie tilted her head so she could see Dane's face when he got out of the car.

Dane stooped over, stuck his head back into the car and smiled. "*We* aren't going to do anything. *I* am going to wait until we finish our milk-shakes and see what those guys do. If they're still just sitting over there at the Mini-Mart, then I'm going to call Lieutenant McCullough and have him run a check on their license plate number."

"Don't you dare start out this relationship by being condescending to me, Dane Carmichael!" Annie stuck her index finger in his face. "Whatever happens in this case, you and I are in it together. So when I say *we*, I mean *we*. Not you!"

Grinning, Dane closed the door and walked away. Annie's initial reaction was to get out of the car, follow him and blast him with a few more well-chosen words. But on second thought, she just crossed her arms over her chest and sat there fuming.

A few minutes later Dane tapped on the window. He held up two large plastic cups. Annie slid across the seat, opened the door and reached up for her drink.

"Our friends haven't budged," Dane told her as he slid into the seat and closed the door behind him. "One of them got out and went into the Mini-Mart. But they're still sitting over there."

"Waiting for us."

"Probably."

Dane started the motor and turned on the radio. After switching through several stations, he stopped on an Oldies station that was playing the best of Roy Orbison.

Annie enjoyed the milk shake. But then, she'd had a love affair with chocolate since tasting her first chocolate Easter Bunny when she was a child. When she finished the shake, she handed the empty cup to Dane, who had already drunk his and was looking into the rearview mirror.

"Are they still there?" she asked.

"Yes." He glanced at her, grinned, then reached over and wiped the corner of her mouth with the paper napkin he held.

Warmth spread from her stomach through her body when he touched her. Involuntarily, she smiled at him. The rat-a-tat-tat of her heart drummed in her ears.

Dane broke eye contact and she wondered if he'd been as ridiculously affected by that slight gesture—by that brush of his fingers against her mouth—as she had been.

He jerked the cell phone from his jacket pocket,

whipped out a white business card, scanned it quickly and then dialed a number.

She listened, waiting patiently for Dane to complete his conversation with Lieutenant McCullough. Hearing only Dane's questions and comments, Annie wasn't able to deduce much, and that irritated her. Suddenly Dane chuckled. Annie eyed him quizzically, wanting him to tell her what was going on. He laughed again, this time longer and more light-heartedly. She punched his arm and glared at him.

She mouthed the words, "What's going on?"

Dane shook his head, cautioning her not to interrupt, then he said into the phone, "Yeah, well, thanks, but you could have saved me some worry if you'd told me." He flipped the phone lid closed and returned it to his pocket, then turned to Annie. "Buckle up. It's safe to head out now."

Dane buckled his seat belt, then started the engine. Annie grabbed his arm and shook him.

"Tell me, dammit!"

He grinned at her. "It seems McCullough's feeling real guilty for not taking you seriously when you first went to him with the story about Halley being murdered."

"So?"

"So, he called in a few favors and got a couple of off-duty Mobile policemen to follow us to Birmingham, where a couple more cops will take over and go all the way to Florence with us."

"That numbskull! Why didn't he just tell us that he had arranged—"

"He didn't think we'd spot our escort." Dane reached over, pulled her safety belt into place and then put the car in reverse.

"Oh, yeah, sure." Annie snorted. "He didn't think a

private security agent, a former FBI agent, would notice. Even I noticed!''

"Are you sure you don't want to go home first?" Dane asked, as they drove through Florence several hours later.

"No. I told Mother, when I called her, that we were going to Halley's apartment first." Keeping watch on the traffic on Florence Boulevard, Annie pointed to the left side of the road at the red light. "Turn here. Halley's apartment is about half a mile down the road."

"Just what do you think we'll find at Halley's?" Dane took a left when the light turned green.

"I have no idea. Maybe a clue of some kind. She has a computer there, so maybe she left some notes on it. Or maybe she sent the package she mailed from Foley to her house, intending to give it to me later."

"If she didn't unearth this story until she arrived in Point Clear and opened the package, then she probably didn't leave anything in her apartment that would point us in the right direction."

"The night Halley called me, not much she said made sense." Annie closed her eyes momentarily as memories of her protégée's pretty, young, smiling face flashed through her mind. "She had just started to explain things when the line went dead."

"Exactly what else did she say to you, other than she had come across the story of a lifetime?"

"Before she mentioned that, she said something about if she'd known what was in the package, she'd have opened it before she'd left home."

"We're back to that package again."

"The apartment is right up there. Turn in. That's Halley's building, the first one on the right."

Dane drove under the decorative metal entrance arch to

Garden Grove, a modern apartment complex consisting of five, two-story brick buildings, each with either a patio or a balcony. The thick, green lawns were immaculately maintained. Spring flowers grew in profusion in neat beds, and young trees stretched toward the sky.

"Apartment A-2," Annie said.

Dane parked in an empty slot, then killed the motor. "Do you want to wait here and let me go check—"

"No!" Annie flung open the door, then jumped out and slammed the door behind her.

Dane shrugged. Foolish question, Carmichael, he reminded himself. This lady doesn't want to be left out, left behind or left alone. And she certainly doesn't want to let a man do the job for her.

Dane locked the car, shoved the keys into his pants' pocket and stepped up onto the sidewalk beside a nervous, toe-tapping Annie. "You lead the way, honey."

She tossed him an eat-dirt-and-die glance, then flounced off toward the steps leading up to the second level apartments. Before they reached the door of A-2, Annie rummaged around in her purse, pulled out the two keys Clay Boyd had given her and chose the larger of the two.

Pausing outside Halley's apartment, Annie inserted the key into the lock, turned it and sighed when she heard a distinct click. She opened the door and entered the quiet, dark foyer. Clutching both keys in her hand, she stood for a moment, unmoving, uncertain what they might find. After following her inside, Dane flipped on the light switch and closed the door.

"My God!" Annie had never seen anything like the disaster that lay before them in the living room, which was an open area directly off the small foyer.

The room had been ransacked. Furniture overturned. Lamps broken. Bookshelves emptied. Pictures ripped from the walls. Knickknacks, photo albums and throw pillows littered the floor.

"Looks like somebody's already been here," Dane said.

Annie allowed her gaze to travel the length and breadth of Halley's living room as she tried to assimilate the gravity of the situation.

"Whoever did this was looking for something," Annie said as much to herself as to Dane. "Probably whatever was in that package."

"I'd agree with you there." Dane turned to the closed door on the left, twisted the brass knob and eased the door open. "Well, they did a thorough job of it."

Halley's bedroom had been struck by the same devastation, even her bed had been striped down to the mattress, which lay sideways across the box spring.

Annie made her way through the wreckage, being careful not to step on any of the broken glass. "Her computer is on her desk, in here. Ah, damn!"

Dane's gaze halted on the mangled computer and smashed monitor lying on the floor. "I'd say somebody took great delight in doing that. My bet is they wiped the computer clean before they demolished it."

"If there was anything to find, they found it before we got here," Annie said.

Annie's shoulders slumped. She felt a sense of defeat, as if she had lost a battle. She had hoped they could find some tidbit in Halley's apartment, something—anything—that could give them a clue as to why someone kidnapped her and probably killed her. And why that same someone wanted Annie dead, too.

"If they didn't find what they were looking for, then they're going to assume you have it or know where it is."

"And we have to assume that whatever they're looking for is in the package that Halley told Jarrod Fines she was mailing to her boss. That means she sent me the information. So, where is it? It hasn't arrived at my office or at my home. Where could she have sent it?''

Coming up behind her, Dane swallowed Annie in his embrace. Bringing her back to rest against his chest, he leaned over, close to her ear and said, ''Come on, Annie, let me take you home.''

She hated herself for loving the feel of Dane's big, strong arms around her, for enjoying the comfort of his caring words. ''We need to call the police,'' she told him.

''I can do that on the way to your house.'' He slipped his arm around her waist and pivoted her slowly, until they stood side by side. ''There's nothing we can do here. You need to go home and get some rest.''

''I want to go to the cottage.'' Annie held up the second key. ''Maybe they don't know about her parents' place on the lake.''

''How far is it to the lake?'' Dane asked.

''It's a forty-minute drive from here,'' she said.

''Then we're not going now.'' Dane tried to lead her forward, but she balked.

''Why not?''

''Because you're exhausted. You need—''

''I need to find out who's trying to kill me!''

He hugged her in the most reassuring way he knew how. ''Listen to me.'' He tilted her chin just a fraction, his touch soothing and gentle. ''If they don't know about the lake house, then it'll be there waiting for us—untouched. And if they know about it, they've probably already given it the same treatment they gave this place.'' Despite knowing she wouldn't like it, he shushed her when she started to protest. ''I'm taking you home. You need a decent meal and at least a nap before we do any more sleuthing today.

And you're getting an appointment to have that knife wound checked.'' He glanced at her side.

"You're very bossy, Mr. Carmichael."

"So I've been told," he replied. "But God knows someone needs to boss you around and make sure you take care of yourself."

"I'm perfectly capable of taking care of myself without any help from you or anyone else." She pulled away from him and rushed from the bedroom, into the foyer and out the front door.

Dane caught up with her on the sidewalk. "This will be a lot easier if you work with me and stop fighting me every inch of the way."

"Our arrangement has to work only until Dundee's can send another agent to replace you," she told him. "I just hope the next agent remembers that I'm the employer and he's the employee—something that you apparently choose to forget."

When he reached out to grab her shoulder, she sidestepped to prevent him from touching her. Huffing loudly, he shrugged. "Part of my job as your bodyguard is to protect you, and that includes taking care of you."

"Your job is to act as my bodyguard, not my caretaker! You aren't my father and you're certainly not my... Just unlock the damn car and take me home."

"You're right. I'm not your father or your husband, but I think you're the one who keeps getting me confused with them."

Dane pulled the car into the four-car garage at the back of the three-story brick home in the historic district. He had grown up in a house similar to this one, its portico supported by Doric columns and massive magnolias shading the structure from the hot Southern sun.

"My mother and her sister inherited this place when their parents died," Annie told him as they headed toward the back door. "She bought out Aunt Vera's share and moved here after my father died."

"I'm surprised you'd live in an old place like this, considering how you feel about tradition and—"

"It isn't old houses I object to, it's antiquated ideas."

Just as Annie reached to open the back door, it swung open and an attractive woman, as petite and slender as Annie, rushed outside. She threw her arms around Annie.

"Thank the Lord you're finally home. I've been simply worried sick." The woman's accent was decidedly Southern, with a hint of superiority to it that reminded Dane of his mother.

Annie draped her arm around the older woman's shoulders. "Mother, this is Dane Carmichael."

"The man who saved your life?" Jennifer Harden surveyed him from head to toe, taking in every inch. "I don't know how to thank you, Mr. Carmichael. Annie means everything to me. She's all I have." Jennifer held out her small hand. Jeweled rings sparkled on several fingers. Her long, oval nails matched the pink in her linen slacks and silk blouse.

"Please, call me Dane." He took her proffered hand into his. "Ma'am, it's a pleasure to meet you. Annie speaks highly of you."

"Well, Mr. Car—Dane, I'm pleased to welcome you to our home."

Fluttering her eyelashes, Jennifer smiled sweetly. Her whole body seemed to soften right in front of his eyes. Totally feminine in a genteel way that flattered a man, Mrs. Harden reacted to Dane's courtesy much as his mother reacted to any gentleman's. Old-fashioned Southern women had a way of boosting a man's ego with nothing more than a look—a look that said she appreciated his masculinity and strength.

So what the hell had happened to Annie? The apple didn't usually fall far from the tree, but in this case, little Annie Apple had rolled a million miles away from Mother Tree.

Dane turned to Annie. "Why don't you go on in? I'll get our bags." He excused himself and went back into the garage.

"You know this is Helen's off day, so there isn't any supper prepared," Jennifer said. "I'm going out to dinner with your aunt Vera and uncle Royce. Why don't you and Dane join us?"

Annie led her mother into the modern kitchen, which had retained the feel of the older home through its mix of wood cabinetry, finishes and oversize crown molding. A six-foot-long, built-in bench was framed by two doors that opened into the sunroom.

Pausing by the gleaming wood table, Annie removed her arm from her mother's shoulders. "I think we'll pass on going out for dinner. We'll fix sandwiches here. I need to phone Dr. Lowery and make an appointment for him to take a look at my side. After that, I'd like to get a little rest, and Dane probably needs to make a few phone calls." She knew she should tell her mother that she planned for Dane and her to drive up to the Robinsons's lake cottage this evening, but she wanted to spare her mother any needless worry.

Falling into step beside Annie, Jennifer followed her into the den. "He seems very nice," Jennifer said.

"I thought you'd like him."

"He's charming and well mannered and—"

"And every bit the gentleman that Daddy was." Annie finished the sentence for her.

"Is he, dear?" When Jennifer tilted her head, her chin-length auburn hair swayed slightly.

"Don't play coy with me, Mother. I'm your daughter. I know you." Annie dropped onto the floral chintz sofa, kicked off her flats and tucked her feet up under her. "Dane is exactly what he seems. My guess is that he was born and raised with a silver spoon in his mouth, just as I was."

"What, other than his good manners, makes you assume that?" Jennifer sat beside Annie, crossed her ankles and smiled pleasantly.

"He was married to Richard Hughes's daughter." Annie wiggled her toes as she stretched her arms over her head and leaned back into the plush sofa.

"Was he? How interesting," Jennifer said, her smile enlarging just a fraction. "I believe Vera told me that Richard's daughter died about ten years ago."

"I don't know. We haven't discussed his wife. All Dane told me is that he's a widower."

"And he's the CEO of a private security agency in Atlanta—is that right?"

"The Dundee agency." Annie entwined her fingers and cupped her open palms behind her head.

"You have no idea how thankful I am that you hired Mr. Carmichael. The very thought that someone is trying to kill you frightens me terribly. I can't believe that poor little Halley might be dead."

"Mr. Carmichael is my temporary bodyguard," she said. "Just until another agent is free."

"Why is that, dear? Does Mr. Carmichael have a previous commitment?" Jennifer stared at Annie, a look of puzzlement in her brown eyes.

Loosening her entwined fingers, Annie sighed, then brought her hands down and around to her lap. She lifted her head from the soft sofa back and looked directly at her mother. "I asked Dane to arrange for another agent. He and I don't—we have a difficult time... I'd feel more comfortable with someone else."

"But why would you be uncomfortable with him? Dane Carmichael is obviously a fine man and a perfect gentleman." Jennifer's eyes grew bright as she uttered a silent, *Ah.* "He reminds you of Preston, doesn't he? You're attracted to him and that upsets you."

"You're much too smart, Mother."

Dane stood in the doorway, suddenly feeling as if he were a voyeur secretly listening to a private conversation. He was about to make his presence known, but Annie made a confession before he could clear his throat or shuffle his feet.

"It would be much too easy to give in to the feelings I have for Dane, and it would be disastrous if I did. The man saved my life and he's been at my side, protecting me, for the past four days. The danger that surrounds me combined with the feeling of safety I have when he's near is getting all mixed up with physical attraction."

Jennifer glanced past Annie, her gaze locking with Dane's for just an instant. She quickly returned her full attention to her daughter.

"Why would it be disastrous for you to give in to the feelings you have for Dane?"

"Good heavens, Mother, stop and think! Dane is cut from the same cloth as Daddy. And yes, of course, he reminds me of Preston. Not physically, of course, since there's no resemblance. But that smooth charm and old-fashioned good manners and—"

"Preston Younger was a fraud. He only pretended to be a gentleman, unlike your father, who *was* a gentleman."

Dane wondered just how long Jennifer Harden would

continue the conversation with her daughter, knowing full well that he was listening. Not liking the feel of being an eavesdropper, Dane cleared his throat.

When both women jerked around, he thought what an accomplished actress Mrs. Harden was.

"I left the bags in the kitchen," he said.

"Do come in, Dane," Jennifer said. "Annie can show you to your room later. My sister and her husband are due here anytime now. I'd like for you to meet them. Royce is a business associate of your former father-in-law's. He owns a substantial amount of stock in Hughes Chemicals and Plastics and I think I might own a few shares, too. I'll have to ask Royce."

As if on cue, the doorbell rang before Dane had a chance to respond.

"That's Vera and Royce, now." Jennifer brushed past Dane on her way out of the room, then paused to look back at him over her shoulder. "Would you be a sweetheart and play bartender for me?" She glanced at Annie. "Show him where things are, will you?"

"The liquor is in the mahogany secretary." Annie inclined her head toward the large antique piece situated along the wall to the right of the sofa. "Nothing for me, thanks. Mother and Aunt Vera will take sherry and Uncle Royce will want whiskey...neat."

Dane nodded, then busied himself at the makeshift bar. Moments later Jennifer reappeared, along with a woman who could have been her twin, except that she was several years older and a few pounds heavier, and a tall, slender man with a shock of snow-white hair and piercing gray eyes.

"Sweetie." With her arms open wide, Vera Layman rushed toward Annie, who stood and went into her aunt's embrace. "We've been worried sick ever since Jenny told us about Halley Robinson's disappearance and the attempt on your life.''

Annie's uncle sized Dane up quickly, then extended his hand. "Royce Layman."

"Dane Carmichael," he replied, and shook the older man's hand.

"So you're the young man who saved our Annie's life. Well, we're mighty grateful, I can tell you that. This girl—" his gaze fell on Annie, the look warm, caring and paternal "—means the world to us."

"Jenny tells us that Annie has hired you as her bodyguard." Vera released her niece and turned to Dane. "If you're playing bartender, I'd like a sherry, please."

Dane poured the sisters's drinks, then took the glasses to them. Each responded with flirtatious smiles of appreciation.

"Dane was married to Richard Hughes's daughter," Jennifer informed her sister.

"Is that right? Oh, my, we're friends with Richard and Gloria," Vera told him. "They're lovely people. Richard is a candidate for governor, you know."

Royce Layman looked at Dane oddly, then nodded to himself and said, "We appreciate your taking the job as Annie's bodyguard. I feel reassured knowing what sort of man you are. I believe Richard's daughter married a young man who was with the Federal Bureau of Investigation, is that right?"

"Yes, sir. I was with the Bureau nearly thirteen years before going to work with the Dundee agency."

"Shouldn't y'all be leaving?" Annie asked. "We don't want to keep y'all from your dinner plans."

"We're just going over to Stillwater," Royce said. "I don't think they'll run out of steaks anytime soon. Besides—"

The doorbell rang. All four people in the den stilled instantly.

"Are you expecting anyone else, Mother?" Annie asked.

"No, dear," Jennifer said.

"Would you like for me to go to the door, Mrs. Harden?" Dane offered.

"I'll get it," Royce said. Taking charge with his usual gusto, he marched out of the room.

Three minutes later he returned, a small package in his hand. "Nothing to get upset about. It was a special delivery for Annie." He held out the small rectangular object to his niece.

Annie eyed the brown paper-wrapped parcel as if it were a poisonous snake. Could this be the *little gift* Halley had mailed to her from Point Clear four days ago, the day Halley had disappeared?

The rush of her heart pumping blood through her body thundered in her ears as she reached for the package.

"Wait!" Dane called to her.

All eyes turned toward him. Annie dropped her hand away.

"What's wrong?" she asked. "This could be the gift Halley sent me."

Dane gave her a hard look, silently rebuking her for mentioning the item Halley had mailed.

"This is my family," she told him, understanding the meaning of his menacing glare. "My mother and aunt and uncle. I trust these people with my life."

"What's going on here?" Royce demanded.

"Give me the package, please, Mr. Layman," Dane said. "I want to have it checked before Annie opens it."

"Checked for what?" Vera asked.

"A bomb," Dane said.

Chapter 8

Royce Layman handed the ominous package to Dane. Their gazes connected briefly, exchanging a silent message. *We must protect the ladies.* Checking the outer covering of the package, Dane noted the return address on the special delivery form had been written in ink and that moisture of some type had obliterated it, leaving only a dark smudge. And the postmark was so faint as to be unreadable.

"Call the police," he told Royce. "Tell them we have a package we suspect might contain a bomb. Then call the post office to see how quickly they can trace the package's origins. I'll wait outside for the police."

Dane left the others in the family room while he made a hasty retreat through the kitchen and out the back door. Despite her mother's nervous cry for her to stay, Annie followed Dane as far as the kitchen.

Jennifer came up behind Annie and laid her hand on her

daughter's back. Annie shuddered. "Our lives aren't ever going to be the same, are they?" Jennifer sighed.

Annie nodded. "No. Not until we find out who is behind Halley's disappearance and the attempts on my life."

"Come back into the den with me." Jennifer tugged on Annie's arm. "There's nothing we can do to help Mr. Carmichael."

"You go, Mother," Annie said. "I'm waiting right here until Dane comes back." The fear within her grew stronger with each passing minute. If there was a bomb and Dane was hurt— No, no! She shouldn't think that way. Dane wasn't some amateur who would take unnecessary chances. He was a professional who could take care of himself.

"I'll stay here with you." Jennifer slipped her arm around Annie's waist.

The two women waited together, the moments ticking inside them with the rapid beating of their hearts.

"What's going on?" Royce asked as he and Vera entered the kitchen. "Have the police arrived yet?"

Both Jennifer and Annie gasped and jumped. "Lord have mercy, Royce, you should have given us some warning you were there," Jennifer said.

"I'm sorry. I didn't mean to frighten y'all." Royce marched across the room and peered out the window. "I can't see him. He must have taken the damn thing as far from the house as possible."

Thirty-five minutes later, Florence Police Chief Milton Holman handed the unopened package to Dane, who waited in the chief's office, Annie at his side. He had done everything he could to persuade her to stay at home with her family, but being the mule-headed woman she was, she'd insisted on coming with him.

"Looks like this was a false alarm, folks," Holman said. "But better safe than sorry, right, Ms. Harden?"

"Right." Annie let out a long sigh. "So, it's safe for me to open the package?"

"Go right ahead," Holman told her.

Just as she took the parcel from Dane, the chief's telephone rang. He excused himself and quietly answered on the fourth ring. With nervous fingers, Annie ripped open the package. She prayed that the contents would be something—anything—that could help them solve the mystery of Halley's disappearance. Inside the thick, brown wrapping paper was a shoe box. Annie's heartbeat accelerated as she opened the lid. Then the air in her lungs swooshed out loudly when she exhaled the breath she'd been holding.

She lifted the envelope lying on top of a pair of leather sandals, which were nestled inside the box. Inserting her fingernail under the edge of the flap, she zipped open the envelope and pulled out the card inside. She scanned the card quickly, then burst into laughter.

"It's a birthday present from my great-aunt Rosetta in Italy." Holding the shoe box in her arms, Annie pressed it against her chest and slumped down into the nearest chair.

"That was Tony Reed from the post office on the phone," Chief Holman said. "The package was sent from a Mrs. Rosetta Pirandello, in Salerno, Italy."

"All this to-do over a pair of Italian leather sandals," Annie said.

"Well, considering what you and Mr. Carmichael have told me, I'd say you're lucky that this was a gift from your aunt." Chief Holman crossed his arms over his broad chest. "If you get any more packages, we'll check them out for you. It takes only a few minutes to X-ray them."

"Thank you, Chief." Annie shook hands with Milton

Holman, then turned to Dane. "I'll call Mother on the way home and let her know that everything is fine. It's nearly seven. They still have plenty of time to go out for dinner."

The minute they arrived home, Annie's family rushed into the foyer to meet them. Royce Layman had a dozen questions, which Dane answered. And her aunt and mother hovered over Annie as if she had just survived a horrible accident.

"Look, y'all go on out to dinner. I'm fine," Annie said. "Right now, I'm going upstairs to try on my new sandals from Aunt Rosetta."

"Annie, wait, dear…" Jennifer called as Annie raced up the stairs to the second floor. When Annie disappeared into her room and slammed the door, Jennifer turned to Royce and nodded.

Royce clasped Dane's shoulder. "Mr. Carmichael, we—that is, Annie's mother, my wife and I—want to hire you as Annie's permanent bodyguard, for as long as her life is in danger. Jennifer explained that your arrangement with Annie was only temporary, but we prefer not to have another agent take over at a later date."

Dane surveyed the threesome—a distinguished gentleman and two lovely ladies, all three products of wealth and good breeding. They were the type of people he'd known all his life, people very much like his relatives. He realized that, in him, they sensed a kindred spirit. He was, after all, one of their kind.

"Annie has been insistent that the first available Dundee agent replace me," Dane explained. "She won't approve of y'all hiring me on a permanent basis."

"Annie can be stubborn," Jennifer said. "An annoying trait she inherited from her father. But the fact is, that when Annie chose to go against my husband's wishes, he disinherited her. She's a working girl, Mr. Carmichael, and although she is successful at her job and has a nice income, she isn't wealthy." Jennifer paused for effect. "But I am wealthy. I can, and will, pay your fees. Annie knows that she'll have to come to me for the money to continue your or any agent's employ."

"So, you're saying that you don't intend to give your daughter a choice in the matter?" Dane thought that perhaps Annie hadn't inherited all her stubbornness from her father.

"That's exactly what I'm saying!"

"And we agree and support Jennifer's decision," Royce said. "While y'all were at the police station, I telephoned Richard and told him what was going on and that his son-in-law was acting as our Annie's bodyguard. He praised you highly and advised me to keep you on the job."

"I'll have to make a point to see Richard while I'm in Florence," Dane said. He had avoided contact with his former father-in-law for years. They had both suffered greatly when Lorna died and seeing each other again was bound to dredge up old memories and open old wounds. Sometimes he wondered if Richard blamed him for Lorna's death. He had to admit that sometimes he blamed himself.

"Then you'll take this case, as my employee, until I terminate our agreement?" Jennifer Harden extended her small, delicate hand.

Annie would be livid if he agreed. But he had to admit that he'd had every intention of finding a way to stay on this case. Despite the fact that he had originally agreed to take the assignment, temporarily, he had known then that he didn't want anyone else keeping Annie safe.

Dane shook hands with Annie's mother. "I'll take the case."

"Good."

"Who's going to tell Annie?" Dane asked.

Laughing, all four people glanced up the staircase.

"You leave Annie to me. I know just how to handle her," Jennifer said, then turned and went upstairs.

Annie lay across her bed, hugging a pink pillow to her body. The open shoe box rested on the floor, the shoes still inside, and the cheery birthday card from Aunt Rosetta stood on the nightstand, propped up against the lamp.

When she'd moved into her grandparents' house with her mother, she had, at her mother's insistence, redecorated the bedroom she'd chosen from the four available rooms. Her mother had taken over her parents' suite on the ground level, leaving the upstairs Annie's domain and allowing her some semblance of privacy.

She'd brought her bedroom suite from the apartment in Memphis, an eclectic mixture of antiques she'd found in little shops and at auctions. The pale pink walls added a soft, rosy glow to the room when late afternoon sunshine flooded through the long narrow windows.

Glancing around the room, Annie sighed as an inner voice chided her. *Get your butt up off this bed, go downstairs and tell Dane that you're ready to drive to the Robinsons's cottage right now. There's no point in waiting.*

If there were any clues at the lake house, she wanted— no, she needed—to find them as soon as possible. She had never been an overly nervous woman nor was she the type to worry needlessly. But recent events had shattered her sense of security and unbalanced her equilibrium. She felt off center, as if her whole world had tilted sideways on its axis.

Only a few days ago she'd been in complete control of her life and now here she was at the mercy of some unknown person determined to kill her for information she didn't even have. But they didn't know she was clueless, that Halley had imparted very little to her in their brief conversation.

A soft rapping on the door startled Annie. Shuddering, she gasped silently, then sucked in a deep, calming breath. "Yes?"

"Annie, dear, it's Mother."

Oh, great. She'd thought her family had left for dinner by now. "What is it, Mother?"

"May I come in?" Jennifer asked. "There's something I have to tell you."

"Please, come on in." She really didn't want to talk to her mother. Didn't want to be lectured. Didn't want to have to listen to the family's opinion of her situation.

After entering the room, Jennifer quietly closed the door and approached the bed where Annie sat on the edge. "Feeling better?"

"I'm fine, Mother."

"This whole affair has been terribly upsetting for you, and for us. We're very fortunate that Mr. Carmichael happened to be in the right place at the right time."

"I don't mean to be rude, but if you're going to dinner with Uncle Royce and Aunt Vera, perhaps you should get to the point."

"Certainly." Jennifer sat beside Annie. "I've hired Dane."

Annie stared at her mother, a sense of dread dropping like a lead weight into her stomach. "What do you mean, you've hired Dane?"

"We—Uncle Royce, Aunt Vera and I—decided that Dane is the best man for the job." Jennifer cleared her throat. "We want him to take this case and remain your bodyguard until there is no longer any danger to you."

"I do not want Dane Carmichael as my bodyguard on a permanent basis." Annie shot up off the bed, her eyes darkening, her mouth set in a grim line. "I refuse to allow you to do this to me!"

"I'm paying the man's salary, so I think it's my prerogative to choose whom I think the best qualified man is." Jennifer folded her hands in her lap.

Annie turned on her mother, her face contorted in rage, "How many times in the past have I been forced to endure the dictates of my family because they thought they knew what was best for me? I married the man Daddy hand-picked for me. I tried to be the dutiful daughter. Even after I found out about Preston's first affair, I stayed with him because you and Daddy thought that was what was best for me."

"Annie, child, you're only hurting yourself to remain so bitter."

"First of all, I'm not a child! I'm a woman! I'll be thirty-five soon." Annie clenched her jaw tightly. Why was she having this conversation with her mother? Why did she feel as if she were pleading for her freedom? She had fought and won that battle years ago. "I'd rather do without a bodyguard than keep Dane Carmichael on the job indefinitely. And I can find a way to pay for an investigator."

Jennifer reached up and took Annie's hand in hers. "My sweet, Annie Sophia. Always so stubborn and independent. Always fussing and fuming and fighting to have your own way. Just like your daddy."

"Good God, Mother, I'm nothing like Daddy!" Annie jerked free of her mother's hold.

Jennifer smiled, the look in her eyes sympathetic and understanding. "Be that as it may, I have hired Dane. And unless you really are desperately afraid you'll succumb to your attraction to him, then I can't imagine why you'd prefer to risk your life without a bodyguard and to hire a less qualified investigator.''

"I am not afraid I'll succumb to Dane. I shouldn't have told you that I find him very attractive or that he reminds me of Preston. The only reason y'all want him on this case is because he's one of you. He belongs to the same good ole boys club that Daddy and Preston were a part of.''

Jennifer stood and faced her daughter's wrath. "Oh, my poor Annie. You must think you'll fall in love with Dane to be so afraid of him.''

"I would never fall in love with—''

"If you're not worried about falling in love with Dane, then what possible reason could you have to object to my hiring him?''

Annie knew when she'd been outmaneuvered. There was no reasonable explanation for why she didn't want Dane to stay on as her bodyguard—none, other than the one her mother had mentioned. And she was not going to admit to her mother that she was afraid of falling in love with Dane. If she did, her mother would be planning a wedding and having invitations printed. Nothing would please her family more than if she wound up with a man who had been born into their world of wealth and privilege.

"Dammit,'' Annie mumbled under her breath. "All right, Mother, you win.''

Jennifer's lips curved into a wide, triumphant smile.

"I have no feelings whatsoever for Dane Carmichael and I'll prove to you that I don't.''

"Yes, dear, you do that.'' Jennifer hugged Annie, kissed her cheek and sauntered toward the door. After opening the bedroom door, she paused for a moment and said, "Thank you for being so reasonable about this.''

Annie glowered at her mother, who only smiled at her as she turned and headed toward the staircase. Annie hurried into her bathroom, brushed her teeth, freshened her makeup, ran a comb through her hair and threw the straps of her bag over her shoulder.

She waited at the top of the stairs until she heard the front door open and close, then she walked downstairs and waited in the foyer until she heard Uncle Royce's Mercedes pull out of the driveway. She rushed into the den, where she found Dane sitting on the sofa, his arms crossed over his chest. He looked right at home, as if he actually lived here. Annie cringed. He will be living here for God only knows how long, she reminded herself.

"Well, am I staying or leaving?" Dane asked, his gaze locking with hers the minute she entered the room.

"You're staying, courtesy of my mother's generosity," she said reluctantly. "Until the mystery is solved and my life is no longer in danger."

Dane frowned, furrowing his brow and widening his eyes. "I thought you'd put up more of a fight. Your mother must have amazing powers of persuasion."

"Let's just say that Mother challenged me and she knew I'd never be able to resist a challenge."

"So this is my case," he said. "You won't be replacing me in a week or two?"

"I think we've established the fact that my mother has hired you for the duration of my problems." Annie tapped her foot on the wood floor. "Are you ready to go now?"

"Go where?" he asked.

"To the Robinsons's lake house."

"It's rather late, isn't it? Don't you think this can wait until morning?"

"Maybe, but I can't wait," she told him. "I want to go

now, and even if my mother is paying your salary, I'm your boss. Got it?''

"All right, boss lady.'' Dane rose from the sofa, his long, leanly muscular body towering over her as she approached him. ''We've still got the rental car.'' He jangled the keys in his pocket.

"We'll take my Navigator.'' She gave him a look that dared him to disagree. ''And I'll drive. I know where we're going. The Robinsons's cottage isn't far from Uncle Royce and Aunt Vera's place on the lake.''

Annie headed toward the back door. Catching up with her, Dane grasped her shoulder. She glanced up at him.

"Did you tell your mother that we wouldn't be here when she returned from dinner?''

"No-oo.'' The word dragged out slowly, laced with sheer aggravation. ''Oh, you're right. I'll leave her a note.''

After disengaging herself from Dane's grip, she stomped across the kitchen. Finding a notepad and pen by the telephone, she jotted down a quick message and stuck it to the refrigerator with a magnet.

Dane read the note aloud. ''Dane and I have gone to the Robinsons's lake house. We'll pick up burgers on the way there. Don't wait up for us. Love, Annie.'''

"She'll worry if she thinks we didn't have dinner,'' Annie explained.

"You're a good daughter.''

"I'm not what she wanted or expected.'' Annie shrugged. ''And she's not the kind of mother I needed. But we both make the best of it.''

Annie had protested vehemently when Dane actually did ask her to go through the drive-up window at a local fast-food restaurant. He'd pointed out that they could eat on the way and not lose any time. Begrudgingly, she had agreed. Besides, she was hungry.

The Robinsons's cottage, located directly on the lake, sprawled out in three directions to form a T with open porches on two sides and a long, wide deck at the back.

No streetlights dispelled the darkness, but a quarter moon shone brightly enough to guide them from the car to the front door. Annie fumbled with the key for several seconds before Dane aimed one of his two flashlights toward the keyhole. Annie inserted the key into the lock. Dane hovered directly behind her, his breath warm on her neck. She opened the door and waited, anticipation shooting an adrenaline rush through her body. Dane reached around her and felt for a light switch. Finding a triple plate conveniently located just inside the door, he flipped all three switches and lights came on in the living room, the adjoining dining room and kitchen.

The cottage was neat—not even a throw rug out of place. Annie sighed. Dane nudged her into the room.

"Doesn't look as if anyone's searched this place," she said.

"There are three possibilities," Dane told her. "One—they don't know about this place. Two—they just haven't had a chance to check it out yet. Or three—they don't think Halley would have left anything here."

"Well, don't just stand there," Annie said. "Let's get started. Where do you think we should begin our search?"

"Since we really have no idea what we're looking for, then I suppose we need to give the whole place the once-over. But we should begin with Halley's room."

"I have no idea which room she used when she came here."

"Then we'll search all of them."

"All of them" turned out to be three regular-size bedrooms and one small room off the screened-in back porch, which held a cot and a nightstand. Being careful not to make a mess as they searched, they checked closets and cedar chests, and under the beds. They took each book from the bookshelves that covered the back wall of one bedroom and rummaged through an old oak desk in another.

"Nothing!" Annie fumed. "I thought for sure we'd find something."

Dane entered the final bedroom, a dejected Annie following closely behind him. "I'll check the closet. You try under the bed and the nightstands."

Annie shone the flashlight under the bed and, as in the other rooms, found nothing but dust. After placing the flashlight on top of the left nightstand, she flopped onto the edge of the bed and pulled out the only drawer. She lifted out a telephone directory and found an odd assortment of pens, pencils and rubber bands. She brushed them aside. There, at the bottom of the drawer, was a small spiral-bound notebook.

Her hand trembled as she reached for the notebook. *Please, dear God, let this be something that can give us a clue. No matter how insignificant. We desperately need something to go on.*

She lifted the notebook out of the drawer and sat on the bed for several minutes, just staring at the object in her hand.

"What have you got there?" Dane asked.

"I'm not sure."

"Open it and find out."

Excitement burst inside her like bottle rockets on the Fourth of July. *Please, please, please,* she silently prayed. After opening the notebook to the first few pages, she groaned. Empty. She flipped through the pages, all of them blank, before suddenly noticing handwriting about halfway through. She spread open the book and scanned the notes.

Dane sat beside her and looked over her shoulder. "Is that Halley's handwriting?"

"Yes, I'm almost certain it is."

"So read it and see if it means anything to you."

Feeling as if she were invading Halley's privacy, Annie hesitated. "What if this is some sort of diary she was keeping?"

"Read the damn thing," Dane said. "Even if it is a personal diary, I don't think the lady would mind if she knew it meant our discovering who kidnapped her."

"You're right."

She read the page, then turned and read quickly through several pages. "These are notes on the stories I assigned her. See—" Annie pointed to the open page "—these are background notes on Judge Weaver's indictment for misuse of state funds. It says here that he's all but admitted his guilt and is trying to work out a deal where he can simply retire and not be prosecuted. Oh, yeah, sure," Annie said. "Why is it that some people think they're above the law?"

"So, why would a man who has pretty much admitted his guilt have anything to hide?"

"Not the Judge Weaver story, huh?"

Dane shook his head. "See what else she's got in there."

Annie continued reading for several minutes before she said, "The story on food poisoning doesn't appear suspicious. All the cases are documented and all the facts seem to already be out in the open."

"What was the third story she was working on, the gubernatorial race?"

"Yes, but I can't see how interviewing the candidates

and their families could have possibly put Halley's life in danger.''

"Maybe one of the candidates or a family member has something to hide," Dane said.

"You mean, a skeleton in the closet?" She clicked her tongue against the roof of her mouth. "It would have to be a really terrible secret for someone to kidnap Halley and try to kill me. What could possibly be that bad?"

"Check out the rest of her notes."

Annie hated having Dane read over her shoulder, but she didn't possess the energy to argue with him over something that was, at this point, trivial.

She read hurriedly, skimming through page after page of handwritten notes on all four candidates for governor. Democrat. Republican. And two Independents. Boring details. Facts and figures that were already public knowledge. Just as her vision began to blur and the words jumbled in her mind, Annie turned the page and there it was—written in large, bold print, and in red ink.

Richard Hughes. Underlined twice. And directly below it, another name. Martin Edwards. Underlined three times. Beside the second name was a word that had been scribbled in blue ink and an arrow that linked the word to the name Martin Edwards.

"What does that look like to you?" Annie asked Dane, pointing to the illegible word. "Daphne? Dauphin?"

"Digital? Or maybe dough."

"No, look the way it ends there. I think that's an *e* and an *r*."

"You're right."

"Daughter!" Annie exclaimed. "I think it's daughter."

"Yeah, looks like it could be daughter." Dane's gaze kept returning to his former father-in-law's name. The word isn't attached to Richard's name, he told himself.

Besides, the facts about Lorna's death weren't a secret. They were a matter of public record. And his guess was that if Richard were to broadcast the story of Lorna's tragic death, it would probably gain him the sympathy of every parent in the state. No, if the word was daughter, it wasn't referring to Richard's daughter. It had to be the other man's daughter.

"I've never heard of Martin Edwards," Annie said. She flipped through the rest of the notebook and found nothing. "This has to be it, Dane. It has to be!"

"Why does it have to be?"

Annie's shoulders slumped. She huffed out a long, disgusted breath. "You're right. It could be meaningless. After all, Martin Edwards could be anybody and he might not even have a connection to Richard Hughes. I guess I'm just grasping at straws."

"Let me assure you that Richard Hughes isn't the kind of person who has anything terrible to hide. I know the man. He was my friend as well as my father-in-law. I admire him. I'd stake my life on his being above reproach."

"Would you stake my life on it?" she asked.

Dane stared into her eyes and realized that she truly was questioning his father-in-law's integrity. "Richard Hughes isn't the bad guy here, so there's no point in wasting time arguing about this. You have no idea if Richard's name beside this other man's and the scribbled word we think is *daughter* has any connection to Halley's disappearance."

"I know. I know. It's just, so far, it's all we've got."

"Then I suggest we search the rest of the house to see what we can find."

An hour later, after inspecting the other rooms, they came up empty-handed, except for Halley's notebook, which Annie had slipped into her purse. They separated and went from room to room, straightening and rearranging, trying to make sure everything looked exactly the way it had before they'd rummaged through cabinets, closets and drawers.

"Ready?" Dane asked when Annie returned to the living room.

"Yes. I just wish we'd found something besides this notebook." She patted her purse.

Dane checked his watch. "It's nearly midnight. Let's go. We'll take another look at the notebook in the morning, after we've both had a good night's sleep."

"Is that a subtle way of saying things will look better tomorrow?"

"We're both too tired to think rationally right now," he said. "We might catch something that we missed on a second reading." Dane opened the door and waited until Annie walked out onto the porch, then closed the door behind her. "Give me the key."

He took the key she gave him, locked the door, turned, and together they moved toward the rock steps that lead down to the driveway.

Dane knew the instant he heard the sound that someone had just fired a rifle. The bullet whizzed past Annie's right shoulder and hit the wooden porch column.

"Oh, God!" She reached out for Dane.

He grabbed her, threw her to the deck and covered her body with his. Another shot rang out and then another.

Annie screamed.

Chapter 9

"Are you hit?" Dane asked.

"No." Her voice quivered. "Are you?"

"No, I'm fine."

The gunman fired again, splintering wood off the shingles on the house. Dane felt Annie shivering beneath him. He heard the boom-boom-boom of his own heart. Adrenaline pumped through his body like water through an open floodgate.

He eased his hand beneath his jacket, undid his hip holster and pulled out his Ruger. "Stay down. Don't move until I tell you to."

Dane scanned the wooded area across the street from the lake cottage. Whoever was out there might be using a rifle with an ungodly range, and that could mean he was a good distance away. But Dane's instincts told him that the shooter wasn't a professional—if he was, he wouldn't have missed. And that probably meant he was close by and using a hunting rifle.

"When I start shooting, we're going off the porch and toward the car." As they dashed from the porch, Dane fired off several shots toward the unseen enemy in the woods. They landed in front of the Navigator just as their attacker retaliated, peppering the porch and house. Then he fired several bullets into the side of Annie's sport utility vehicle. Dane maneuvered Annie down to the ground, keeping his body between her and the shooter.

He exchanged more fire with the gunman. Suddenly an odd sound, like a muffled cry, came from the woods, followed by the crunch of footsteps over dry leaves and underbrush. And then everything went eerily quiet. Deadly still. A faint rustle of wind through the trees. A whispery mumble from the lake behind the cottage. The hum of springtime insects.

And the roar of a car's engine.

"I must have hit him," Dane said.

"Is he gone?"

"Yeah, I'd say he's leaving." Dane grabbed Annie's arm and brought her to her feet along with him, when he stood. "We're going after him."

"We are?"

"Give me the keys," he demanded.

She didn't think twice, didn't question his barked order. She just dug into her purse, pulled out the keys and handed them to him.

He unlocked the doors, shoved her into the passenger seat, fastened the safety belt and then rounded the hood. He jumped in the Navigator, slammed the door, swung the safety belt around him, and started the motor.

"Is there more than one road out of here?" Dane asked as he backed the vehicle into the road.

"No, just this one, coming from town and going farther out into the country."

"Then he'll have to leave by this road."

"But how can we know which way he went?"

"We'll have to guess." Dane turned the car in the direction that lead to town. If the guy was shot, he'd go toward civilization, go to someone who could discreetly take care of his wound.

Pressing his foot on the accelerator, Dane put the Navigator's V-8 engine to the test. He glanced at Annie. She looked as if she were holding her breath.

"Hang on, honey. I see taillights up ahead."

"Do you think it's him?"

"We'll find out."

Dane increased the speed and within minutes they were overtaking the car in front of them.

"Can you make out the license plate numbers?" he asked.

"Not yet."

When Dane pulled the Navigator closer, the car in front of them began swerving from one side of the road to the other, as if the driver were intoxicated. Either the guy's injury was seriously affecting him or he was playing some kind of deadly game. Every time Dane tried to get close to the car, which he now recognized as a dark blue older model sports car, the driver increased his speed and veered off toward the side of the road.

"What's he doing?" Annie laid her hands over her stomach.

"Are you getting sick?"

"Queasy, but I'm okay. What's he trying to do?"

"Keep us from getting his plate number and stop us from passing him to get a look at his face."

Without warning, the sports car drove off the road, shrieked into reverse and came back toward the Navigator. He rammed the side of the sports utility vehicle with his back bumper. Annie gasped. Dane clutched the steering wheel with white-knuckled strength, trying to avoid another direct hit.

Suddenly Dane noticed something shiny in the driver's side window, the moonlight reflecting off the object. A gun! Damn! One of the bullets entered the front wheel. Double damn! Dane thought. The tire would be flat in no time.

"He hit the tire, didn't he?" Annie tried to concentrate on the license plate of the attacking car. "A four and a one," she said. "It's a Lauderdale County tag."

The sports car roared, shifted into drive and flew away, leaving the Navigator crippled. Dane pulled off to the side of the road, then got out. Cursing under his breath, he unlocked the tailgate.

Annie hopped out, grateful to be alive, glad she hadn't thrown up and mad as hell that she hadn't been able to get more than four-one off the license plate.

"Did you get a look at him?" she asked as she watched Dane roll the spare tire around to the front fender.

"No, it was too dark and he kept moving." Dane laid the tire on the ground and turned to Annie. "Are you sure you're all right?"

"I'm okay, just a little shaken."

The Navigator's headlights shown like two luminous balls, casting beams of illumination out into the darkness. Overhead, the moon glowed brightly and stars littered the black sky. Dane reached out, slid his hand under her hair and around her neck, then pulled her toward him. She looked up at him and saw the concern in his eyes. "I'm going to keep you safe. I promise."

Leaning down, he pressed his forehead against hers, his breath warm on her face. His big fingers threaded through her hair, inching upward to cup the back of her head. She lifted her face. He kissed her. An I'm-so-damn-glad-you're-alive kiss. The kind that was hot and wet and thrusting from the moment their lips met.

He ended the kiss abruptly, released her and stepped away. "Get one of the flashlights and hold it for me while I change this tire."

She couldn't move for a couple of seconds. She was still reeling from Dane's passionate kiss. But he didn't seem the least bit affected by it. He was as cool as a cucumber.

She pulled her purse off the seat, delved inside and found a flashlight. "Where do you want me to shine it?" She hated that quivery note in her voice.

"Shine it on the tire," he said, his lips curving into a smile.

She laughed, a nervous, agitated little laugh. "On the tire. Of course."

Annie saw the lights flashing atop the police cars half a block away from her house. Her heart leaped into her throat. Dear God, what had happened?

Dane slowed the Navigator and pulled it up to the curb. Two police vehicles blocked the driveway. He reached over and grabbed Annie's arm. "You stay here. Let me see what's going on."

At that very minute Annie saw her mother, wearing a yellow satin robe, and Uncle Royce standing in the yard, talking to Chief Holman. Aunt Vera sat on the portico steps, her hands folded in her lap. Disregarding Dane's order to stay in the car, Annie flung open the door and ran across the lawn.

A young, bright-eyed officer threw out his arm in front of her. "Sorry, ma'am, you can't—"

"Let her through, McNabb. That's Mrs. Harden's

daughter. She lives here," Holman said. "And him, too."
He nodded at Dane, who was only a couple of feet behind
Annie.

Annie rushed to her mother's side. Jennifer opened her
arms and embraced her. "Oh, Annie, Annie, where were
you?" Jennifer asked, her voice quivering. "I've been
scared to death that something dreadful had happened to
you. Someone broke into the house while we were out to
dinner and—"

"I'm fine, Mother." Hugging Jennifer and patting her
on the back, Annie offered comfort. "Didn't you see the
note I left?"

"What note?" Jennifer lifted her head and stared at Annie. "We didn't find a note, did we, Royce?"

"No note," Royce Layman said. "Where did you leave
it, Annie?"

"On the refrigerator where I always leave notes."

"Then I don't understand why it wasn't there." Jennifer
looked to her brother-in-law, her gaze questioning.

"Was the house ransacked?" Dane asked.

"No, why?" Chief Holman asked.

"Just curious. Was it a burglary or—"

"They broke in through the kitchen door." The puzzled
look on Jennifer's face was a silent proclamation of her
disbelief that anyone would have done such a terrible
thing. "They made a bit of a mess in the kitchen and the
den…" She shuddered, apparently unnerved by the memory of what she'd seen. "And they stole several items from
the den. The VCR, the small TV, the CD and tape player,
along with some CDs and tapes."

"Is that all that's missing?" Dane asked.

"Seems to be," Holman said. "We've had Mrs. Harden
take a quick look through the house and it appears that the
only rooms touched were the kitchen and den."

"Don't you think that's odd?" Dane said.

Annie glanced over her shoulder and cast her gaze up at Dane. She knew what he was getting at. Someone had broken into her house, read the note she'd left for her mother, and then faked a burglary by taking the TV, VCR and CD player. Her gaze locked with Dane's and they exchanged a mental acknowledgment. *So that's how he knew where we were!* Their attacker had read the note and followed them to the Robinsons's cottage. But how had he known where the cottage was located?

"How did he know—" Annie said.

"Didn't your security system work tonight?" Dane asked, cutting Annie off midsentence.

She glared at him. He lifted his eyebrows and cut his eyes to the side. He didn't want *someone* to know what had happened at the lake house. Who didn't he trust? she wondered. The local police. Or a member of her family! But how could he distrust her mother? Or her aunt and uncle?

"We don't have a security system," Jennifer said. "And it's my fault. Annie's been after me for over a year now to have one installed, but I hate those things. It always seemed to me that they're more trouble than they're worth."

"I'll call first thing tomorrow and have one installed," Dane informed them.

Chief Holman placed his hand on Dane's shoulder and led him aside. "We've done all we can here. No fingerprints. No clues of any kind. None of the neighbors saw or heard anything."

"What time did Mrs. Harden and the Laymans come back from dinner?" Dane asked.

"They said around ten-fifteen," Holman told Dane. "But the Laymans left and went home. It was about thirty minutes later, when Mrs. Harden went back downstairs, after she'd changed into her gown, that she discovered the break-in. She called 9-1-1 immediately and then phoned the Laymans."

"Annie Harden and I were at the Robinson family's lake cottage tonight." Dane lowered his voice to keep the conversation between himself and the police chief strictly private. "Someone driving a dark blue sports car with a Lauderdale County license plate shot at us. I returned fire and I'm pretty sure he took a bullet."

"Another attempt on Ms. Harden's life," Holman said. "You think this staged burglary and what happened out at the lake are connected, don't you?"

"Yes, I think someone broke in here, looking for something, and found the note Annie had left for her mother. Whoever did this knew where the Robinson family's lake house is because he showed up there before midnight."

"That means someone local."

"Either that or he's working for someone local, someone who knows the Robinsons and probably the Harden family, too."

"I'll give Sheriff Brewer a call and he'll send somebody out to the Robinsons's place on the lake." Chief Holman rubbed the back of his neck. "This isn't going to look good in the local papers or on WOWL-TV tomorrow."

"Dane!"

Annie motioned for him to come to her. She stood on the front portico, her arm around her mother. Royce Layman sat beside his wife on the steps, holding her hand, their fingers entwined.

"Annie's Navigator has a few bullet holes in it and there's a bullet in the tire I had to change." Dane handed the car keys to Holman. "And there's probably paint off the sports car on the driver's side. It wouldn't hurt to have things checked out, would it?''

Holman nodded, stuffed the keys into his pocket and started issuing orders for his men to finish up and clear out. He went over to speak to Royce Layman, assuring him they'd do their best to find the culprit.

Dane passed Royce on the steps. Annie's uncle glanced up at him. ''We're counting on you, my boy.''

When Dane joined Annie on the portico, he found her arguing with her mother.

''But why must I leave my own home?'' Jennifer's mouth drooped in a pitiful little pout.

''It isn't safe here, Mother,'' Annie said. ''Dane will have a difficult enough time keeping me safe without our having to worry about you.''

''Annie's right,'' Vera said. ''You should come home with Royce and me tonight and stay until this whole mess with Annie is straightened out.''

''I don't want to leave you, when you need me.'' Jennifer grasped Annie's hand tightly, as if letting go would summon some horrendous disaster. ''A mother is supposed to take care of her child…and you're the only child I have. Nothing must happen to you.'' Tears streamed down Jennifer's cheeks, streaking her creamy, translucent skin.

Dane gently eased Annie's hand from her mother's tenacious grip, then he brought both of Jennifer's hands together in his. ''If you want to help Annie, and I know that you do, then you pack a bag and go home with your sister. I'm not going to let anything happen to Annie. I'll guard her with my life.'' He gazed directly into Jennifer's moist, worried eyes. ''I give you my word.''

As a gentleman. He didn't say it, but Annie knew, as her mother did—as her aunt and uncle did—that that was what he'd meant.

"All right then, if you think it best for me to stay with Vera for a while, I'll go pack a bag." Jennifer's mouth lifted in a fragile smile. "I trust you, Dane Carmichael. I trust you with my only child's life."

Annie leaned back against the white Doric column on the left side of the portico, shook her head in amazement and covered her mouth to silence a stupid little chuckle that she couldn't control. Dane had handled her mother the way she'd seen her father handle her time and time again during their marriage. Earl Harden had always known just the right thing to say to make his wife do whatever he wanted her to do. She had never questioned his orders or his suggestions. And she'd never questioned his right to take charge of every situation.

No doubt Dane had learned from his father just how to handle a sensitive, delicate Southern belle. And God knew Jennifer Lee Forrest Harden was as sensitive and delicate a Southern belle as the New South had ever bred.

"I'll go with you, Jenny," Vera said, then followed Jennifer inside the house.

"Would you care for a drink, Mr. Layman?" Dane asked. "I think I saw a bottle of bourbon in the liquor cabinet earlier."

"I could use a drink," Royce said. "I'm afraid my old heart isn't used to so much excitement. First Annie's problems and now this break-in. What's this world coming to when people aren't safe in their own homes?"

Thirty minutes later, when the grandfather clock struck the half hour, Annie stood in the doorway, waving goodbye to her mother, who was tucked snugly between Aunt Vera and Uncle Royce in the front seat of their Mercedes. Annie closed the door and turned, then gasped. Dane stood directly behind her.

He caught her shoulders to steady her. ''It's late. We both need to get some rest.''

Her breathing quickened. Dane was close—too close. She could smell the masculine heat of his body, could feel the soft, warmth of his breath, could almost hear the beat of his heart.

''Don't you think we should talk?'' She wished he would release her and yet at the same time something inside her longed for him to pull her closer, to bring her up against his hard body and give her the feeling of being safe and secure.

''There's nothing that won't wait until morning.'' Dane dropped his hands from her shoulders. ''I told Chief Holman what happened at the cottage earlier tonight and gave him the keys to your Navigator. He's getting in touch with the county sheriff.''

She nodded, then swallowed. She was bone weary. Her body ached from the tumble and roll on the front porch of the Robinsons's cottage. A hazy fog of exhaustion clouded her mind as tiny fragments of memory tormented her. The rifle shots. Dane protectively covering her body with his. The godawful fear!

''Annie?''

''Yes?''

''Staying here really isn't safe, you know,'' Dane told her. ''The smartest thing for me to do is take you into hiding somewhere.''

''No! Absolutely not.'' She sought understanding when she stared directly into his eyes.

''You don't have to set yourself up as bait, honey. It's far too dangerous.'' He reached for her, but she sidestepped his grasp. ''Annie, I won't let you deliberately set yourself up this way.''

''You have no choice.'' Her voice possessed the calm,

cool control of a determined woman. "The decision isn't yours to make. I want whoever kidnapped Halley—whoever is trying to kill me—to come after me again. It's the quickest and best way to bring him out in the open. You know that as well as I do."

"By putting yourself in this position, you'll be making my job twice as difficult." However, Dane knew she was right. Using Annie as bait to draw out the man behind Halley Robinson's disappearance and the attempts on Annie's life was the quickest and perhaps easiest way to capture him. But it was also the most dangerous way for Annie. If he thought, for one minute, that he could dissuade her from remaining in her mother's home, making herself easily accessible to the would-be killer, he would whisk her away tonight. But he was smart enough to know when he was fighting a losing battle. Annie was damned and determined to do this. Now, all he had to do was keep her safe, while she risked her life to lure their attacker out of the shadows.

"I'm staying here," she said.

"I'll do everything within my power to protect you."

"I know you will." Their gazes met and held. The look they exchanged silently voiced his concern and her appreciation. "Take the room across the hall from mine. It has its own private bath…and if anyone comes upstairs, they'll have to pass that room before they come to mine."

"Try to sleep," he told her. "Take something, if necessary."

She moved up the staircase, then paused after a few steps, but she didn't look down at him. "I don't have anything I can take. Nothing except the pain pills. I never have a problem sleeping."

"Then maybe you won't tonight. I'll see if I can rig

something up to cover the broken pane in the back door and then I'll be on up. If you need me, just call out and—''

"And you'll come running?" Annie asked as she climbed the stairs.

"Yeah, honey, I'll come running," Dane said so quietly that he knew Annie didn't hear him.

Dane tossed and turned, flopping from one side of the bed to the other. He reached out in the darkness, groping on the nightstand in search of his watch. Grabbing it in one hand he held it up and checked the time on the illuminated face. Three forty-five!

Dane didn't think their attacker would make another "house call" this soon. The guy was probably holed up somewhere, nursing his wounds and either trying to figure out his next move or putting in a call to his superior. If he had a superior. And that was the problem—the main reason Dane couldn't sleep. If the guy who'd broken into the Harden house—the guy in the woods—was working for someone else, then the boss man could have already called in another employee.

Until a security system was installed, this house remained vulnerable to unlawful entry by anyone from a petty thief to Annie's stalker. But even if he fell asleep, there was little chance anyone could enter the house and come up the stairs without his hearing them. He was a light sleeper, awakened easily, and trained by years as a bodyguard to listen in his sleep.

When Dane laid his watch back on the nightstand, his hand encountered his hip holster. His instincts told him that they were safe—for tonight. But regardless of his certainty, he couldn't sleep. He hated the idea that Annie was putting herself in more danger than necessary by staying here. But he understood her reasoning and admired her courage. There wasn't anything weak or fragile about Annie. She didn't run from her fears—she met them head-on.

Dane laced his fingers together and cupped the back of his head with his palms. He kicked the sheet and lightweight blanket down to the foot of the bed and stretched. His toes touched the footboard of the antique bed. He tried to concentrate on relaxing, but the harder he tried the more tense he became.

He couldn't stop thinking about Annie. The way she'd laughed and smiled aboard the *Sweet Savannah*. The way the sunlight had highlighted the silky blue sheen of her jet-black hair. The way her eyes widened when she was angry. The sweet feel of her body pressed against his. And the hot, hungry way she had returned his kiss.

Dane's body grew hard as blood pumped heavily below his waist. He supposed Ellen Denby had been right when she'd said he needed to have sex. It *had* been quite a while since he'd been with a woman. But just any woman wouldn't do. Not now. Not since he'd meet Annie. The most stubborn, independent little cuss he'd ever known.

What was it about her that got him all hot and bothered just thinking about her? She was pretty. She had a nice figure. She was intelligent. But he'd known his share of women who possessed those same attributes. No, Annie was different. She was smart and sassy. Independent and alluring. Poised and passionate.

And every time she looked at him, he knew she wanted him. She might not like it much, might even hate the very idea of it, but it didn't matter. She could no more control her feelings for him than he could his for her. Even though they shared common backgrounds, Annie had made it perfectly clear that she despised the traditions and customs of the society into which she'd been born. And he embraced his heritage. He followed in the footsteps of his father, grandfather and countless Carmichael men before him. He was proud of his lineage and felt comfortable in the role of a Southern gentleman.

But a Southern gentleman needed a true Southern belle as his mate. Lorna had been his perfect counterpart. She had been all that was sweet and gentle and pure.

Annie Harden was nothing like Lorna. But then, he had no intention of mating with Annie for a lifetime. Wanting to make love to a woman didn't mean you had to make a commitment. And he was sure Annie would run from any permanent entanglement with him. But they could become lovers. An affair for as long as it lasted. Until the fiery passion burned itself out.

Dane shot up, turned on the bedside lamp and ripped off his pajama bottoms, which he'd only worn as a concession to his duties as Annie's bodyguard. He unzipped his bag, yanked out a pair of old jeans and shimmied them up his legs and over his hips.

He couldn't have an affair with a client! It was against all the rules, against his own principles. Getting personally involved with Annie could endanger both her life and his. He needed to be thinking with his head and not his groin.

Annie prayed for sleep, for just a few hours of rest. No worries, no troubles, no thoughts. But her mind wouldn't shut off and her body wouldn't relax. She had gone over everything that had happened since Halley's telephone call. Nothing made sense. Nothing added up. Nothing except the fact that Halley had disappeared and ever since she had gone to Point Clear four days ago in search of Halley, someone had been trying—repeatedly—to kill her.

What had she overlooked? she wondered. There had to be something, some clue, to help her solve the mystery. How had Halley's kidnapper known who she was talking to that night? Redial! Annie thought. Or had the man already been in Halley's room and listened to their conversation? Just what did these people think she knew? Whatever it was, had it cost Halley her life?

It has put your life in danger, an inner voice warned Annie.

What would she have done that night on the beach if Dane hadn't been there? And later, in her hotel room, what if Dane hadn't come back to check on her? And what if he hadn't suspected that there might be a bomb under her rental car? And what if she'd been alone at the Robinsons's lake house when the shooter had opened fire?

You'd be dead! she told herself.

She owed her life to Dane and all she'd done since she'd run into his arms on the Point Clear beach was argue with him, resist his kindness, and fight the urge to surrender to him. She hadn't shown any appreciation at all.

Her mother was paying him a small fortune to protect her. This was just a job to him. She didn't owe him anything! *Okay, so he's strong and brave and fearless, but he's not a man you want to get involved with,* her conscience warned her. *No way, no how. You've been down that road before, Annie ole girl. And you know where it leads—straight to heartbreak.* To-die-for good looks and courtly manners and impeccable breeding can camouflage a domineering tyrant or a philandering playboy.

But you want him, that inner voice taunted her. *You want him so bad you're—*

Annie sat straight up in bed. Perspiration moistened her body, causing her coral silk gown to adhere to her skin. Her femininity throbbed. Her nipples peaked. You're just horny, she told herself. You haven't been with a man since—

She turned on the bedside lamp, hunted down her coral

house slippers and matching silk robe. No use wearing out the bed, she thought. And no use lusting for a man who was so very, very bad for her. But there was also no use trying to pretend that she didn't want to go across the hall and climb into bed with Dane Carmichael!

Once out in the hall, she paused by Dane's open door. Tiptoeing into the room, she held her breath. His bed was empty. Where was he? Had something happened? Maybe he couldn't sleep, either. Maybe he went downstairs to get a drink or find a book to read or...

She made her way down the stairs. Not a sound. Then she noticed a dim illumination coming up the hallway from the kitchen. She glided along the hall, stopping when she reached the den, which opened up onto the kitchen.

Dane stood at the counter, barefoot and bare-chested, wearing nothing but a pair of faded jeans. Her eyes scanned him, glancing at his tousled, sun-streaked brown hair and moving slowly down to his muscular chest. Thick swirls of curly brown hair created a triangle that began just below his throat and traveled all the way downward, tapering at his navel and disappearing inside his unbuttoned jeans.

Annie swallowed hard. He was a beautiful sight. Magnificent manhood in all its glory. Everything feminine within her reacted to his blatant masculinity. She ached from the sheer pleasure of looking at him.

Turn and run back upstairs, she warned herself. He hasn't seen you. It's not too late.

She took several steps backward, inadvertently backing right into the wall. A loud gush of air escaped from her lungs.

Dane lifted his sky-blue eyes to her, his gaze raking over her, burning her with its intensity.

''Annie.'' On his lips her name was an endearment.

Oh, God! Oh, God! She couldn't let this happen. She just couldn't.

Chapter 10

Annie eased away from the wall. Dane stepped forward, his movements slow and easy, yet purposeful. *He was coming for her.* She knew this as surely as she knew her name. She had to get away before it was too late, before she surrendered to him.

Like a panther on the prowl, he stalked her. She crept backward, step by step, praying she had the strength to escape his predatory grasp. But when she looked into his eyes, she became transfixed by the blatant desire she saw.

"Annie." He said her name again as he approached her.

"I'm...I'm going back upstairs." She groped for words, for an explanation that would fend him off. "I noticed you weren't in your room, so I just came down here to check on you. Now that I see everything is all right—"

In two long strides he was in front of her. He reached out, grasped the back of her neck and pulled her to him.

Her startled cry didn't deter him nor did her barely audible plea. "No, Dane, no." She pushed against him, her efforts weak and halfhearted.

"Yes." He mouthed the word against her lips just before he captured them in a blazing kiss that turned her world upside down.

She tried not to respond, tried valiantly not to give in to her own wanton needs, but the moment he touched her, she'd been lost. She knew it—and so did he. This incredible hunger inside them had been building since that night on the beach when she'd run into his arms. Had it really been only days ago? Somehow it seemed as if she'd wanted this man all her life, that the passion ripping her apart inside had been growing for aeons. Not once in all her nearly thirty-five years had she experienced anything like this raw, uncontrolled need to mate with a man. To give herself completely and to take him in the same unconditional way. She'd never wanted anyone to the point of madness. Not until now. Not until Dane.

As his mouth devoured hers, hot and hungry, he cupped the back of her head in his palm. Opening his other hand, he spread it across the small of her back and pressed her into him until her mound rested against his swollen sex. Her body clenched and unclenched, shooting currents of desire from her core. She lifted her arms around his neck and gave herself over to the moment, to the utter pleasure of their sensual embrace.

She pushed herself intimately against him, glorying in the animalistic growl that erupted from his throat. His tongue lunged into the damp, dark cavern of her mouth, tasting and tempting, delving and retreating in an exciting imitation of the sex act.

Pure primeval need controlled her—mind and body—dictating her actions, giving orders to satisfy the raging hunger.

Her tongue thrust and parried in an unchoreographed mating dance with his. They couldn't get close enough. Couldn't taste enough. Couldn't feel enough. They wanted more. Much more.

Dane grabbed her hips and lifted her up and into him. She clung to him, mindless with passion. Raising her leg, she rubbed against him. Heat suffused her body as the fire in her belly burned white-hot.

Dane knew he had to have this woman and have her now! Nothing mattered except appeasing the beast inside him. The animal instinct that lay buried deep within controlled him. He had needed before, wanted before, and had even loved once. But nothing compared to this mindless obsession to possess a woman—this one woman. Annie.

He wanted to see her body, to touch and taste her until her essence was embedded so deeply in him that she would be a part of him. Lust ruled him as it never had, not even in the hormone-crazed days of his youth.

While his mouth ravaged hers, he lifted his hands to the lapels of her coral silk robe, grasped and tugged them apart. Then he removed the robe, letting it drop to the floor behind her. He kissed her chin, her throat, the swell of her breasts above her gown. She trembled and moaned when he raked his fingers across her jutting nipples. When he lowered his head and took one tight point into his mouth, Annie held his head, encouraging him. He moved to the other breast and paid it equal attention. And while he suckled her through the thin silk, he grabbed a handful of her gown and, inch by inch, raised it up the back of her legs enough for him to slip his hand inside and caress her bare buttocks.

He eased the straps of her gown down her arms, drawing it over her breasts and to her waist. Her breasts were high and round and full. Sweet temptation. He covered them, then cupped them and finally stroked them with his thumbs. Annie reached out and unzipped his jeans, then tugged them down his hips. When they fell to his feet, he kicked them aside and quickly pulled her gown up and over her head. He tossed it aside and took one long, appreciative look at her. She was beautiful. Not even the small, white, sterile strip that covered the length of her wound detracted from her perfection.

He skimmed his finger around the top edge of the bandage. "I don't want to hurt you."

"You won't."

Her assurance released him. They went at each other like savages. Touching, tasting, grunting and groping. Dane lifted her by her hips. She swung her legs around him as he hoisted her up and onto his straining sex. She cried out with pure sweet joy, reveling in the sensation of being filled completely.

Dane thought he'd die, so overwhelming was the pleasure of taking her, of burying himself deeply inside her. He wanted it to last, but knew the feelings were too powerful to endure.

He brought her hips backward and forward, pounding her against him, knowing that their movements were attending to her needs as well as his. Her muscles contracted, gripping his sex in her hot, wet sheath. He increased the speed of his plunges, unable to stop the raging tide of fulfillment sweeping over him. Her raspy, pleading cries sent him over the edge and he jetted his release into her.

She shuddered, the pressure building, higher and tighter inside her. Her climax hit her with hard, unrelenting power that sent shards of wild, sweet pleasure through her whole body and left her weak and her flesh ultra-sensitive. She clung to Dane, wanting them to remain a part of each other, needing this perfect moment to go on forever.

Dane kissed her tenderly, disengaged them from their intimate joining and swept her up into his arms. She laid her head on his shoulder and said nothing when he carried her out of the den, down the hall and up the stairs. He walked through her bedroom and into her private bath. After putting her on her feet, he kissed her, then reached into the shower to turn on the water.

He held out his hand and she accepted without reservation. Together they stepped into the warm shower and bathed each other, glorying in their renewed arousal. They dried hurriedly, dropping the damp towels on the floor in their haste.

Dane tended her wound and covered it with a new dressing, then she led him to her bed. Lying before him, she opened her arms. He stood over her, big, powerful and completely male, his erection telling her how much he wanted her.

Joining her on the bed, he caressed and kissed every inch of her body and when she thought she couldn't bear another minute of his loving attention, he parted her legs and taught her just how much she could bear. With each stroke of his tongue, he brought her closer and closer to fulfillment. She squirmed and twisted as the sensation intensified until finally she exploded with release. While she was still quivering with completion, Dane mounted her. When he entered her, she lifted her hips to meet him, taking him completely, wantonly, urging his conquest.

She wanted to be taken again, to be ravaged and plundered and dominated. She wanted nothing more than to be the woman who belonged to this man—and the woman to whom he belonged. No past. No future. No need for independence. No fear of being subjugated. Only the moment. The beautiful, perfect moment of unparalleled joy.

Their second mating was less frenzied, but equally in

tense. The hunger they had fed downstairs returned full force, demanding to be fed again. Dane made sure they didn't repeat the frantic, hurried joining they'd shared the first time. This time he made love to her as if they had forever. He brought her to the brink time and again, only to stop and build her frustration until she was begging for release.

And when completion claimed her, she fell apart in his arms, crying his name. The words *I love you* were on the tip of her tongue, but she managed, just barely, to refrain from saying them out loud.

Minutes later, Dane hammered furiously into her, then groaned like a roaring lion when his release came. His big body shuddered convulsively and then collapsed on top of her. He eased off her, pulled her up into his arms and held her. They lay side by side, their breathing ragged, their hearts beating rapidly, sweat glistening on their bodies.

"Dane?" She lifted her head to look at him.

He nuzzled her cheek with his nose. "Go to sleep, Annie. We don't need to talk about it now."

She kissed his shoulder, cuddled against him and closed her eyes. Dane was right. Whatever needed to be said could wait. All she wanted now was to sleep in her lover's arms this one time.

The ringing telephone jarred Annie from the most restful sleep she'd had in ages. With her eyes still closed, she groped across the top of the nightstand, searching for the phone. She accidently knocked the receiver off the hook. Damn! She opened her eyes, scooted toward the edge of the bed, picked up the receiver and put it to her ear.

"Hello?" Her voice was groggy.

"Ms. Harden?"

"Yes."

"This is Lieutenant McCullough."

Annie's eyes flew open. She shot straight up in bed, sending the sheet and blanket to her waist. Suddenly realizing she was naked, she dragged the sheet up far enough to cover her breasts.

"Yes, Lieutenant, what can I do for you?"

She glanced over at Dane, who had just opened his eyes and was staring at her.

"Ms. Harden, I'm afraid we've got some really bad news for you."

Annie's heart ached with the foreknowledge of what he was going to tell her. "It's Halley, isn't it?"

"Yes, ma'am. The body of a woman fitting Ms. Robinson's description was pulled out of Mobile Bay early this morning. The Mobile police department has already gotten in touch with her family. Her boyfriend, Mr. Boyd, identified the body about thirty minutes ago."

"H-how was she…" Tears lodged in Annie's throat. She looked at Dane through a haze of moisture.

Dane prized the phone from her hand and spoke to McCullough. "How was Ms. Robinson killed?" he asked.

Annie covered her face with her hands as tears racked her body. She'd known all along, deep down inside, that Halley was dead, but she had clung to the possibility that her young protégée had just been kidnapped and the police would find her alive. But now there was no hope. Clay Boyd had identified Halley's body.

"Yeah, I know. Thanks for calling," Dane said, then placed the receiver back on the telephone base. He turned and pulled Annie into his arms. He stroked her hair away from her cheek and tilted her damp face up so that she had to look at him. "Ah, Annie, honey, you knew."

She nodded. "Why didn't I just let her stay in that safe little world her parents had given her? Why did I have to encourage her to follow in my footsteps and break free?'' Tears streamed down Annie's face.

Dane caressed her cheek. ''Don't do this to yourself. You aren't to blame for Halley Robinson's death. If she hadn't wanted a different kind of life than the one her parents offered her, she wouldn't have taken a job on your magazine and—''

''I want to find the person responsible!'' Annie jerked away from Dane, her eyes afire with anger and determination. ''I want them punished for what they did. I want…''

''We'll find whoever was behind Halley's murder. I promise.''

''How—how was she killed?'' Annie asked.

''Honey, you don't—''

''Tell me!''

''He cut her throat.''

''Oh, God!'' Annie realized that Halley's killer would have done the same thing to her if she hadn't escaped and if Dane hadn't helped her.

She saw the look of concern and affection in Dane's eyes and knew he longed to comfort her. She understood that it was in his nature to care for others, especially the women in his life, whether they were friends, clients or lovers. An odd sensation zinged up Annie's spine. Complete realization of just how intimate they were dawned on her. And memories of the time they had spent making love in the hours before dawn came back to her all at once.

As if reading her thoughts, Dane said, ''We lost our heads, didn't we?'' He ran his gaze over her face, down her throat, and stopped on her uncovered breasts.

Warmth spread through her as she looked at Dane and remembered that he was naked under the sheet. ''I've been on the pill for years, if that's what you're worried about,'' she blurted. "The doctor put me on them to regulate my irregular period. I'm not promiscuous, or anything. I haven't had sex with anyone since…in years and years. So, you don't have to worry about other stuff. And—"

Dane gently cupped his palms around her face. "Shh… I'm not worried about anything, except taking care of you. My first priority is to keep you safe, and I'm afraid that when we made love, I didn't do that. I'm sorry, honey."

She closed her eyes, wanting to block out the sight of him. That tender, loving look. She bit down on her lower lip, then felt his lips on hers. Her eyelids flew open. He ended the gentle kiss and released his hold on her face.

"By becoming your lover, I've jeopardized my effectiveness as your bodyguard," he told her. "You realize that, don't you? This case has become personal because I have feelings for you. Instead of thinking logically, I might let my emotions make decisions for me."

"We couldn't help ourselves," Annie admitted. "It has never been like that for me. I have never lost control."

"I've never lost control so completely, either. It's almost frightening to think someone else has that much power over you." Dane's gaze met hers and locked, the truth of what had happened between them exchanged in that one long look.

"We probably got it out of our systems, didn't we?" Annie forced a fragile smile. "I mean, you can't feel like that about someone all the time. If you did…"

"It was great. Fantastic. The best either of us has ever had, but it can't go any further." Dane's eyes narrowed as a frown wrinkled his brow and tensed his jaw. "That is what you're saying, isn't it?"

Annie nodded. "Yes, that's… We've only known each other a few days. And what we do know is that you're the wrong type of man for me and I'm the exact opposite of what you find appealing in a woman.''

"So, what happened between us this morning was a two-time thing, not to be repeated. Right?"

"Right!"

"From now on, our relationship is strictly business," Dane said. "I'm your bodyguard and you're my client."

"We just have to forget about our making love."

"Sure. Just pretend it never happened."

"Uh-huh."

They both knew they were lying to themselves. Neither of them would ever forget what had happened or how they'd felt. Even now, while they were so adamantly denying their feelings, desire stirred inside them.

Annie tugged the blanket off the bed as she stood. She wrapped it around her and nearly tripped over the hem when she took her first step. She righted herself, lifted the blanket and smiled triumphantly at Dane.

"I'm going to take a bath and get dressed," she said. "I'll stop by Dr. Lowery's office to get my stitches checked, then I need to go over to see the Robinsons." She wanted a long soak in a hot bath to ease the soreness out of her body, but she'd have to settle for another shower. During their rowdy lovemaking she had used muscles she'd forgotten she had. And she just hoped she hadn't broken loose any of the stitches in her side.

Dane got out of bed, totally at ease with his nudity. "I'll catch a quick shower and meet you downstairs for—" he glanced at the clock on the nightstand "—brunch. I was going to say breakfast, but since it's nearly eleven—"

Annie's eyes widened in disbelief when she looked at the clock. "I never sleep this late!"

"We wore ourselves out," he said, then picked up his

jeans, stepped into them, turned around and left her bedroom.

Most of the town turned out for Halley Robinson's funeral, the overflow crowd gathering around outside the church. Annie wasn't sure she could have gotten through the ordeal without Dane's strength to lean on. Although they had kept to their agreement—that their relationship return to a professional one only—she knew that the strong emotions they'd shared nearly a week ago had formed an unbreakable bond between them. It was always there, even though they never spoke of it again or acted on the desire that neither could totally disguise.

Dane stood at her side during the graveside ceremony that followed the elaborate service at the church. He was the only person who understood the depth of her feelings. He was the only one to whom she had confided her guilt over helping Halley achieve her dream of independence from a family who had smothered her in the same way Annie's family had once done her.

The look of anguish on Mrs. Robinson's face was nearly Annie's undoing. Dane gripped her elbow and held her steadily on her feet as she spoke to Halley's parents. They stared at her through bloodshot eyes, thanking her for being there, for caring about their daughter. Annie felt no anger, no hostility or blame coming from Dennis and Amelia Robinson. Only a grief almost too great to bear.

Dane had suggested that she forego Amelia Robinson's invitation to join the family at their home after the interment, but Annie had insisted on going.

The Robinsons's Colonial beige brick home in Florence held the upper echelons of local society and the atmosphere, although subdued, retained the flavor of one of Amelia's gala parties. People shook hands, exchanged dainty little hugs and kissed the air at one another's cheeks. Two uniformed waitresses served hors d'oeuvres and a waiter attended the bar.

"There she is now." Jennifer Harden waved to Annie from across the room. "Come over here, dear. Look who we have with us."

Dane recognized his former father-in-law, Richard Hughes, and his second wife, Gloria, whom he'd married when Lorna was twelve. Richard looked the same—thick, steel-gray hair, lean physique, movie-star-handsome face—as if time had passed him by and left him a perpetual fifty, although Dane knew the man was well over sixty. Richard Jr. was a pale carbon copy of his father, only lacking in the original's charisma and easy charm. Dane and Dickie had never been friends, but they'd never been enemies, either.

He had remained in contact with Richard and Gloria for a while after Lorna's death, but it had been easier on all of them to gradually lose touch. He had missed the close relationship with Richard. They'd once been as close as father and son. Indeed he had thought of Lorna's father as a role model—a gentleman who epitomized all that Dane admired. There had been a time when he had aspired to emulate his father-in-law's sterling qualities as an upstanding citizen, a devoted husband and father, and a caring human being.

Richard thrust out his hand as he grabbed Dane by the shoulder. "Dane, my boy. How good to see you." He pumped Dane's hand and patted his shoulder. "Terrible thing, isn't it, poor little Halley Robinson being murdered that way? We know what her family's going through, don't we?" A fine mist of tears glazed Richard Hughes's stormy gray eyes.

When Gloria wrapped her arm around her husband, he released Dane's hand and stepped back to his wife's side.

Dickie held out his hand. "Hello, Dane."

Dane shook his former brother-in-law's hand. There was a weakness in Dickie's handshake just as there was a weakness in the man himself.

"We had no idea that Dane had once been married to your daughter, Richard," Royce Layman said as he and Vera closed ranks around Annie. "He certainly was a godsend for our girl." Royce gave Annie an affectionate squeeze. "He's going to take good care of her for us until this whole nightmare is over."

"When did you leave the FBI?" Dickie asked. "I can't imagine you as anything but a G-man."

"I've been with the Dundee agency for several years now."

Gloria Hughes reached out and took Annie's hand in hers. "It's unbelievable that Halley is dead and that someone is trying to harm you, too. Do you have any idea who or why?"

"We have some theories," Annie said, but didn't elaborate. Dane had instructed her to trust no one and not to share information with others, even her mother.

Your mother might accidently let something slip, Dane had told her.

"What sort of theories?" Richard asked.

"Just theories," Dane answered. "Nothing worth discussing."

"Well, if there's anything I or my family can do to help, just let me know," Richard said.

"Thank you. I'll keep that in mind."

An hour later, after a tearful goodbye to Mr. and Mrs. Robinson, Halley's eighteen-year-old brother and fifteen-year-old sister, Dane led Annie through the milling crowd of mourners. Just as they entered the black-and-white, marble-tiled foyer, Dane sensed someone staring at them. He glanced to the right just in time to catch a glimpse of a husky-built man with a military-style haircut, glaring at them. What caught Dane's immediate attention was the sling in which the man's arm rested. The moment the man realized Dane had caught him staring, he averted his gaze and maneuvered his way back through the horde.

"Who was that?" Dane asked.

"Who? Where?"

"The guy with his arm in a sling," Dane told her. "Over there, next to the lady in the wide-brimmed hat."

Annie searched the crowd. Her gaze rested on the man in question. "Oh, that's Jason Webber."

"Exactly who is he?"

"He's your father-in-law's employee," Annie said. "Well, actually, he works for Dickie at Hughes Chemicals and Plastics. I understand that he's been with the company for years."

Before Dane had a chance to react, Royce Layman came up behind them. "What's this about Jason?" Royce asked.

"Dane was just wondering who he is," Annie replied.

"Jason's the security chief at Hughes Chemicals and Plastics. He plays golf with us sometimes when Richard and I get together," Royce said. "Odd sort of man. A bit on the unfriendly side, but then, he's a Yankee, you know. Came from somewhere in Illinois or Indiana years ago."

"Is he a friend of the Robinsons's?" Dane asked.

"Jason? Why, no. But he's never far from Richard and Gloria, now that Richard is running for governor."

"Are you saying he acts as Richard's bodyguard?" Annie focused her gaze on her uncle.

"In a manner of speaking," Royce said.

"What happened to his arm?" Dane noticed that Jason Webber had disappeared.

"I asked Richard about that." Royce chuckled. "Seems he accidently shot himself while he was cleaning his rifle last week. He won't be able to use that arm for a few more days. Good thing it's not deer season. Jason's quite the hunter, you know."

Dane grabbed Annie around the waist before her silent gasp acquired sound. "Ready to go?"

"Uh, er, yes, I'm ready." She waved at her uncle. "'Bye Uncle Royce. Tell Mother that I'll call her later."

When they reached the sidewalk leading from the porch to the driveway, Annie halted. "Do you think Jason Webber is the man you shot at the Robinsons's lake house?"

Dane surveyed the area, checking to see if anyone was around who might have overheard Annie. Several people milled around on the porch, but he didn't think they were close enough to have heard her.

"We'll talk in the car." He grasped her elbow and led her out to her Navigator.

Once belted into her seat, Annie turned to Dane. "Well?"

"I don't know," he said. "It could be a coincidence that Jason Webber has a gunshot wound that he acquired last week and it could be that he was staring daggers through us because he just didn't like the way we look."

"Jason Webber works for Richard Hughes, and one of the two names on the last page of Halley's notebook is Richard Hughes. She underlined it twice."

"Jason works for Dickie," Dane said. "Richard Hughes Jr."

"Okay, I'll agree that it's possible the Richard Hughes in Halley's notebook referred to the junior and not the senior Hughes. So what could Dickie and Jason Webber be trying to hide?''

"I have no idea. But once the agency completes the search for Martin Edwards, we might have our answer."

Annie cooked shrimp and filet mignon on the indoor grill, while Dane prepared their salad. They sat together in the kitchen and discussed a hundred and one scenarios while they ate. They carried their after-dinner coffee into the den and Annie put a Stan Getz CD on the new CD player she had purchased. The music wrapped around her, got inside her and soothed her. She kicked off her shoes and tucked her feet under her when she sat on the sofa. Dane placed his coffee cup on a coaster atop the end table and sat beside her.

"Don't forget to call your mother," he reminded her.

"How often do you call your mother?"

"Once a week," Dane said.

"Ever the dutiful son, aren't you?" She grinned. "But then, what else could I expect from a true gentleman."

You weren't a gentleman last week. You were a brute, who acted just as savagely as I did, she thought. She realized by the way he was looking at her that he knew what she was thinking.

The doorbell rang. Annie jumped. Dane tensed.

"Just sit still. I'll get it," he said.

When he headed toward the foyer, she followed him. "It could be Mother stopping by, since I forgot to call her."

"Will you just stay here!" Dane's voice reeked with aggravation.

"Oh, all right." Annie huffed, crossed her arms over her chest and leaned against the wall at the base of the staircase.

Dane opened the door to find a young woman holding a huge flower spray, similar to the ones that had been piled on Halley Robinson's grave this afternoon.

The girl smiled. "I have a delivery for Annie Harden."

"These are for Ms. Harden?" Dane stared at the huge floral arrangement of bloodred roses.

"Yes, sir. There's a card." The woman pointed to the sealed envelope attached to the spray, which had a large satin ribbon draped across it with the words Rest In Peace emblazoned on it.

Dane took the flowers from her. "Thank you."

She smiled warmly and left. Dane waited until she got in the delivery van marked Flowers by Margaret before he turned toward Annie. He kicked the door closed.

"Someone sent me a funeral spray?" Annie touched the flowers, yelped and pulled back her hand.

"What's wrong?" Dane tossed the flowers to the floor.

"Nothing, I just pricked my finger on a thorn."

Dane lifted her injured finger, brought it to his lips and kissed the tip.

"She said there was a card." Annie glanced down at the wreath.

Dane released her hand, bent over and jerked the card off the spray. He ripped it open. Annie grabbed it out of his hand and read it quickly. All color drained from her face.

Dane caught the card as it fell from her limp fingers, then scanned it quickly. "You're next" was the succinct but frighteningly clear message.

Chapter 11

"The florist said the arrangement was paid for in cash and the money was delivered by a messenger," Dane told Annie when he hung up the phone. "She said that she and her assistants were so busy with flowers for Halley's funeral that they didn't have time to question an odd request. Neither she nor any of her employees even remember what the messenger looked like."

"Another dead end." Fingering the bloodred roses on the wreath, Annie's hand trembled.

She had made it through Halley's funeral without collapsing, without giving in to her emotions and crying her heart out, the way she'd felt like doing. Having Dane at her side had made it easier somehow. Strange as it seemed to her, she had felt as if she'd been drawing from his strength.

Don't fall into that trap, she cautioned herself. Strong men make it easy for you to lean on them. But in return they want your undying adoration and obedience. Father had demanded it and Preston had expected it. And Dane was cut from the same cloth, wasn't he?

Thunder rumbled in the distance. Annie glanced out the windows. Gray rain clouds swirled around in the sky, forewarning of the approaching storm.

Dane lifted the wreath away from the wall in the den where he'd placed it while he phoned the florist. "I'll dump this out back by the trash," he said. "Why don't you go on upstairs and take a bubble bath and I'll put on a pot of coffee and—"

"Don't give me orders!"

Dane stared at her, puzzlement in his eyes. "Sorry. I didn't intend for my suggestion to sound like an order."

Annie hung her head, smoothed her hands over her forehead and back over her hair. Then she glanced up at Dane, who had picked up the wreath and was carrying it toward the kitchen. "Dane!"

He paused, but didn't turn around. "Yes?"

"I'm the one who's sorry. I overreacted. I know you weren't giving me an order."

"Yeah, sure."

Annie slumped onto the sofa, forked her fingers through her hair, tugged down on the ends and growled a cry of disgust and aggravation. Why did she keep doing that to Dane? Maybe he was an old-fashioned Southern gentleman. Maybe he was a member of the good ole boys' club. But that didn't mean he was a carbon copy of her father. And she knew he wasn't an imitation of Preston Younger. Just having known Dane for less than two weeks, she could see the differences in him and her ex-husband. She sensed that there was an honesty and goodness in Dane that had been lacking in Preston. And not at any time during their marriage had Preston made her feel the way Dane had the night they'd made love. Preston had known how to take, but not to give. Dane, on the other hand… Annie sighed.

"Would you like some coffee?" Dane called from the kitchen.

She took a deep, relaxing breath. "Yes, thank you." She rose from the sofa, took a few tentative steps toward the kitchen, then paused. "I think I will go upstairs and take that bubble bath you suggested."

"I'll have the coffee waiting for you," he said without glancing her way.

Dane listened to her footsteps as she left the den and went out into the hall. After removing his coat and tie and loosening the first button of his shirt, he began preparations for the coffee.

A smart man would get himself out of this assignment any way he could, he told himself, even by hiring a replacement from another security firm. A smart man would never have made love to a client.

Why am I sticking around, taking Annie's verbal attacks, when I know I should leave?

Because you don't trust anyone else to take care of her, an inner voice acknowledged. *You cannot bear the thought of anything happening to her. You've committed a bodyguard's unforgivable sin—you've become emotionally involved with your client. Hell, you've done more than that— you've made love to her.*

And you want to make love to her again.

Just as he flipped the switch to start the coffeemaker, the phone rang. He lifted the receiver from the wall base.

"Harden residence."

"Dane?" the feminine voice asked.

"Yeah. Is that you, Denby?"

"I've got some information on Martin Edwards," Ellen Denby said.

"Have you found him?" Dane asked.

"In a manner of speaking. But, Dane, I've got to warn you—"

"Martin Edwards is somehow connected to the Hughes family." Dane felt as if a large lead weight had dropped into his stomach.

"How did you know? Anyhow, it seems that Martin Edwards is dead. He's been dead for twenty years."

Dead for twenty years! Dane did some swift calculations in his head and came up with the answer—twenty years ago, Dickie Hughes had been only eighteen. What kind of mischief had Dickie been into back then?

"So Edwards is dead," Dane said. "What's the connection?"

"Edwards was the plant manager for Hughes Chemicals and Plastics in Florence, Alabama, which is one of four companies your former father-in-law owns in the southeast."

"Right. And?"

"And twenty years ago, that particular plant in the Shoals area did a little illegal dumping of PCBs into a nearby river, thus causing death to wildlife and illness to some residents." Ellen paused, took a deep breath and continued. "Hughes paid some hefty fines on behalf of the company, but Martin Edwards was the one held legally responsible for what happened and shortly thereafter, he committed suicide."

Dane's mind whirled with the information, processing it and combining it with other things he knew—and with his gut instincts. Why would Halley Robinson have been interested in a twenty-year-old suicide? And no one would have been interested in a PCB dumping scandal that had been resolved so long ago. If this was the story that had cost Halley her life, there had to be more to it.

"Did Edwards have a family?" Dane asked.

"A wife and daughter," Ellen replied. "They moved out of state a few weeks after Edwards's death."

"Where are they now?"

"We're working on it," she told him. "I expect we'll have that information for you by tomorrow."

"Thanks. By the way, have y'all unearthed anything interesting about Clay Boyd?"

"Not so far," she said. "It appears that Mr. Boyd is as clean as a whistle. But we did find out something about Royce Layman that may or may not have anything to do with this case."

"What?"

"It seems Mr. Layman and several prominent Florence businessmen own quite a bit of stock in Hughes Chemicals and Plastics."

"Yeah, I knew. Jennifer Harden owns some Hughes stock, too. Any leads on the other two stories Halley Robinson was working on?" Dane had hoped that one of the other stories would remove any suspicion from his former father-in-law. He couldn't—wouldn't—believe that Richard was involved in Halley's murder or in the attempts on Annie's life. Lorna had adored her father, and Dane had become fond of him. And more importantly, he had learned to respect him and trust him. If there was any connection between the Hughes family and Halley Robinson, then Richard Hughes Jr. was the person involved. Dane would bet money on it.

"The other two stories were pretty cut-and-dried," Ellen said. "There doesn't seem to be anything suspicious about either."

"I want y'all to do a little more digging into Dickie Hughes's life, especially what was going on with him twenty years ago. See if there's a personal connection between Dickie and Martin Edwards.''

"I'll get on it right away." Ellen cleared her throat. "Dane?"

"Yeah?"

"Murdock will be winding up his case in a couple of days, about a week sooner than he thought, so if you still want another agent to take over—''

"Annie's family wants me to stay on the case," he said.

"Mmm-hmm. And what does Annie want?"

Damn Ellen Denby! Dane thought. The woman had a sixth sense when it came to reading between the lines. "Annie agrees with her family."

"Mmm-hmm. Give me a description of Annie Harden."

"What! Give you a— Stop being a smart-ass, Denby."

"A sweet Southern belle, is my guess. Fragile and dainty and very helpless. And, of course, old-fashioned. And probably beautiful, to boot."

"You're out of line," Dane said.

"Did I describe her to a T or not? I can't see you giving up a long overdue vacation for a woman who wasn't—''

"Annie Harden is nothing like you described her." She's nothing like Lorna, he thought. "Annie's her own person—tough, smart and independent. And before you say it, no, she isn't my usual type. But then, Annie is a client, not my date for the cotillion."

Dane grimaced when he heard Ellen's smothered laughter. He realized too late that he had overreacted. Ellen had added two and two and come up with a definite four.

"Annie sounds like just the kind of woman…er, client, you need right now. I'll give you a call when we get that information on Edwards's wife and daughter."

Dane hung up the receiver, poured two mugs of coffee, doctored Annie's to her tastes and headed for the stairs.

When he reached Annie's room, he found the door closed. He paused, lifted his foot and tapped several times.

"Coffee's ready," he said.

"Be right there," Annie called through the closed door. "Who was on the phone?"

"My office."

Annie swung open the door and ushered Dane into her bedroom. His gaze skimmed her quickly from head to toe, taking in everything, from the towel wrapped around her head to the gleaming red of her toenails. He couldn't help but wonder just what she had on beneath that red-and-gold-striped silk robe. He knew her body intimately, every sweet curve, every tempting inch. His sex hardened at the memory of their lovemaking.

"Any news?" Annie reached out and took the mug from Dane's hand.

"Martin Edwards was the plant manager at Hughes Chemicals and Plastics here in Florence, about twenty years ago."

Annie sat in one of the two pink-and-white-checked upholstered chairs in front of the window alcove. She lifted the mug to her lips and sipped. "Where is he now?"

"Dead." Dane crossed the room and sat across from Annie in the matching chair. "He committed suicide after he was held legally responsible for the company dumping PCBs into the river."

"I was only a kid then, fourteen, but I vaguely remember hearing my grandparents talking about that one summer when I visited them here. But I didn't remember any details or names of the people involved."

"I've got Denby checking on Edwards's family. He had a wife and daughter." Dane leaned back in the chair, spread out his legs then crossed his ankles as he relaxed and drank his coffee.

"You still don't think Richard Hughes could possibly be involved in Halley's death or—''

"Richard is one of the finest men I've ever known."

"I agree that Richard is a fine gentleman, who seems to be just what he presents himself to be," Annie said. "But everyone has their dark side. Very few people live to be Richard's age without having a secret or two buried in their past. Or at the very least, something they would prefer the rest of the world not know."

Dane knew Richard Hughes's secret—the one thing he didn't want anyone else to know, something he hadn't told his wife or his son. A sad, heartbreaking secret that only Richard and Dane shared.

Dane placed his coffee on the table. He sat up straight, bringing himself to the edge of the chair. Dangling his arms between his parted legs, he thumbed his fingers together in a repetitive beat. "If Martin Edwards has any connection to Halley's death, then I'd say the Hughes we need to investigate is Dickie."

Annie noticed the change in Dane's facial expression and the faraway look in his eyes. "Dickie couldn't have been much more than a kid himself when Edwards died," she said.

"He was eighteen."

"You know something about Richard Hughes, don't you? Something no one else knows." Annie focused on Dane, narrowing her gaze to center on his profile.

Without answering her, Dane stood and turned toward the shuttered windows. He opened one of the shutters and looked outside at the front lawn.

"It's nothing that has any connection to this case," he said, his voice distant and forlorn.

Annie sensed some great sorrow weighing heavily on Dane's shoulders, some tragedy that still resided in his heart. She rose from the chair and moved toward him. When she came up behind him, her hand raised to touch his back, he turned abruptly and stared at her. Instinctively she took a step backward. The look on his face told her that he was in pain, but he didn't want her comfort.

"What I'm about to tell you must never go any further," Dane said. "Do you understand?"

She nodded. What secret did Dane share with his former father-in-law that could be so terrible that Dane was still suffering from its aftereffects?

"Lorna..." He paused, as if saying her name hurt him. "My wife was beautiful and kind and gentle. She was so delicate and fragile and sensitive. She was everything I'd always wanted in a wife. I thought she was a lot like my mother—a genteel Southern lady. And in that respect she was. But..." He hesitated, as if he couldn't bring himself to speak ill of the woman he had loved. "The first couple of years after we married, Lorna was very happy, making a home for us and participating in all the clubs she belonged to and enjoying life in Alexandria, where we had bought a house."

"Dane, if this has nothing to do with the case—my case—then you don't have to tell me." She grabbed his arm. She didn't think she wanted to know any more about Lorna Hughes Carmichael. Dane's beautiful, perfect, beloved wife.

Dane pulled Annie's hand off his arm and clasped it in his. "After we'd been married several years, she decided she wanted a child. Nothing could have pleased me more, so... She couldn't get pregnant. We tried a dozen different doctors, went through numerous procedures. The more she tried, the more obsessed she became with getting pregnant.

"I watched my wife slip from unhappiness into a deep depression. Richard assured me that all she needed was time to accept the facts, mourn her inability to have a baby and...he said she needed a child. So we started adoption proceedings. And Lorna began seeing a psychiatrist. I'd insisted that she needed help. But nothing helped. Nothing.''

Annie squeezed his hand. The fine sheen of moisture in Dane's eyes tore her apart inside. Here was this big, strong man almost in tears. She wanted to wrap her arms around him and comfort him. ''Dane, you don't have to tell me. Please, I really don't want to know.''

He grabbed her chin and forced her to look directly into his eyes. ''Lorna killed herself.'' He spoke the words calmly, with no emotion, as if he'd been reading the sentence from a book.

''Oh, God! Oh, Dane.'' Unable to go against her need to comfort him, she reached out and wrapped her arms around him.

''I came home from work and found her in our bedroom. She'd taken an overdose of sleeping pills.'' Dane stood there in Annie's arms, the pain inside him tightening harder and harder until he could barely breathe.

Tears formed in Annie's eyes. ''My poor, poor Dane.'' Standing on tiptoe, she kissed the side of his face.

He ached with the memory, dying inside once again, the way he had when he'd found Lorna that evening ten years ago. ''She looked so pretty, so peaceful, lying there on our bed.''

Annie clung to Dane as his big body trembled, memories flaying him, slicing into his heart, cutting deeply into his soul. He pulled Annie closer, holding on to her, sensing that this woman was his lifeline. He had never told another soul the truth about Lorna's death. Not even his own family.

''I called Richard.'' Dane's voice became quieter,

calmer. "Before I called the police. Even though he was in Georgia and we were in Virginia, he told me not to do anything, to leave it all to him. And so I did exactly what he told me to do.

"I don't know how long I sat alone in our bedroom, at Lorna's side, but eventually a doctor—someone Richard had contacted—came to the house. He handled the entire situation. Lorna's death was ruled an accidental overdose of prescribed medication."

"Why did Richard want Lorna's suicide covered up?" The moment she asked the question, she felt Dane's body tense in her arms.

"I suppose I was in shock at first and then in some sort of grief-stricken fog later," he said. "Otherwise I might have questioned Richard sooner. But it was weeks later before we really talked about what had happened. I felt so guilty because I hadn't been able to do something to prevent Lorna from taking her own life."

"It wasn't your fault." Annie held Dane like a fierce tigress protecting an endangered cub. "I know you did everything you could have done."

"That's what Richard told me." Dane eased out of Annie's embrace, turned away from her and closed his eyes. "You see, Lorna's mother—Richard's first wife—had a history of mental problems and, when Lorna was just a little girl, she killed herself. She hung herself in her bedroom and—" Dane swallowed hard. "Lorna was seven years old when she found her mother."

Cold shivers washed over Annie. "Richard covered up his wife's suicide, too, didn't he?"

"Yes." Dane rubbed the back of his neck, then opened his eyes and turned to Annie. "Richard's secrets are personal tragedies."

"I'm so very, very sorry." Annie had never wanted anything so much as she longed to encompass Dane in a safe, loving circle of peace and happiness. She wanted to erase the pain she'd seen in his eyes, longed to help him forget the past, to help him let it go and forgive himself for crimes he'd never committed.

"You'd never..." Dane let the words trail off, as if whatever he'd been about to say was somehow wrong.

"No, I'd never do what Lorna did," Annie said. "But then, I don't have a family history of mental illness and I didn't have to grow up with the memory of finding my mother's body after she'd committed suicide."

"It was unfair of me to compare the two of you," Dane told her.

"Like comparing apples to oranges."

"Two Southern-bred women from similar backgrounds," Dane said. "But nothing alike. No more alike than your ex-husband and I."

"I know I was wrong thinking you and Preston were two peas in a pod," Annie admitted. "You're far more than a gentleman, Dane Carmichael—you're a good man."

Her arms opened of their own volition, in an invitation to come and find solace within her embrace. She noticed the indecision on his face, the uncertainty in his eyes.

Annie held her breath and waited.

Dane came forward, slowly, hesitantly, as if he were unsure of himself and of her. When he was only a couple of feet away from her, he stopped, and she somehow knew that he was trying to resist the lure of her comforting arms.

Then suddenly, he reached for her, slipped his arm around her and tenderly eased her up against him. Leaning down, he nuzzled her neck. "You smell so good, honey."

She held him close, savoring his nearness, accepting the gift of his trust. "I need you, too," she whispered, and gave herself over completely to the moment.

He clung to her, breathing in the scent of her, taking strength from her as he'd never done from any other woman. Knowing that he was safe with Annie. He could find peace in the haven of her body. A passion that could soothe. A gentleness that could inflame.

He kissed her neck, then moved lower to her chest, seeking her breast. He suckled her through the thin silk of her robe. Her nipple beaded instantly.

''Dane,'' she sighed.

He backed her away from the windows, his hands fondling her, his mouth devouring hers. He jerked the towel from her head and tossed it to the floor. He speared his fingers through her damp hair. The minute the back of her legs encountered the side of the bed, Annie began undressing him. First, his shirt came off and floated to the floor. Then she reached for his belt. By the time she had him completely naked, he had stripped the red-and-gold robe away from her body and left her naked, too. She reached for him, trying to entice him back into her arms, but he would have none of it. Instead, he worshiped her with his touch, his lips and fingertips exploring her thoroughly.

Outside the wind howled, swaying the trees, as lightning streaked the black sky with jagged illumination and earth-trembling thunder shattered the nighttime solitude. Perspiration glistened on Dane's big, hard body, dampened his hair and blended with the moist glow on Annie's skin as they tossed and turned on the bed.

Annie lay on her belly, Dane straddling her. He rubbed her neck, her shoulders and her back, then eased his hands slowly downward to massage her hips. While his fingers worked their magic on her body, he kissed, licked and nipped her heated flesh from neck to heels. Every rational thought disappeared from his mind—the past, the present and the future—as he concentrated on Annie. She was the beginning and the end of his world.

Their heated passion melted away the pain from Dane's soul, releasing him from the past. Now, here, in Annie's bed, making love with her and sharing the ultimate pleasure he had found with no other woman, Dane said farewell to his grief. Farewell to Lorna. Relief filled his mind and heart. He was free.

When Annie writhed beneath him, moaning with the aching heat of longing boiling inside her, he turned her over onto her back and began a frontal assault. First her mouth and then her ears. Sweet, savage kisses. And all the while, his hands moved over her damp skin, caressing her breasts, tormenting her nipples, sliding between her thighs. He urged her legs apart just enough to seek and find the entrance and work two fingers inside her burning depths.

Annie reached for him, wanting him to take her and end this glorious torture. But he eluded her grasp. When he licked a path from her navel to the apex between her thighs, she tensed like a coiled spring. The minute his tongue moved closer to its destination, she gave herself over to him completely, aware of the ecstasy to come.

She melted into mindless pleasure as he made love to her with his mouth. Release came in a sudden blaze of fiery light that ignited inside her the same moment a lightning bolt hit the earth somewhere nearby. Her breathing quickened, her heartbeat accelerated and perspiration dotted her forehead and upper lip. She cried out. With her cry of fulfillment echoing inside him, Dane came to the brink of release.

While ripples of continuing satisfaction danced along Annie's nerve endings, Dane lifted her hips. But she jerked away from him and shoved him down on the bed. Surprised by her actions, he started to protest, but before he could complain, Annie circled his erection and caressed him intimately. He groaned as her hand pumped him with a slow, steady beat. But when she skimmed fervent kisses down his body and stopped to allow her mouth to replace her hand, Dane growled, forked his fingers through her hair and held her head in place. He urged her to love him as he had loved her.

Mindless with pleasure, Dane moaned and grunted. Then he uttered a few incoherent words that indicated how thoroughly he was enjoying her ardent attention. His groans grew louder and his movements more fierce. He warned her that his completion was near, but she chose to continue, to carry this special loving to its conclusion.

Dane exploded and splintered into shards of unparalleled satisfaction. When the spasm of intense release eased off to quivering aftershocks, he brought Annie up and over him and took her mouth in a hungry, appreciative kiss. He held her close, kissing her, telling her how wonderful she was and how much she had pleased him.

They fell asleep in each other's arms, while the stormy night was held at bay, as was the reality that tomorrow would bring.

Chapter 12

Annie lifted the bacon from the skillet, laid it on the paper towel to drain, then turned her attention to the scrambled eggs in another skillet. It had been a while since she'd prepared breakfast. She and her mother had become accustomed to Helen being around to take care of the meals and the housework on a daily basis. Of course, until the present situation was resolved, Helen would be helping Aunt Vera's housekeeper. No one was safe in this house or anywhere Annie stayed. Not as long as someone was trying to kill her. She'd come to realize that the only thing that stood between her and death was Dane Carmichael.

Before dawn, Dane had awakened her. She had opened her eyes drowsily and smiled at him, then opened her arms and welcomed him into her embrace and into her body. They'd made love slowly, maddeningly, driving each other to the breaking point, then retreated to form a new attack. When release had claimed them, they had absorbed every ounce of satisfaction and then fallen asleep again.

Just remembering what she had shared with Dane, the passion and the pleasure, aroused Annie anew. She had never experienced anything like this, not with anyone. Certainly not with Preston. She couldn't explain exactly what it was. A hunger. A desperate need. A madness. Whatever it was, it rode her hard, and the more of Dane she got, the more she wanted. She knew it was the same for him.

Even though she wasn't sure what it was—this wild, uncontrollable thing between Dane and her—she knew it really wasn't love. She'd known him less than a week. It couldn't be love. She'd never believed in love at first sight, even as a teenager and certainly not now that she was nearly thirty-five. No, it wasn't love. Lust maybe. Lust! That was it. And unlike love, lust didn't last. It burned itself out and left nothing but ashes.

The doorbell rang. Annie tensed. Dane was upstairs in the shower. She felt safer in her mother's house now that a security system had been installed, but whoever was at the door wasn't trying to break in. Don't go to the door, she warned herself. But you could go and see who it is, and if you don't know them, you don't have to open the door.

She pulled her robe securely across her body and made sure the tie belt held the silky material together. Just as she started up the hall, she heard Dane running down the stairs. Fully dressed in a brown sport coat, tan slacks, cream shirt and striped tie, he looked every inch the professional businessman. Of course, Annie knew better. Beneath his jacket, he wore a gun. And behind that gentlemanly facade was a warrior. And a primitive man.

Dane glanced back over his shoulder as he paused at the front door. "You weren't going to answer it, were you?"

"I was just going to see who it was!"

Dane peered through the viewfinder. Royce Layman stood on the porch. Dane eased the door open and stepped aside to allow Annie's uncle entrance. Royce came into the foyer, shook hands with Dane and smiled when Annie approached.

"Is something wrong?" Annie asked. "Is Mother—"

"Your mother's fine," he replied. "She and your aunt Vera wanted me to stop by and check on you. They were afraid you might be upset after Halley's funeral yesterday."

Annie hugged her uncle. "Would you like to join us for breakfast?"

"No, thank you, dear." Royce patted her affectionately on the back. "I've already eaten."

"Please, assure Mother and Aunt Vera that I'm fine." She glanced meaningfully at Dane. "My bodyguard is taking very good care of me."

Royce turned to Dane. "Any new leads in the case? The sooner you catch this person who's trying to harm our Annie, the better for all of us."

"My agency is working on it full-time, Mr. Layman," Dane said. "And I assure you that we'll find out who killed Halley and who's behind the threats to Annie."

"Just keep us informed." Royce shook hands with Dane, gave Annie another hug and started to open the door.

The ringing telephone delayed Royce's departure. He closed the front door and waited while Dane hurried into the living room and picked up the extension. Annie and Royce joined Dane, their full attention focused on his conversation.

"Morning," Dane said to Ellen Denby as he smiled at Royce Layman. It wasn't that he didn't trust Layman or that he actually thought the man might somehow be involved. It was more a nagging worry in the back of his mind—a concern that Layman might let some information fall into the wrong hands.

"We found out where Edwards's wife and daughter moved after his suicide," Ellen said.

"Where?"

"A small town in Ohio. Rogersville. The wife's name is Wilma and the daughter is Rene. We're tracking down more specifics about both women, but we do have a current address—412 Tunstill Avenue."

"Thanks for calling," Dane told her. "I'll be in touch."

"I take it that you're not alone," Ellen said. "I'll just wait for your call, unless we uncover something vital in the next ten minutes."

Dane placed the receiver on the telephone and turned to his audience. "My office," he said. "They just wanted to report in and let me know they're checking out a few leads."

Royce smiled. "I'll be going, then. If you need me, just call."

"I will," Annie assured him. "Give Mother and Aunt Vera my love."

When Royce Layman's Mercedes pulled out of the driveway, Dane followed Annie into the kitchen. While he poured two cups of coffee, she filled two plates with bacon, scrambled eggs and toast, then they sat opposite each other at the table.

Dane took a sip of coffee. "Martin Edwards's wife and daughter live in Rogersville, Ohio. I think we should fly up there today and talk to them."

"Was that the information your office gave you over the phone?"

"Yes."

"Why didn't you tell Uncle Royce?" Annie's eyes widened. Her mouth formed a perfect oval. "Oh, you don't trust my uncle! How could you possibly distrust Uncle Royce?"

"The same way you distrust my former father-in-law, a man I trust as much as you trust your uncle."

"Touché," she said. "I suppose we can't trust anyone except each other at this point, can we?"

"Probably not." Dane nodded to her plate. "Finish up breakfast and then get dressed. And pack an overnight bag. While you're getting ready, I'll call and get us a flight to Rogersville and make hotel reservations."

"Do you think Edwards's wife really might have some pertinent information?" Annie asked.

"Guess, we'll find out later today, won't we?"

They rented a car at the Dayton New Lebanon Airport and drove the fifty miles to Rogersville. They picked up a city map, ate a hurried lunch of burgers and fries and set out in search of Tunstill Avenue. Located in a middle-class area of town, with tree-lined streets and homes built in the sixties, Tunstill made a circle that was comprised of neat lawns and well-kept homes.

The house at 412 was a redbrick ranch-style, with white shutters and a two-car garage. A large For Sale By Reliable Realty sign perched in the center of the green lawn.

Dane pulled the rental car into the driveway, parked and got out. Annie followed him up onto the front porch and to the door. Dane rang the doorbell. No answer. He tried the storm door. Locked.

"Let's try the back door," he said as he stepped off the porch and rounded the side of the house.

He knocked at the back door. Nothing. He knocked again. Harder. "Mrs. Edwards?" he called.

Annie peeped into the kitchen window. "Furniture and appliances are all there, but there aren't any lights on."

"The electricity is still connected," Dane said. "They haven't pulled the meter."

When Dane and Annie came around the side of the house, a tall, slender, redheaded woman waved at them from the front porch of the house next door. Annie waved back at her.

"Nobody's there," the redhead said. "If you want to see the house, you'll have to call the Realtor."

"We're looking for Mrs. Edwards and her daughter, Rene," Dane said.

The woman shrank back into the afternoon shadows falling across her porch. "Mrs. Edwards died a few months ago and Rene...she...Rene's selling the house."

"Do you know where we can reach Rene?" Annie asked.

"She moved. Left the state," the woman said.

"Do you have any idea where she moved?" Dane asked.

Before the woman could reply, a burly, partially balding man joined her on the porch. "My wife and I don't know anything," he said. "Rene didn't tell us anything!"

"In case you remember something, you can contact us at the Serenity Inn downtown," Dane said. "My name is Dane Carmichael and I'm a private investigator."

"I told you—we don't know anything!" The man grabbed his wife's arms, urged her back into the house and slammed the door.

"Well, what do you think that was all about?" Annie shared a they-know-something glance with Dane.

"Let's check with a few other neighbors and then go by Reliable Reality to see what they can tell us."

* * *

Five hours later, after questioning neighbors, checking with the Realtor, and exploring every possible avenue to unearth Rene Edwards's whereabouts, Annie and Dane checked into the Serenity Inn in downtown Rogersville.

Annie dropped down on the bed, kicked off her shoes and fell backward. "Well, we accomplished a whole hell of a lot today, didn't we?" she said sarcastically.

"There's something very wrong with the scenario," Dane said as he removed his jacket, hung it over a chair and sat. "Rene Edwards seems to have vanished off the face of the earth. She put her house up for sale and didn't even leave the Realtor a number where she can be reached."

"That is very odd." Annie closed her eyes and sighed as fatigue overcame her. "Mrs. Freeberg said that Rene told her that she'd contact her when she got settled."

"And that was nearly three weeks ago." Annie dragged a pillow from beneath the spread, doubled it over and stuck it under her head. "Wonder why she was in such a hurry?"

"Good question. One I wish I knew the answer to. If I did, we might be able to figure out if there's any connection between Martin Edwards's suicide and Halley Robinson's murder."

"What are we going to do now?" Annie asked.

"Go back to Florence in the morning." Dane loosened his tie, removed it, tossed it on the small table beside him and unbuttoned the top three buttons of his shirt. "I'll call Denby and have her contact an Ohio investigation agency to see if they can do some legwork for us."

"I'm beat," Annie said. "My feet ache, my back aches, and I've got the beginning of a headache."

"Why don't you take a shower and go to bed?" Dane

smiled mischievously. "I'll be glad to join you in the shower and wash your back. And later…"

"A tempting offer." Annie rolled off the bed, stood and sauntered over to Dane. She slid down onto his lap and wrapped her arms around his neck. When she rubbed her cheek against his, she groaned and pulled away. "You shave first and then you can scrub my back."

When she tried to stand, Dane pulled her back onto his lap and wrapped his arms around her. "I've never had a, uh, a physical relationship with a client before. And getting intimately involved with you is wrong, but—"

Annie covered his mouth with her hand. "But you can't help yourself any more than I can." She gave him a quick kiss, then smiled as she laid her head on his shoulder. "We've got it bad, you know. We're going to have to work this out of our systems and the only way to do that is by having sex as many times as it takes for the fire to burn itself out."

"I like that idea." Dane cupped her breast and squeezed gently.

"Shave first," she told him. "And then we can play in the shower."

Dane stripped down to his briefs before he drew water in the sink and began shaving. Annie removed her jacket, slacks and blouse and folded them into her overnight bag, then took off her knee-highs, bra and panties and shoved them into a small plastic laundry bag. She slipped into her red-and-gold silk robe.

When she entered the bathroom, Dane splashed his face with water, removing the remaining shave cream, and reached out for her. He caught the belt of her robe, pulled it loose and slid his hand inside and around her waist. The robe fell open. She leaned into him, allowing her breasts to rake his chest.

Dane sucked in a deep breath, tugged the robe off her shoulders and tossed it on the floor. After reaching inside to adjust the water, he lifted Annie and set her under the shower. He stripped off his briefs and joined her.

They bathed each other, savoring each touch, enjoying the foreplay that soon led to the lovemaking they both wanted—both needed. The fire between them burned hotter and higher, showing no signs of dying out anytime soon.

An hour later, Dane, in his wrinkled slacks and unbuttoned shirt opened the door for pizza delivery, while Annie blow-dried her still damp hair.

"Pizza's here," he told her, and held up the large box.

Annie finished with the dryer, laid it on the vanity and ran a comb through her hair. "I can smell it all the way in here. I'm famished."

Dane set the box on the table, flipped the lids on the two colas and spread out napkins. "Dinner is served, madam."

Annie emerged from the bathroom, wearing her robe and nothing else. She grabbed a piece of pizza and plopped down into the chair. "I'm so hungry, I could eat a horse."

"I think that's pepperoni and sausage," Dane said teasingly. "But if you'd prefer horsemeat, I can toss this pizza in the garbage and call them to order another one."

Cutting her eyes toward him, Annie gave him a hard look. "Don't you dare touch this pizza."

A soft rap at their motel room door ended Annie and Dane's teasing. Annie held the pizza halfway to her mouth. Dane dropped the piece he'd just picked up back into the box.

"I'll go," he told her.

Dane glanced through the viewfinder and saw Rene Edwards's redheaded neighbor standing on the other side of the door. He unlatched the safety catch, unlocked the dead bolt and opened the door.

"Hello again, Mr. Carmichael," the woman said, a tense smile on her face. "May I come in?"

"Of course."

Dane stood aside to allow her into the room. He glanced over at Annie, who laid her piece of pizza down into the box, stood up and secured the tie belt on her robe.

"I'm sorry about this afternoon," the redhead said. "I wanted to talk to you, but my husband wouldn't let me."

"Won't you sit down, Mrs., er, Mrs.?"

"Franklin. Tina Franklin." She crossed her arms at her waist and rubbed her elbows nervously.

"Do you know where Rene Edwards is?" Annie asked as she approached their visitor.

"Are you really a private investigator, Mr. Carmichael?" Tina asked.

"Yes." He reached inside his jacket, which hung on the back of the chair where he'd been sitting, and pulled out his ID. "If this isn't enough, I can give you a number to call to verify my identity."

Tina inspected Dane's ID, then handed it back to him. "What about her?" She nodded toward Annie.

"This is Annie Harden. She's my client. Mrs. Harden is the publisher of a regional magazine in Alabama. Recently one of her reporters was murdered and since then someone has been trying to kill Ms. Harden. We have reason to believe—"

"They killed Rene's cousin? Oh, God! Oh, God!"

"Rene's cousin?" Annie asked.

"Mrs. Franklin, please, calm down and tell us—"

"I had to make sure you weren't one of them," Tina interrupted. "If someone killed Rene's cousin and they're trying to kill her—" Tina glanced at Annie "—then it must be them, the same men who warned Don and me to keep our mouths shut.''

Dane and Annie exchanged questioning looks, then Dane asked, ''What men are you talking about, Mrs. Franklin?''

''About two and half weeks ago, a couple of men came snooping around Rene's house, just like you two did this afternoon.''

When Dane noticed how shaky their guest looked, he pulled out a chair. ''Won't you sit down, Mrs. Franklin?''

''Thanks.'' She took the seat, placed her hands in her lap and glanced from Dane to Annie. ''These guys were looking for Wilma, and when I told them that she was dead, they wanted to know how they could get in touch with Rene.'' Tina rubbed her shaky hands together. ''I told them I didn't know where Rene had gone, just that she had recently put the house up for sale and moved away.''

''Did you get their names?'' Dane asked.

''They didn't give me their names, they just told me that if I knew where Rene was that I'd better tell them. They—they threatened me. I think they could tell I knew something because...well, they told me to keep my mouth shut if anybody else came around asking questions and that if I knew where Rene was I'd better tell them or I'd be sorry.''

''Do you know something?'' Annie asked.

''Did you tell these men anything else?'' Dane laid his hand on Tina's shoulder.

''Yeah, I told them.'' Tears sprang into Tina's hazel eyes. ''They scared me. I was afraid not to tell them.''

''Just what did you tell them?'' Dane bent down on his haunches in front of Tina and took her hands into his. ''It would help us a lot if you told us.''

Tina sucked in a deep breath. Tears trickled down her

cheeks. "Rene and I were friends. She's a good person. She took care of her mother after Mrs. Edwards got sick." Tina nibbled on her bottom lip. "All Rene told me was that she'd gotten hold of some information that proved her father's suicide twenty years ago had actually been murder. And she was scared because the person responsible for her father's murder knew she had the information and had called to warn her to keep her mouth shut. She was afraid they might kill her, so she—she told me that she sent the information to her cousin in Alabama."

"Her cousin?" Annie came over to Tina and looked directly at her. "Did she tell you who her cousin was?"

"No, she didn't mention her cousin's name. But she did tell me that her cousin was a reporter."

"Halley was Rene Edwards's cousin?" Annie looked at Dane. "Is that possible? I've known Halley for several years and I thought I knew most of her relatives."

"They might not have been first cousins," Dane said. He released Tina's hands and stood. "Mrs. Franklin, do you have any idea where Rene Edwards might have gone?"

"No, I swear. I don't have the foggiest notion. I think she's in hiding somewhere and she's not going to show herself as long as she thinks her life is in danger." Tina hung her head. "I told those men about Rene sending that information to her cousin. I didn't mean to tell them, but…but I was so scared."

"We appreciate so much your coming here tonight." Annie grasped Tina's hand and shook it, then draped her arm around the woman as she stood and hugged her. "I promise you that we are going to find the person responsible for putting Rene on the run and we'll make sure the whole truth about her father's death comes out."

"I've got to go." Tina backed toward the door. "I

waited until Don went bowling with his friends before I
came. I want to get home before he does. He'd be awfully
upset if he knew I'd talked to you. He's afraid for me.''

"Before you leave, could you tell me what the two men
who threatened you looked like?'' Dane asked.

"Sure. One guy was tall and dark and wore sunglasses.
I figure he was in his thirties. The other guy, the one who
made the threats, was older—early fifties, I'd say. He was
stocky and had a real short haircut. And his accent was
like yours. Very Southern.''

"Thanks.'' Dane walked Tina outside. "If Rene con-
tacts you—'' he handed her his business card "—call this
number and they'll know how to reach me. Day or night.''

Tina nodded, then ran down the corridor and out to her
car. Dane returned to the room and locked the door behind
him.

"If Martin Edwards didn't commit suicide, then who
killed him and why?'' Annie asked. "Could it have been
that he wasn't responsible for the illegal PCB dumping and
was going to turn in whoever was?''

"He was the plant manager,'' Dane said. "He was the
man in charge. He had to have known what was going on
and was probably the person who ordered the dumping.''

"But he had to answer to the company owner—to Richard Hughes!'' Annie took a hesitant step toward Dane.
"Maybe Edwards was just following orders.''

"Richard owns several companies in the Southeast, but
twenty years ago he was headquartered just outside Savannah. He started sending Dickie around to the various
plants when he was just a teenager. He wanted his son to
learn the business from the ground up. Maybe Dickie—''

"You just aren't willing to explore the possibility that
Richard Hughes could be behind everything, are you? You
think hc's too much of a Southern gentleman to order an

illegal PCB dumping or to let one of his plant managers take the rap. You don't think he's capable of ordering someone's murder." Annie's face flushed with anger. "Well, he was capable of covering up his wife's suicide and his daughter's."

She almost wished the words back when she saw the look on Dane's face. He couldn't have looked more stunned or saddened if she had slapped him.

"There's a big difference in trying to protect those you love from scandal and in committing a crime—to being responsible for having someone murdered."

"Then if it wasn't Richard Hughes who—"

"First of all, we don't know for sure that Martin Edwards was murdered," Dane told her. "And if he was murdered because he was about to blow the whistle on someone else who was responsible for the PCB dumping, then there are other possible suspects. Dickie, for one. Even if he was only eighteen, he was the boss's son and would have used his position to do whatever he wanted to. And Jason Webber definitely comes to mind. He was the chief of security at the plant, and Tina Franklin's description of the man who threatened her could fit Webber."

"We aren't going to find out any more staying here in Ohio," Annie said. "Why don't we see if we can get a flight out tonight? We need to talk to Richard as soon as possible. If he's innocent, maybe he can shed some light on this and even help us."

"He's innocent," Dane said.

"I hope you're right. After all, you're not the only person who thinks highly of Richard. My aunt and uncle are close friends with Gloria and him. And practically the whole town of Florence is working on his election campaign. Your former father-in-law has a great deal to lose, if he turns out not to be the man you think he is.''

He accepted the drink offered him. He actually preferred his whiskey on the rocks, but his employer served the bourbon straight.

''So, Dane and Annie flew to Ohio this morning,'' his boss said. ''Do you think the Franklin woman will talk?''

''I think we scared her enough to keep her quiet, if she actually knows where Rene Edwards is.''

''And what if she tells Dane Carmichael what she does know?''

''Isn't that the reason we wanted Carmichael to take Ms. Harden's case?'' he asked.

''Dane is one of our kind, that's for sure, but he's an honest man. And truly honest men can be dangerous.''

''Are you saying that, if it comes down to it, you're willing for me to eliminate both Annie and Dane?''

''If it comes down to it, then, regrettably, yes, eliminate both of them.''

Chapter 13

Dane stood in the partially open door of Annie's bedroom and watched her while she slept. They'd arrived back in Florence at dawn, both exhausted from their whirlwind trip to Ohio. He'd awakened an hour ago, at eight, showered and shaved and gone downstairs to start the coffee and make a few phone calls. Denby would get in touch with Dundee's associates in Cincinnati and employ them to investigate Rene Edwards's whereabouts. She would also dig for more information about Hughes Chemicals and Plastics here in Florence—twenty years ago, around the time of the PCB dumping and Martin Edwards's death.

Watching Annie as she lay in the center of the bed, her arms wrapped around the pillow on which he'd slept, as if she were hugging him, stirred some deep emotions within Dane. Emotions he'd rather not deal with. Not today. Not ever.

He had loved only one woman in his whole life. Lorna. And he had failed her miserably. If only Lorna's father had been honest with him about the mental illness that ran in her mother's family—the illness that had led both Lorna's mother and her to take their own lives. He would have done anything to save her. If only he'd known. Maybe the psychiatrist could have helped her more, if he'd known the truth about her family's mental health history.

Lorna had been born and bred to be a Southern gentleman's wife, the kind of woman he had wanted and expected to marry. He had thought she was perfect for him, perfect in every way. And she *had* been perfect—except for one fatal flaw.

In the ten years since Lorna's death he hadn't loved another woman, didn't think he could ever care deeply for someone else. But here was Annie. Sassy, rebellious, independent Annie. He'd known the woman two weeks, yet he felt as if he'd known her forever. What he felt for her wasn't what he'd felt for Lorna and it certainly wasn't love. But he did care about Annie. He cared deeply.

He thought they'd been right to admit their attraction to each other, to call it by its proper name—lust—and to agree that the best way to handle it was to accept it, give in to it and allow the fire to burn itself out. And it would burn out sooner or later. Something that powerful wouldn't last.

He couldn't get enough of Annie or she of him. This hunger between them possessed them in a way neither could resist. He was drawn to her, and she to him, on the most primitive, basic level.

Dane wanted to go to her, wake her and make love to her again. Selfish bastard, he rebuked himself. He needed to be thinking about finding the person who had ordered Halley Robinson's murder, the person intent upon seeing Annie dead, instead of using his energy to contemplate the pleasures of having sex with his client.

He eased the bedroom door closed, went downstairs and looked up the number for Hughes Chemicals and Plastics. Just as he reached for the telephone in the den, it rang.

"Harden residence," Dane said.

"Dane?" Ellen Denby asked.

"Yes. What's up?"

"I've followed through on your instructions," she told him. "And I have some information that you might find interesting."

"What?"

"It's about the summer, twenty years ago, that all hell broke loose at Hughes Chemicals and Plastics in Florence, after the discovery that the plant had been illegally dumping PCBs into the river. Guess who was working there between his senior year of high school and the beginning of his freshman year of college?"

"Dickie Hughes." He'd known it! Damn, he'd known that if anyone had been involved in that mess it was Dickie. Not Richard.

"Right. While he was working at the Florence plant, he and Jason Webber became friends. They were a couple of young bachelors who partied together. And—" Ellen paused for dramatic effect "—Richard Jr. was dating sixteen-year-old Rene Edwards!"

"Webber and Dickie and Edwards. All together at the plant at the same time." Dane's mind went into overdrive as he tried to sort through the possibilities. But nothing added up. There had to be more. A missing piece of the puzzle.

"One other thing," Ellen said offhandedly. "I don't know if it means anything, but that summer Dickie spent in Florence, he lived with Royce and Vera Layman."

"Layman!" Webber, Dickie, Edwards *and* Uncle

Royce. Were they all involved? They had to be, if he could just figure out how.

"I'd say you need to talk to Richard Hughes Sr. to find out just how much he knows about that summer and about Martin Edwards's death."

"I don't think Richard was involved," Dane said. "In any way. He probably wasn't even in the area that summer."

"Dane, don't let your loyalty to your former father-in-law cloud your vision. Even if he wasn't actually involved in the PCB dumping, or in forcing Edwards to take the rap, or in Edwards's so-called suicide, he has to know something. Remember, he's the man in charge. The big boss. At the very least, he allowed the coverup."

"Thanks, Denby. Keep me informed as soon as you get anything new on this case."

"Sure thing," Ellen said. "By the way, how is Annie?"

"Annie's fine."

"Glad to hear it. I'm really looking forward to meeting the lady who finally got through that thick hide of yours. She must be some woman!"

"Stuff it, Denby!" Dane hung up the phone.

Ellen was right. Annie had gotten to him, in a way no other woman ever had. But he'd be damned if he'd admit that to Dundee's only female agent. Ellen had been needling him for a long time about his lack of a love life. *A guy like you should be married and raising a family,* she'd told him. *You shouldn't waste the rest of your life mourning your dead wife.* He could have turned the tables on her and asked her why she wasn't married, why he never saw her with the same guy twice. But nobody pried into Ellen's private life. No one dared.

Did he want to get married again? Did he want children? Maybe. Probably. But despite his relationship with Annie, he knew a future with her was probably out of the question. After all, they were totally unsuited. And they weren't in love, just in lust.

She would probably never see him as anything other than a duplicate of her father and ex-husband. And even if the day came when she could accept him for the man he really was, could he ever let go of the past, of his dream of the perfect wife, of his memories of Lorna?

Shaking off his thoughts about Annie, about marriage, and how the two didn't mix, Dane dialed the number for Hughes Chemicals and Plastics. He wanted to ask Dickie Hughes a few questions.

Annie absentmindedly tapped her foot on the floor as she and Dane sat in the waiting area of the executive offices at the Hughes plant. Dickie's secretary, Judy Cantrell, had asked them to wait, that Mr. Hughes would see them directly. That had been twenty minutes ago.

Dane had awakened Annie at ten and shared with her the information his agency had given him over the phone earlier that day. Afer she'd showered and dressed, she had gone downstairs and found breakfast waiting for her. Waffles and sausage links. And a good cup of coffee. Dane Carmichael could cook, something no self-respecting good ole boy would dream of doing. Other than barbecuing, which was an acceptable manly chore. Every day she spent with Dane, she saw a new facet to his personality, a new trait she found endearing.

Fidgeting, tired of waiting, Annie checked her watch. One forty-five! Just as she rose from her chair to protest to Dickie's secretary, the outer door swung open and her uncle Royce entered.

He paused, smiled at her, nodded to Dane and then told Judy that he was there to see Dickie.

Judy glanced past him and smiled nervously at Annie. "Ms. Harden and Mr. Carmichael are waiting to see him, too."

Royce turned to them. "What business do y'all have with Dickie?"

"We just need to ask him a few questions," Annie said.

"We've come across some information that we think might be linked to Halley Robinson's murder," Dane told him.

"Really?" Royce asked. "What sort of information?"

"It seems that Halley might have been given some evidence concerning the suicide of a man who was the plant manager here twenty years ago." Studying Layman's reaction, Dane noted a tightening in his facial muscles. "Do you remember Martin Edwards? He was supposedly guilty of allowing PCBs from the plant to be illegally dumped into the river."

The color drained from Layman's face. His shoulders slumped. He cast his gaze to the floor.

"Did you know Martin Edwards, Uncle Royce?" Annie asked.

"Yes, I knew Martin. He was a fine man. A family man." Royce walked across the room and gazed out the windows that overlooked the parking lot. "I suppose he just couldn't live with the disgrace. Such a pity he chose that way to end things. We would have stood by him and seen him through. Richard had told him that the company would support him, pay all the legal costs. I've never understood why he..." Royce turned abruptly. Color splotched his cheeks. "What possible connection could Martin's suicide have to Halley Robinson? What sort of information do you think she had?"

The door to Dickie Hughes's office opened. Jason Webber, his arm no longer in a sling, stood guard just inside the door. Dickie emerged, went straight to Royce Layman and shook his hand.

"I'm afraid I'll have to postpone our appointment a few minutes," Dickie said. "It seems Annie and Dane have something urgent they want to discuss with me."

Annie had never paid much attention to Dickie Hughes. He was attractive enough, she supposed, if you liked the tall, slender type. However, his delicate features bordered on the feminine. In most instances, Dickie seemed to fade away alongside his handsome, manly, charismatic father.

"They've got some ridiculous notion that Halley Robinson's death might be somehow connected to Martin Edwards's suicide," Royce said. "You remember, don't you, Dickie, you were staying with us that summer?"

Jason Webber cleared his throat loudly. All eyes turned to him.

"I think this discussion is best suited for the privacy of Mr. Hughes's office," Webber strongly suggested.

Five minutes later, with everyone seated in Dickie's office—everyone except Jason Webber, who stood behind Dickie's chair, his pose that of a guardian protecting his charge—Annie felt a strange undercurrent in the room. For the first time since Dane had suggested the possibility that her uncle might somehow be involved, she wondered if Dane could be right. No, it wasn't possible. Uncle Royce wasn't the kind of man who would be involved in murder.

Dickie Hughes placed his clasped hands atop his desk, straightened his shoulders and looked directly at Dane. "I have no idea how you made a connection between Martin Edwards's suicide twenty years ago and Halley Robinson's murder, but I can assure you that whatever your source of information, it's incorrect."

"You remember Rene Martin, don't you, Dickie?" Dane asked, and was rewarded with an indiscreet blush on his former brother-in-law's hollow cheeks. "You and she dated that summer, before her father died."

"Yes." Dickie cleared his throat. "I dated her a few times that summer. But I don't see—"

"Rene Edwards was in possession of some information that, according to her, proved her father's death was not a suicide."

"That's preposterous," Jason Webber said, his voice deadly calm. "Martin was depressed and despondent. He was so ashamed of what he'd done, how he had betrayed Richard and the company, that he took his own life. The coroner ruled his death a suicide."

Suddenly a memory flashed through Dane's mind. *Let me handle this,* Richard Hughes had told Dane when Lorna died. *The coroner will rule Lorna's death an accident. There's no need to tarnish her family's good name or put any of us through the humiliation. Believe me, son, Lorna would want it this way.*

If Richard Hughes had possessed the power to change a coroner's findings from suicide to accidental overdose, then was it possible he'd had the power to have other findings altered from murder to suicide? No, Richard wouldn't have covered up a murder! Unless— Dane knew that nothing was more important to Richard than his family's good name. What if Richard had been protecting Dickie?

Annie waited for Dane to speak up, but he remained silent. When she glanced at his face she realized his mind was a million miles away. Something Webber had said must have triggered a memory of some kind. Was he, at long last, questioning his former father-in-law's integrity?

"We have reason to believe that Rene Edwards sent Halley Robinson the proof she claimed she had," Annie explained. "Whoever murdered Martin Edwards found out that Halley had this proof and he hired someone to retrieve the evidence and murder Halley to keep her quiet. But the killer didn't get to Halley before she called me and told me…'' Annie glanced at Dane. She took his nod as a signal to continue. "Halley mailed a package to me and I'm sure that package contains the information Rene gave her."

"If you have this information, then why haven't you turned it over to the police?" Webber asked, his keen dark eyes narrowed on Annie.

"I haven't received the package, yet," Annie admitted. "But that isn't going to stop us from finding out the truth."

"If there is any truth to this wild story of yours, why would Rene send the information to Halley Robinson? Why not a newspaper reporter?" Dickie asked. "And why haven't you contacted Rene and asked her if she sent Halley any type of evidence that her father's death wasn't a suicide? She'll tell you that someone is fabricating vicious stories. Probably one of Father's political opponents."

"Rene's mother and Halley's grandmother were first cousins," Royce Layman said, as if thinking out loud. "I thought everyone knew. It's common knowledge. If any such information exists, then Rene would have known she could trust her cousin."

"Whatever you think Rene knows, you're wrong," Dickie said. "I worked here the summer the PCB dumping scandal hit and Martin took all the blame for it. He held a plant meeting and told the employees that he and he alone was at fault. He couldn't face a trial and more scandal for his family, so he killed himself. It's that simple. There can't be any proof that his death wasn't a suicide!"

"Rene Edwards has vanished, so we can't ask her anything until she's found," Dane said. "She put her mother's house in Ohio up for sale and disappeared. I think she's afraid for her life.''

"Why should she be afraid?" Royce asked. "Why didn't she just go straight to the police with her so-called evidence?"

"Maybe she thinks that whoever she's afraid of has the power to influence the police," Annie suggested.

"Just what are you implying?" Dickie shot up out of his chair. His face flushed and perspiration dotted his upper lip. He glowered at Annie. "I hope you're not implying that my father was somehow involved."

"Of course she wasn't implying that Richard was involved," Royce said hurriedly, as if he were trying to calm Dickie.

"Ms. Harden can't possibly think Richard Hughes would do anything illegal." Jason Webber placed his hand on Dickie's shoulder and urged him back down into his chair.

"I'd like to talk to Richard," Dane said. "We can probably clear up this matter with a simple conversation."

"Richard is out of town," Webber said.

"He and Gloria got away for a few days of vacation before he goes off to Birmingham for a rally there this weekend," Layman explained.

"You of all people should know the kind of man my father is." Dickie looked directly at Dane.

"I do," Dane said. "But Richard may be able to help us uncover the truth about Martin Edwards's death. I'm sure if he knew that there's evidence floating around out there somewhere that Edwards might have been murdered, he would want to do whatever he could to help us find the killer and bring him to justice."

"Of course he would." Webber kept his hand on Dickie's shoulder, as if making sure he stayed put and kept quiet. "I'll be joining Richard this weekend in Birmingham and I'll tell him about your concerns. I'm sure he'll want to talk to you as soon as he comes back to town."

"And when will that be?" Annie rose to her feet.

"He's due back in the Shoals area for the big Fourth of July celebration at Spring Park in Tuscumbia," Webber said.

"If you'll give me a number where I can reach him, I'll call him and explain the situation myself." As he stood, Dane's gaze locked with Webber's.

"I'm afraid I can't give out Richard's vacation number. Not even to you," Webber said. "He and Gloria gave strict instructions not to be disturbed."

Dane nodded. "Then when you speak to him, ask him to call me."

"Certainly." Webber gave Dickie's shoulder a squeeze, then rounded the desk and went over to Annie. "May I escort you out, Ms. Harden?"

Instinctively, Annie backed away from Jason Webber. Dane moved between them and took Annie's arm in his.

"We'll see ourselves out," Dane said.

When they reached the hallway, Annie started to speak, but before she could do more than open her mouth, Dane stopped her.

"Don't say anything until we're in the car."

"But—"

"Wait!"

Once Annie was seated behind the wheel of her Mercury Navigator, she started the engine before Dane had a chance to buckle up. He knew she was upset that he'd asked her to stay quiet until they got outside the plant. But he had been afraid that in her exuberance over her suspicions, she might talk a little too loud and be overheard. Besides, she was liable to go off the deep end with her speculations.

Something told him that Richard was still her chief suspect. He had to admit, reluctantly, that Richard's name now appeared on his mental list of suspects. But Dickie's name was still at the top, followed by Royce Layman's. And his gut instincts assured him that whatever else he didn't know for sure, he did know that Jason Webber was an accomplice.

One of the first things he'd had Denby do after Halley's funeral was run a check on Webber.

"I'm pretty sure Webber is the man who shot at us when we left the Robinsons's cabin," Dane said.

Annie kept her gaze focused on the road, but Dane noticed her eyelids flicker and her jaw tighten.

"I had the office check him out." Dane waited for Annie to comment. She didn't. "His record is clean as a whistle. Not so much as a traffic ticket."

Annie pulled up at a red light on Court Street. She tapped her neat, French-manicured nails on the steering wheel. "You know as well as I do that they were hiding something. They're scared spitless. Even Uncle Royce seemed nervous." The light turned green. Annie pressed her foot on the gas pedal.

"Are you acknowledging the possibility that your uncle could be involved?" Dane asked.

Annie sucked in a deep breath. "Yes." She glanced quickly at Dane and then back at the street in front of her. "Are you willing to admit that your former father-in-law might be involved?"

Was he? Dane wondered. He had mentally added Richard's name to the list of suspects, but was he ready to voice his suspicions out loud? Somehow admitting that Annie could be right about Richard seemed paramount to admitting that his own life was a lie, that all he believed in was false. If a man like Richard, whom Dane admired and trusted, could be involved in the deaths of two people, then Dane could no longer have faith in his own judgment.

Annie whipped the Navigator into the driveway, then eased it into the garage. She killed the motor, unbuckled her safety belt and turned to Dane.

"You still can't accept the truth, can you? A Southern gentleman, a leading member of the good ole boys' club, just might not be the noble man you think he is. The golden god may actually have feet of clay."

Dane sat silent and unmoving, trying to come to terms with the possibility that Annie was right. Even if Richard hadn't been involved in Martin Edwards's death, he could have—and probably would have—been involved in the coverup. Especially, if it meant saving his son.

Annie opened the door and started to get out. Dane grabbed her arm. "It's possible that Richard is somehow involved."

"Oh, Dane." Annie saw the lost look on his face, the pain etched around his eyes and mouth. "I know what it cost you to admit that—"

"Even if Richard did something illegal to help protect Dickie, I can't believe he was behind Halley Robinson's murder or the attempts on your life." Dane released Annie's arm. "I need to talk to Richard to find out for myself just what he knows."

"For your sake, I hope I'm wrong about Richard. And I hope I'm wrong about Uncle Royce, too. I can't believe he's capable of doing anything illegal any more than you can believe the worst of Lorna's father."

When they got out of the Navigator, Dane rounded the vehicle and fell into step alongside Annie. Just as they emerged from the garage, Dane noticed a car slowing down on the street in front of the house. One of the car's darkly tinted windows eased down a fraction. The afternoon sunshine hit the tip of the metal object inserted through the partially open window.

Dane grabbed Annie, threw her to the ground, covered her body with his and rolled her off the driveway. That's when Annie saw the rifle that was aimed directly at them.

"What—" Annie cried, then heard the shots whizzing through the air, several peppering the garage door. All the while the shots rang out, Dane sheltered her body with his as he moved her farther and farther away from danger.

Relying on Dane completely, she didn't move and barely breathed. The rifle shots continued for several seconds, then the car sped away, tires screeching and the motor roaring. Loud, piercing screams came from somewhere nearby. When Dane lifted himself up and off her, she saw two of her neighbors running toward them. Stacy Kimball and Andy Porter. Undoubtedly, Stacy had been the one screaming.

Using his left hand, Dane lifted Annie to her feet. When she grabbed his right arm and leaned into his body, he groaned.

"What's wrong?" she asked, then she saw the rip in the sleeve of his jacket. She lifted her hand to the tear and felt the moist stickiness of fresh blood. "Oh, God, Dane, you've been shot!"

Chapter 14

As Dane had been rolling on the ground, one of the bullets zinging past him had ripped through his jacket and shirt and tore through the flesh of his upper arm. He'd tried to pass off the wound as nothing, but Annie would have none of it. She wouldn't allow him to swagger and act all macho on her, despite his efforts to assure her all he needed was a bandage.

"You're going to the hospital," she told him.

"We're calling Chief Holman." Dane grabbed Annie's chin. "Are you all right?"

"My God," Stacy Kimball said as she approached Annie and Dane. "Someone tried to kill y'all. Right here in Florence, in broad daylight. I can't believe it. Are y'all okay?"

"I'm fine," Annie said. "Dane was hit."

"Andy got the license number on the car. He's gone to call the police. I'm sure they'll send an ambulance," Stacy said. "Who in the world would do something so awful?

A person isn't safe anywhere these days. Not even at home.''

"When the police get here, tell them that I've taken Mr. Carmichael to ECM hospital," Annie said. "They can find us in the emergency room."

Dane protested, but Annie insisted. Her will was every bit as strong as his and he knew it. Besides, his arm hurt like hell, so he didn't put up much of a fight.

Annie waited in the ER, talking to Milton Holman, while the doctor cleaned and sutured Dane's wound. She wasn't sure just how much she should tell the police chief. She knew he was one of Richard Hughes's staunchest supporters and that he and Dickie were golf buddies, but that didn't mean the police chief would do anything illegal to protect the Hughes family. Deciding to play it safe, she told Chief Holman only about Rene Edwards's connection to Halley Robinson. She also gave him the license plate number that Andy Porter had written down. He made a call and within ten minutes received his answer—a quick check on the vehicle showed it was a stolen car.

"I've issued an all-points bulletin on the car, but my guess is he's already ditched it somewhere. And we'll look your place over good to see if we can find some bullets in the garage," Holman told her. "If we find any, I'll have them checked against the bullets Sheriff Brewer found at the Robinsons's lake house."

Dane emerged from the ER cubicle an hour later, his shirt partially unbuttoned and his jacket draped over his arm. Annie ran to him, but stopped before throwing her arms around him. She reached up, caressed his face and smiled.

"I'm okay," he told her, then nodded to the police

chief. "We have to keep the bandages changed and the wound cleaned and I get the sutures out in about a week."

"Annie told me that she didn't get a good look at the shooter," Milton Holman said. "How about you, Carmichael?"

"He never lowered the window enough to enable me to get a good look at him. All I saw was the rifle."

"Well, we questioned your neighbors, Ms. Kimball and Mr. Porter," Chief Holman said. "They heard the rifle shots and came outside just in time to see the car speeding away. I just wish somebody had gotten a look at the guy's face."

Dane wasn't a hundred percent sure Jason Webber had been their attacker the night at the lake cottage or today, but his gut instincts told Dane that it had been Webber. And if he was right, then someone was giving Webber his orders? Who? Dickie Hughes? Maybe Royce Layman? Or even Richard?

"I'll keep y'all posted," Holman told them. "Sheriff Brewer and I want to find the person who's been using y'all for target practice. I'm going to put more men on the case and I'll suggest to Dwight he do the same. Together we'll crack this case."

Chief Holman escorted them home and made sure they were safely ensconced inside, then he posted one of his men outside and told Annie that he could spare the man for twenty-four hours.

Dane shook hands with Holman and thanked him. "I'll have another Dundee agent here by morning."

Annie snapped her head around and stared at Dane. "Another agent? Why? Besides, I didn't think anyone was available."

"Until this wound heals, I won't be a hundred percent effective. Ellen can get in touch with Sam and, if necessary, he can round up one of his former agents to help us out. He can either come here or he can take over the office for Ellen so she can fly in tomorrow.'' Dane walked through the kitchen and into the den. He laid his coat across the back of the sofa and sat.

"We'll keep a man posted outside until you get reinforcements, Carmichael." The chief held his hat in his hand and shifted his weight from foot to foot. "We have to get this case solved as soon as possible. The newspapers and television stations will have a heyday with this one. They're still making a big deal out of the lake house shooting."

"Find out just where that car was stolen from and when, and let me know," Dane said. "I have a hunch on this one." Dane would bet money that the car had been stolen from the parking lot at Hughes Chemicals and Plastics. He just wondered if, after his and Annie's visit, *someone* had reacted too quickly and issued a hotheaded order? Or had Webber acted on his own and gone off half-cocked?

Holman nodded to Dane and then followed Annie into the kitchen. She walked him to the back door, thanked him for his help, securely locked the door and adjusted the security system.

"I called Mother from the hospital," Annie told Dane as she returned to the den. "But I need to call her again to let her know that we're home and—"

"Talk to your uncle," Dane told her. "See if he has any idea where Richard is or how I can contact him."

"Even if Uncle Royce knows and shares that information with us, what makes you think Richard is going to talk to you?"

"I don't know for sure, but if he refuses to speak to me, then I'll know he's somehow involved."

                              *   *   *

A sultry blonde and a man the size of a Mack truck walked into Annie's house. "Sam has taken over the office for me," the blonde said to Dane. "And Murdock's case wound up late yesterday."

"Annie, I'd like for you to meet Denby and Murdock," Dane said.

"How do you do?" Annie had pictured Ellen Denby as an unfeminine, rough-looking gal who walked and talked like a man, not as a beautiful young woman with a sexy voice and curvaceous body.

Denby nodded, but didn't offer a smile. However, Murdock grinned broadly and said, "Nice to meet you, ma'am."

"Sam told us to stay here as long as you need us," Denby said. "Or if you'd like to return to Atlanta—" Denby glanced casually at Annie "—we can take over completely."

"I don't think that will be necessary. I just got a scratch on the arm," Dane said. "Besides, I plan to see this thing through to the end."

"Is that what you want, Ms. Harden?" Ellen Denby trapped Annie with her hard stare.

Momentarily taken off guard by the woman's question, Annie fumbled for words. "Uh, ah, yes, that's what I want—for Dane to remain as my bodyguard until we solve the case and put whoever killed Halley behind bars."

"Dane told me that you were originally opposed to his taking this case. So you've changed your mind about him, huh?" Denby gave Dane the once-over. "He can be a real pain in the ass, sometimes, but I have to admit he does have a few redeeming qualities."

Denby smiled then, a smirky grin that told Annie the woman knew there was something going on between Dane and her.

* * *

Annie had thought she wouldn't like Ellen Denby, but she'd been wrong. Within two days they'd become friends. Ellen might be beautiful and sexy, with the kind of body most women would kill to have, but she was a tough, independent lady—and she had no personal interest in Dane, other than as a friend.

The week had been uneventful, with the removal of Dane's sutures the highlight of the entire seven days. Chief Holman and Sheriff Brewer were no closer to finding the shooter than they'd been a week ago, but the chief had confirmed Dane's suspicions that the car used in the drive-by shooting had been stolen off the parking lot at Hughes Chemicals and Plastics. Dane had surmised that Webber had panicked and done something stupid, something he now regretted.

"Tonight's my night to cook," Ellen called from the kitchen. "My speciality is beef Stroganoff. I've checked the pantry and refrigerator. All the ingredients are here. How does that sound?"

Murdock licked his lips in that silly, playful way that always made Annie laugh. The guy's size and rugged appearance was enough to scare the devil, but underneath that intimidating facade, he was just another Southern good ole boy, but without the polish Dane possessed.

"Sounds fine to me," Dane said.

"Would you like some help?" Annie asked.

"I'd love it," Ellen replied.

Dane watched the two women through the open doorway to the kitchen. He wasn't sure he liked the idea of these two becoming so buddy-buddy. He got the distinct impression that, whenever they were alone together, they were plotting his demise.

"Afraid Denby will give away some of your secrets?" Murdock asked teasingly, as if he'd read Dane's thoughts.

Before Dane could answer, the phone rang. He reached over on the end table and lifted the receiver. "Harden residence."

"Dane?"

The thunder of his heartbeat temporarily drowned out all other sounds. "Richard?"

"I understand you've been trying to get in touch with me," Richard Hughes said. "I'm sorry Dickie didn't give you my number. That son of mine is a puzzle to me sometimes. Gloria and I have been in Jamaica resting up before hitting the campaign trail."

"How is Gloria?"

"Rested, relaxed and tanned." Richard chuckled.

That chuckle reassured Dane as nothing else could. His former father-in-law didn't sound like a guilty man worried about being caught. "Did Dickie tell you what I needed to talk to you about?"

"Well, I didn't actually talk to Dickie," Richard said. "I called Royce Layman earlier today and he's the one who told me that someone had taken shots at you and Annie again and that you were anxious to talk to me."

"Did Royce explain what's going on?"

"Yes, and I'm shocked, Dane. Absolutely shocked. I can't imagine why anyone would think that poor Martin Edwards was murdered. His death was ruled a suicide. Gloria and I were in Europe at the time, but we flew back immediately for the funeral. And of course, I saw to it that Wilma and Rene were taken care of."

This sounded like the Richard that he had known and respected for so many years. A sense of relief settled over Dane. "We have reason to believe that there's some sort of proof that Edwards's death wasn't suicide and that somehow Rene Edwards got hold of that evidence and passed it along to her cousin, Halley Robinson."

"So, you're saying that you believe Halley Robinson was murdered because she was in possession of that evidence?"

"I hate to ask you this, but…" Dane hesitated, fighting an inner battle with himself. "Richard, if you know something—anything—I'll understand. If you're protecting Dickie—"

"You think Dickie killed Martin Edwards! That's ridiculous. Dickie was just a boy when Martin died."

"Are you saying that to your knowledge no one associated with the local Hughes plant was involved in Edwards's murder or a coverup afterward."

"Dane…son…you know me. You know the kind of man I am. Do you honestly think I'd allow you or Annie to be harmed if I knew anything that could end the threats on Annie's life?"

"No. The Richard Hughes I've known since I had my first date with his daughter wouldn't be capable of harming another person or putting someone's life in danger."

Richard's sigh was audible. "You don't know how much that means to me, my boy." There was a long, silent pause, then he said, "Lorna wouldn't want the two of us to ever be at odds. She loved us both as we loved her."

Dane would have believed him. He'd have swallowed the lie, hook, line and sinker, if Richard hadn't overplayed his hand. If only he hadn't tried to use Dane's love for Lorna as a bargaining tool. He knew Richard well enough to understand the desperation in his plea. Reminding Dane that Lorna wouldn't have wanted the two of them to be at odds was the act of a man calling in a marker. He might as well have said he expected Dane to take his side in this matter, regardless of the truth.

"Yes, you're right," Dane said. "I'm glad you called and straightened me out."

"No problem, son. I'm just relieved to know that you still have faith in my word as a gentleman."

"Give Gloria my best." Dane felt as if he'd been dropped into a vat of boiling oil, as if his skin was melting away, his muscles dissolving, leaving nothing but bare bones.

"We'll see you at the Fourth of July picnic in Spring Park," Richard said.

"Yes, see you then."

Standing in the doorway, Annie watched Dane crash and burn before her very eyes. What had Richard Hughes said to him? she wondered. What had his former father-in-law done to create such a reaction in Dane? He realized that Richard Hughes is somehow involved, either by direct action or by protecting someone else, she thought. Dane's hero has shown his true colors at last!

Just as Annie rushed toward Dane, the telephone rang again. They both stared at the phone as if it were some hideous monster growling ferociously, preparing to attack.

Murdock picked up the receiver. "Harden residence. Yeah. Uh-huh. How about that. Mmm-hmm. You don't say. Isn't that interesting. Thanks, Sam. I'll tell them."

When the brief conversation ended, Murdock hung up the receiver and glanced at Ellen, who had walked into the den and stopped directly beside Annie.

"Looks like our investigators hit pay dirt." His gaze locked with Dane's. "You know, don't you, that Richard Hughes has to be involved in some way?"

"Yes." The admission caused Dane a great deal of personal anguish. To be the man Annie needed—both professionally and personally—Dane was forced to face some hard truths. And the most painful truth was that he knew, without a doubt, that Richard was a liar and could no longer be trusted.

"Our people have been going over information about Hughes Chemicals and Plastics in Florence with a fine-tooth comb, everything and anything that might give us a clue." Murdock rubbed his mouth and chin with his cupped palm, as if hesitating before dealing a lethal blow.

"Out with it!" Dane knew the hesitancy on Murdock's part was for his sake.

"It seems Martin Edwards had a private secretary named Alice Renegar, who, though only thirty-seven at the time of Edwards's death, retired a week after the funeral. She drew a monthly check for…" Murdock paused. "Ten thousand dollars, until the day she died, last month."

"Ten thousand dollars a month!" Ellen whistled loudly.

"Blackmail money," Dane said.

"She died last month?" Annie asked.

"Yep." Murdock nodded his head. "She had cancer. And by the way, Hughes Chemicals and Plastics picked up the tab for her medical bills."

"Rene Edwards went into hiding not long after Alice Renegar died, then right after Rene disappeared, Halley Robinson was murdered." Ellen lifted her eyebrows as she widened her eyes in a speculative look. "Correct me if I'm wrong, but I'd say in this case, one plus one plus one definitely makes three. Three women, two dead and one missing."

"Alice Renegar is the one who had the proof that Edwards's death wasn't a suicide," Dane said. "She used that proof as blackmail and when she died, the evidence was sent to Edwards's daughter." He turned to Murdock. "Call Sam back and tell him to find out if Alice Renegar had a lawyer."

"He's one step ahead of us," Murdock said. "The lawyer's name is Herrald Gravett, in Nashville. Sam's flying over tomorrow to speak to him personally."

* * *

By the Fourth of July, Ellen Denby had been gone for several days, having returned to Atlanta to relieve Sam of the managerial duties at the Dundee agency. Murdock was staying on until tomorrow, after the annual picnic in Tuscumbia's Spring Park, where it was a custom of long standing for the state's political candidates to speak.

Since Richard had called Dane from Birmingham, another missing piece of the puzzle had fallen into place. Herrald Gravett, once informed of the complexity of the situation and the legal consequences to himself in aiding a blackmailer, had confirmed that he had held a package and a letter in safekeeping for Alice Renegar. And per her instructions, he had mailed that package to Wilma Edwards upon Ms. Renegar's death.

"I'm going to speak to Richard Hughes today!" Annie's feisty pace matched her aggravation as she marched from the parking area into the heart of the park. "He's been back in town two days now and he's been deliberately avoiding our phone calls. We've given him enough time to come clean." She glanced sadly at Dane. "I'm sorry it's turned out like this, but—"

"I've never been so wrong about a person," Dane said. "I trusted Richard. I… Whoever he's protecting, I hope it's worth it to him to have lost his integrity."

"And lose the upcoming election, too," Annie said. "Even if he's only helped cover up the truth, he's still guilty."

Dane wondered just how long Richard thought he could continue with the charade, the pretense that he didn't know anything about Martin Edwards's death, other than that the coroner had ruled it a suicide. If Richard wasn't hiding something, then he would have taken Dane's calls once he and Gloria had returned to Florence.

But the Hughes's housekeeper as well as Richard's personal secretary had undoubtedly been ordered to take no phone calls from Dane or Annie. Did Richard actually think that because he was Lorna's father, Dane would protect him, no matter what?

If Richard didn't give them some satisfactory answers today, Dane knew he couldn't continue putting off the inevitable. They would have to share everything they knew with the police, regardless of what happened to Lorna's brother or her father. Or to Annie's uncle Royce.

"You know, this little town reminds me of where I grew up in Mississippi," Murdock said as he took his position at Annie's left. "We had a park something like this."

Dane kept in step on Annie's right. He was glad Murdock was free to stay on another day, thus giving Annie the added protection of a second bodyguard. Sam Dundee had immediately approved Dane's request for a second agent to stay on. He suspected that Ellen Denby had told Sam that Dane's interest in keeping Annie safe had become personal.

"Between Jason Webber and Dickie running interference, we're going to have a difficult time getting to Richard, without making a scene," Dane said.

Annie halted suddenly, tilted her head to one side and, shielding her eyes from the sun with one hand, smiled up at Dane. "I've been known to make scenes. I've been making scenes since I was a child. Just ask my mother." Annie waved toward the picnic table where Jennifer Harden was seated with Vera and Royce Layman.

"You're my kind of gal, Annie," Murdock said, his broad grin somewhat softening the hardness of his rugged face.

Dane cast Murdock a deadly look. "She's enough of a target as it is. Coming here today and confronting Richard publicly just puts her more at risk."

"If I didn't know better, I'd think you were worried about Richard Hughes's reputation." Annie defiantly stuck out her chin. "Oh, look, there's Richard and Gloria taking their seats on the podium. Why don't we go over and say hello?"

"Annie!" Dane had two choices—either grab her and hog-tie her or follow her into the fray.

Choosing the latter, Dane stayed at her side, as did Murdock, while she stormed forward toward the speaker's podium. Jason Webber headed her off before she reached the steps.

"Good afternoon, Ms. Harden," Webber said. "May I help you?"

"You can tell Richard that I want to speak to him." She angled her head to one side to glance past Webber and stare straight at Gloria Hughes. Annie waved at the gubernatorial candidate's wife, who smiled warmly and waved back at Annie.

"I'm sorry, but Richard can't be bothered right now. He's going to be speaking in just a few minutes."

"What I have to say to him won't take but a few minutes," Annie said.

When Annie tried to move past Webber, he reached out to stop her, but before his hand touched her arm, Dane grabbed Webber's wrist and twisted it behind his back. Murdock moved between Dane and the crowd in front of the podium.

"Don't ever try to touch her again," Dane warned Webber.

Taking advantage of the moment, Annie ran for the podium steps. But after she'd taken only one step up, Dickie Hughes loomed in front of her.

"Father can't speak to you right now, Annie," Dickie told her.

"Look, it's like this," Annie said. "Either your father speaks to me alone now or I'll ask my questions in front of this crowd when Richard finishes his little campaign spiel."

"Wait here."

Annie nodded and waited while Dickie scurried up the steps and across the podium to whisper into his father's ear. Richard looked down at Annie, his gaze deadly cold, then he said something to Gloria, got up and came across the podium alone.

"What's this all about, Annie?" Richard asked as he joined her at the foot of the steps.

Dane stood guard at Annie's side. She glanced back and saw that Murdock's big body blocked Jason Webber from approaching.

"Why haven't you taken our calls for the past two days?" Dane asked. "We've uncovered some more information that leads us to believe that Martin Edwards's secretary used some type of evidence that the man was murdered to blackmail someone in authority at Hughes Chemicals and Plastics."

A pulsing vein in Richard's neck bulged. Although he controlled his facial muscles so that his expression didn't change, he could not disguise the darkening of his eyes or the slight flush that colored his neck.

"This isn't the time or place to discuss such a delicate matter." Richard looked past Annie, straight into Dane's face. "Son, I know nothing about any evidence or any blackmail. Martin Edwards's secretary left our employ right after his death. If Alice Renegar has told you anything—"

"Ms. Renegar died last month." Annie thought Richard Hughes had to be an excellent actor to put on such a good performance.

"I'm sorry to hear that," Richard said. "But the fact remains that I am in no way involved in a murder or a coverup and I know nothing about either."

"Then why did Hughes Chemicals and Plastics pay Alice Renegar ten thousand dollars a month for nearly twenty years?" Dane asked.

Richard's face crumbled. His jaw sagged. His mouth drooped. His eyes shut as if he were uttering a silent prayer. And then, as suddenly as he'd lost control, he regained it and said, "If this is true, then I'll get to the bottom of these accusations. If someone in my company has committed a criminal act, I'll find him and—"

"Even if it's your own son?" Annie asked.

"Yes." Richard squared his shoulders. "Even if it's Dickie."

"You have forty-eight hours," Dane told his former father-in-law, and at that precise moment, he felt sorry for the man. "After that, we'll go to the police with everything we know."

"Then you have the evidence?" Richard asked.

"We have a great deal of information," Dane said. "And we have every reason to believe that the evidence Halley Robinson sent Annie will be in our possession before the week's out." Dane was bluffing, of course, but Richard had no way of knowing that.

Dickie called down from the top edge of the steps. "Father, they're going to announce you in a couple of minutes."

"I have to go," Richard said. "Give me that forty-eight hours."

When Annie and Dane walked past Jason Webber, he all but hissed at them. His dark gaze bored a hole into Annie.

"You have no right to cause trouble for Richard," Webber said to Dane. "He thought he could trust you."

"And I thought I could trust him," Dane said. "Seems we were both wrong."

"This isn't over, Ms. Harden." Webber snarled at Annie.

Dane got up in Webber's face and said, "That sounded like a threat. For your sake, I hope it wasn't."

As Annie walked away, Dane and Murdock flanking her, she sighed. "Well, they've got to make a move now," she said. "We've thrown down the gauntlet."

"You just have to be right in the middle of it, don't you?" Grasping Annie's arm, Dane halted her before she reached her mother's picnic table. "You couldn't let me take care of it. Why not, honey? Do you still think I'd let Richard off the hook if he is guilty."

"*If* he's guilty! Glaring at him, Annie planted her hands on her hips. "*If?* Do you honestly still have any doubts? He's guilty of something, even if it's just protecting his son."

"Or protecting your uncle," Dane said.

Annie nodded, knowing that Uncle Royce was possibly involved. He'd been a major stockholder in the local Hughes business for years and had even served on the board of directors for as long as Annie could remember.

"Let's go on over and say hello to your mama." Murdock lifted Annie's arm out of Dane's grasp and laced it through his. "There's no reason why we can't join your family for lunch and enjoy this beautiful day. I don't think anybody's going to be taking any pot shots at you, not with this crowd around."

Turning her back on Dane, Annie allowed Murdock to escort her to her mother's table. Dane joined them a few minutes later, but remained silent and brooding, even when Jennifer used all her Southern belle charm in an effort to bring him into the conversation.

When Royce Layman tried to question Dane about their little confrontation with Richard Hughes, Murdock stepped in and answered with an out-and-out lie.

"Oh, they were just wishing Mr. Hughes good luck with his speech today."

Annie noticed the concerned look on her uncle's face and once again wondered just how much he knew. She was having as difficult a time accepting the possibility that her uncle might be involved in a crime as Dane was accepting that Richard Hughes could be.

Annie paced the floor. She couldn't sleep. She and Dane hadn't said a word to each other since she'd demanded to know if he still had doubts that Richard Hughes was up to his eyeballs in the coverup of Martin Edwards's murder. In retrospect, she admitted to herself that she'd been wrong to practically accuse him of stupidity, of his being unwilling to accept the possibility that Richard was involved. She knew better. She knew that despite how painful it had been for him, Dane *had* accepted the undeniable truth. But she had lashed out at him, and even when she'd seen the hurt look in his eyes, she hadn't taken back her accusation.

A part of her was afraid to totally trust Dane, to believe he truly was different from her ex-husband. That he'd never betray her, not even to protect his beloved Lorna's father.

Annie gasped when her bedroom door opened. Dane hadn't knocked before he entered her room and invaded her privacy. He paused, looked directly at her and then closed and locked the door. Annie trembled.

"We're going to settle this once and for all," he said. "No matter how your father or your ex-husband treated you, no matter how they hurt you, you've got to know that I'm nothing like them." He came toward her, his steps slow, steady and deliberate. "Regardless of what it costs me and no matter what I have to give up, I'm on the side of truth. I'm on your side, Annie, one hundred percent."

"I know." The words rushed out of her on a whispery breath.

"I'm going to see this thing through to the end, regardless of how it turns out," he said as he moved closer and closer to her. "You, and only you, are what's important to me. You're what matters. Not Richard Hughes. Not generations of tradition. Not my pride. Not…" He stood directly in front of Annie, but didn't touch her. "Not even Lorna."

Annie swayed toward him. She knew what it had cost him to make that declaration. He had cut his ties to the past, to the woman he had loved and to his unfaltering faith in a gentleman like Richard.

"Oh, Dane." Her hand lifted, as if she had no control over it, and caressed his cheek.

Taking her touch as an invitation, he lifted her into his arms, and carried her across the room. She clung to him, one slender arm draping his neck. The minute he eased her down onto the bed, he began undoing the pearl buttons on her black silk robe.

She looked up at him, her big brown eyes smoldering with desire.

"I trust you completely," she said.

Her breathy words curled about him like velvet cords, binding him to her and hardening his already rock-solid sex. He finished undoing the buttons and removed her robe, revealing the skimpy red teddy she wore underneath.

She reached up to unbutton his shirt. "I've missed being with you."

She lifted her hand to his belt. Noting the way her hand trembled, he knocked it aside and undid his belt. Without hesitation, he undressed hurriedly, down to his briefs.

Annie sat there waiting for him. She sucked in her breath when he eased the straps of her teddy down her arms and to her waist, exposing her luscious breasts.

Dane straddled her hips and brought his mouth down to cover one begging nipple. She moaned. Deeply. Harshly. As if the touch of his tongue against her flesh had hurt her. But he knew better. He knew every nuance of Annie's moans and cries and whimpers.

He wanted to take all night with her. And he would. But not the first time. He needed her too much right now and she needed him just as desperately. Later, they could torment each other slowly and pleasure each other until they were spent. But right now, he wanted instant satisfaction.

Lifting himself up, he stood, then removed his briefs. When he hovered over her, Annie smiled and he grinned back at her.

She knew she was staring at him—at his large, blatant erection—but she couldn't help herself. He was a glorious sight. She forced her gaze upward, across his flat stomach and muscular chest and on to his face. Her body zinged with excitement. Anticipation built a hot, heavy flow of liquid inside her. Having experienced the pleasure of Dane's possession, she longed for the fulfillment only he could give her.

Dane cupped her mound through her teddy. She lifted

herself toward his caressing hand. He breathed as hard as she did. A flush of arousal stained his face and neck. Perspiration coated his body, curling his chest hair.

"Now!" she told him. "Please, Dane, now."

Dane slid her teddy down and off, then flung it to the floor. Lowering his body over hers he said, "I'm going to give you what you want...what we both want."

She cried out when he thrust into her—hot, hard and filling her with his need. Her body clutched his, holding him, taking him completely. She clung to his shoulders as he withdrew and plunged again, deeper still. He grabbed her hips, lifting her, working her back and forth until she was filled with an incredible ache that grew stronger and stronger with each lunge of his big body.

Sweet heaven! She thought she was dying. Within seconds the strongest, most intense climax of her life ripped her apart. And in that instant she knew she had indeed died. The little death of sexual pleasure.

Her completion signaled his and he followed her over the precipice, headlong into a release that elicited an animalistic cry from his lips.

Later, after they had both recovered, Dane lifted the covers up and over them and brought Annie into his embrace. He kissed her left temple.

She sighed. "I love you." She hadn't meant to tell him, hadn't known she was going to voice her feelings aloud. When he didn't respond, she wished she could take back her declaration.

"Annie, I—"

She covered his lips with her hand. "It's all right. Don't say anything. I didn't mean to fall in love with you. It just happened."

"You think it's love, but it's not," he told her. "Women

fall in love with their bodyguards all the time. But it doesn't last.''

''Mmm-hmm, I suppose you're right.''

''After this is all over and you're safe, tell me again that you love me and we'll both know it's for real.''

''I'd be a fool if I really were in love with you, wouldn't I? After all, why would I want another domineering Southern gentleman trying to run my life?'' But despite her words, Annie was all wound up inside. Dane had rejected her, damn him! She had told him she loved him and he'd told her what she felt wasn't love. But she knew the truth—what *he* felt for *her* wasn't love!

''You do realize that anything permanent between us would end up in disaster,'' Dane said. He didn't want Annie's love. Hell, he probably didn't deserve it. He had spent the past ten years in love with a ghost—with a dream of the perfect wife, which Lorna had never really been. But something within him wouldn't allow him to let go of the past, of the guilt, the remorse and even the fear. If he chose to love Annie, he would not only have to give up the memory of Lorna, but he would have to take a chance on loving and losing again, a chance that history might repeat itself. He didn't think he was that brave.

''I'm sorry I got sentimental on you,'' Annie cuddled close to Dane, suppressing her feelings in an effort to gain back the intimacy they'd just shared. ''Let's forget about anything permanent and enjoy what we have right now.''

He kissed her tenderly as he held her close. ''What we have right now, is pretty damn good.''

Annie sighed, then closed her eyes and absorbed the warmth of Dane's big body.

They slept for a while, then woke and made love again. They took their time, exploring each other's bodies, teasing, tempting and tormenting. And when fulfillment claimed them the second time, it was even better than the first. Making love with Dane was unlike anything Annie had ever known. Sheer unadulterated pleasure. Hot, hungry and all-consuming pleasure.

Afterward, Annie lay awake a long time, wondering what tomorrow would bring.

Chapter 15

Annie had tried to put her mother off when she'd invited them to dinner. But Jennifer had been insistent that since it was Annie's thirty-fifth birthday, she didn't think it was asking too much that mother and daughter share some time together. Annie preferred to forget that this July the fifth was the halfway mark of her thirties. After all, thirty-five was a passage, as Annie saw it—a passage from the last vestiges of youth to the portals of mid-life.

In twenty-four hours, Richard Hughes's forty-eight hours would be up and, so far, they hadn't heard a word from him. The waiting had made Dane tense and her irritable. They were playing a dangerous game. If Richard saw through Dane's bluff, the most they would accomplish by sharing all they knew with the police would be sullying Richard's good name, by revealing a scandal that would be fodder for the news media. Without Alice Renegar's *evidence,* which was out there somewhere in the package

Halley Robinson had mailed, they had no real proof against anyone.

While she stood on the veranda of her aunt and uncle's Victorian home, waiting for someone to answer the doorbell, Annie had the sudden urge to turn and run.

Dane slipped his arm around her waist. "It's only dinner with your family."

"I know," Annie said. "And my mother is bound to remind me that I'm thirty-five, single and childless."

"I take it she wants grandchildren," Dane said.

"Oh, yes, she most definitely wants grandchildren."

"My sisters have already provided my mother with grandchildren, but she won't be satisfied until I remarry and give her a few more."

"Mothers can be so—"

The door swung open and Vera Layman greeted them in the foyer. "Come in, come in." Her voice tittered with excitement and a silly grin created soft creases in her cheeks. She motioned them inside with a wave of her hand.

The minute they entered the foyer, Vera closed the door behind them and grabbed Annie. "Oh, Annie, love. Happy Birthday!"

On cue, a loud chorus of "Happy Birthday, Annie" rose from the crowd of people who poured out of the living room and surrounded Annie. She looked to Dane for help, but all he could do was shrug, thus informing her that this surprise party was news to him.

Vera led Annie through the living room and into the dining room, where an enormous birthday cake dominated the table. Sitting high atop the three-foot creation were numeral candles. A three and a five, announcing her age to one and all. Virginia, the Layman's housekeeper, lit the candles and stepped aside. Jennifer Harden motioned for Annie to come forward. When she moved into center stage, alongside her mother at the dining table, Dane shadowed her.

Jennifer smiled warmly, leaned over, hugged Annie and whispered, "Happy Birthday. Please, don't be too terribly upset. Your aunt Vera has been planning this party for months now. We can't disappoint her, can we?"

"No, of course not, Mother." *No matter what—famine, pestilence or death—one must never forget one's social obligations.* Annie knew that was Jennifer Harden's creed.

"Then say a few words, dear, and blow out your candles."

Jennifer nudged her around just enough so that she faced the group of friends and family who had gathered to celebrate a birthday she would have preferred to forget. "Thank y'all for coming tonight," Annie said, forcing a feeble smile. "It means so much to me to share this special occasion with such wonderful people."

"Now blow out your candles and while Virginia and Helen are serving, you can open your gifts." Jennifer turned with Annie and pursed her lips as if she were the one who was going to blow out the candles.

The minute Annie accomplished the deed, Jennifer led her into the living room and placed her in a wing-back chair by the fireplace. Only then did Annie notice the stack of gifts arranged on the hearth.

"And you mustn't worry about the gifts," Jennifer said directly to Dane, but loud enough so that Annie heard her. "I had everyone drop off their gifts early so that we could take them over to the police station and have Milton Holman check each one of them."

"That was very wise of you," Dane said.

"Oh, we didn't want anything spoiling Annie's birthday surprise," Jennifer said.

Placing himself behind Annie's chair, Dane scanned the

room. Many of the faces seemed familiar and he realized
he'd seen most of them at the Robinsons's home after Halley's funeral. The two people he didn't expect to see were
Richard and Gloria Hughes. They stood across the room,
champagne flutes in their hands. Richard nodded at Dane
and gave him a broad, politician's smile.

One by one Annie opened the gifts, dutifully thanked
each person as she gushed and gooed over the individual
items. She dreaded the thought of spending hours writing
out appropriate thank-you notes. But despite her abhor-
rence of many old Southern customs, thank-you notes were
an ingrained part of her personality.

Three gifts remained. Jennifer handed her a small rectangular box, covered in plain white paper, with no bow
or ribbon.

"We want to save my gift and Aunt Vera and Uncle
Royce's till last," Jennifer said.

Annie ripped open the paper and tossed it into the sack
at her side where she'd placed the other wrappings. She
held a plain brown cardboard box in her hand. Someone
certainly hadn't gone to any trouble or expense, she
thought, then lifted the lid. A stack of five cassette tapes
lay nestled inside. Annie dumped them into her hand and
looked through them. An eclectic assortment of music
tapes—from country to classical. The tapes looked as if
they'd been well used.

A shiver raced up Annie's spine. There was no note to
acknowledge the gift, but she had an odd feeling she knew
who had sent it.

"Isn't there a card?" Vera asked.

"No, there isn't." Annie grabbled in the sack at her
side, pulled out the crumpled white wrapping paper and
turned it over. Her heart skipped a beat as she recognized
the handwriting on the back side of the paper.

"It's from Halley Robinson, my dear," Vera said innocently. "She mailed the birthday gift to me before—" she sighed "—before she died. I've kept it in a safe place for three weeks, knowing how much it would mean to you."

Annie sensed the tension in the room and noticed that Richard Hughes had disappeared. Uncle Royce edged his way toward Annie.

"Goodness, Vera," Jennifer said, agitation in her voice. "Didn't you know that Annie has been expecting a package from Halley, something to do with a story she was working on when she was murdered?"

"Oh, my!" Vera swooned. "I had no idea. No one told me. Did they? Besides, those tapes aren't evidence of any kind. They're a birthday gift."

Royce Layman planted a sturdy arm around his wife and patted her consolingly. "No harm done. It would appear that this is indeed what it appears to be—a birthday gift—and nothing more."

"Does that mean that the package Halley mailed from Point Clear was this birthday gift and not some sort of criminal evidence?" Jennifer asked.

Gathering all her strength, Annie forced herself to reply calmly, "Looks that way, doesn't it?"

Dane knew something was amiss. Annie might fool everyone else, including her mother, but she couldn't fool him. Leaning over the arm of her chair, he said softly, "Want me to take care of those tapes for you?"

She nodded, then handed him the tapes and the wrapping paper, which he promptly slid into his pockets. Afterward, Annie opened the two remaining gifts. She gasped when she lifted the lid from the velvet box that held her aunt and uncle's gift.

"It's your grandmother's cameo," Vera said. "You're

the only grandchild, so it's rightfully yours. Something you can pass down to your own daughter someday.'' Using a lace handkerchief, Vera wiped the tears from her eyes.

Annie hugged her aunt, thanked her profusely, then tore into her mother's gift, which turned out to be a week's vacation in Paris.

"After all this is over, you'll need to get away for a while," Jennifer said.

Annie counted the minutes until she thought it wouldn't seem odd that she wanted to leave her own birthday party. But after several guests bid the family good-night, Annie tugged her mother up to her side and said, "Would it be rude if Dane and I left now? I'm tired and—"

"Was there something in Halley's gift?" Jennifer asked.

Annie nodded.

"Y'all go on. I'll make your excuses. But be sure you thank Aunt Vera again. She worked very hard to make tonight perfect for you."

Within fifteen minutes, she and Dane were inside the Navigator, the first of the five tapes playing as they drove through the Florence streets toward Annie's house.

"I can't believe that Aunt Vera had the package this whole time. And bless her sweet heart, she had no idea what she had."

"Read Halley's note again," Dane said.

Annie smoothed out the wrinkled paper.

"'Happy Birthday. I'm sending you my favorite tapes. Hope you don't mind that they're slightly used or that I didn't have time for ribbon and a card. I thought it wise to send these tapes to your aunt Vera, disguised as a birthday present. That way, if anything happens to me, you'll be sure to have the evidence you need to make things right. My cousin Rene still

has the original, by the way. Hope I'm there to celebrate your birthday with you.

Love, Halley.'"

"Your uncle Royce and Richard both know that these
tapes are from Halley," Dane said. "There's a good
chance that they suspect what we do—that there's some
sort of evidence on one of these tapes."

"We have to find the evidence before..." Annie blew
out a tense breath. "You know what? I am scared to death.
Afraid the evidence isn't here and even more afraid that it
is."

Dane pulled his cell phone from his pocket and dialed
a number.

"Who are you calling?" she asked.

"Milton Holman." Dane spoke into the phone, "Yes,
this is Dane Carmichael, will you please contact Chief
Holman and ask him to get in touch with me as soon as
possible at Ms. Harden's home. It's urgent."

Dane replaced the cell phone just as he drove into Annie's driveway. He scanned the area for anything suspicious and when he found nothing, he quickly ushered Annie into the house.

They spent the next hour and a half listening to music.
Annie fidgeted in her chair. Dane paced the floor. Then he
removed the third tape from the player and inserted the
fourth. Marty Robbins's distinctive voice drifted through
the den, telling of his love for a Mexican girl. Annie
groaned as she continued tapping her foot on the floor.
Dane cursed under his breath. About halfway through the
tape, in the middle of a song, the voice of two men interrupted the musical rendition. The two voices were instantly
recognizable.

"Richard, it was the only way. Martin was going to blow the whistle on you. If we hadn't stopped him, the whole world would have known that you authorized the illegal PCB dumpings."

"I wish there had been another way, Jason. Did you have to kill him?"

"No one will ever know that his death wasn't suicide. I made sure of that and with the coroner in your hip pocket, there won't be any questions asked."

"I don't want Gloria or the children to ever know. Lorna is so delicate, so much like her mother was. And I don't want Dickie involved. He's just a kid."

Annie glanced up at Dane. She could tell that the mention of Lorna's name had affected him. "Dickie wasn't involved," Annie said.

Dane nodded. The tape continued, Richard Hughes's and Jason Webber's words a confession of murder.

"Jason, I think Hughes Chemicals and Plastics should give Mrs. Edwards a nice fat check and perhaps a couple of one-way plane tickets for herself and her daughter to somewhere up north."

"Consider it done. What about Alice Renegar?"

"How much do you think she knows?"

"I doubt she knows that her boss took the rap for you, if that's what you're asking. She may have her suspicions, but she could never prove anything."

"Give Ms. Renegar two months' severance pay and glowing recommendations, and if she makes a fuss about leaving, give her reasons to keep her suspicions to herself."

Dane didn't know Richard Hughes—the real Richard Hughes. He had never known him. He had loved, admired and trusted Lorna's father, a man of integrity and kindness. The man on this tape was a stranger to Dane.

"I'm so sorry, Dane." Annie rushed over to him, wrapped her arms around him and hugged him fiercely. "I know how I'd feel if it had been Uncle Royce."

Dane held on to Annie. "I have to accept the unacceptable. Richard knew that Jason had killed Martin Edwards and he is no doubt responsible for Halley Robinson's murder, as well."

The telephone and the doorbell rang simultaneously. Annie looked to Dane, who motioned for her to answer the phone.

"Harden residence."

"I got Dane Carmichael's message. What's up?" Chief Holman asked.

"I think you should come over to my house right now. We've—" The phone suddenly went dead.

The insistent doorbell ringing echoed through the house. Dane peered through the viewfinder. Richard Hughes and Royce Layman stood on the other side of the door. Dane removed his Ruger from his hip holster, checked it and then returned it to the holster, leaving the flap undone. He opened the door.

"We must speak with Annie, immediately," Royce said. "It's urgent."

Dane allowed the two men inside. "Go into the den," he said, and followed them when they walked down the hallway.

Annie stood by the windows, the telephone receiver in her hand.

"Annie, I don't know what you believe of me at this precise moment," Richard Hughes said. "But you must believe that whatever evidence you have has been somehow faked. I'm being framed.''

"Richard isn't the kind of man who'd order someone's murder," Royce told his niece. "I've known him for the better part of thirty years and I—"

"Move away from the windows," Dane ordered Annie, his voice deadly soft.

Just as Annie absorbed Dane's order and acted to obey, Dane noticed a shadow outside the window. Simultaneously, he drew his Ruger and knocked Annie to the floor. A shot cracked a glass pane in the window on its path into the house. Dane shoved Annie to the other side of the large mahogany desk in the corner of the den nearest the kitchen.

"Aren't you going after him?" Royce Layman crouched behind an armchair.

Richard Hughes stood in the center of the room, ramrod straight and unmoving, his vision focused on the window.

Annie jerked open the bottom drawer in the desk, pulled out a revolver and a box of bullets. Her hands shook as she loaded the gun, but she accomplished the task quickly.

"Go get him," she told Dane. "If Richard makes a move, I'll shoot him with my father's old Smith & Wesson."

Dane's lips curved in a hint of a smile before he nodded and hurried through the French doors that lead out onto the patio. When Annie rose to her feet, she noticed Richard Hughes fumbling with the CD and tape player on the wall shelf.

"Turn around, Richard," she ordered. "Slowly and carefully. I have a gun. And it's loaded."

"Annie? My dear?" An ashen-faced Uncle Royce grasped the arm of the chair to steady himself as he rose to his feet. "I don't understand any of this."

Richard turned. He clutched the Marty Robbins tape in his hand. About three inches of tape had been pulled loose from the cassette.

"Lay the tape on the floor," Annie told him. "And stay right where you are."

"You can't call the police," Richard said smugly, overly self-confident.

"Why? Did Jason Webber cut the phone wires while you and Uncle Royce were ringing the doorbell?"

Richard smiled like the cat who'd eaten the canary, then when realization dawned, the smile vanished. "How did you know?"

"What is she talking about?" Royce asked, his eyes filled with puzzlement.

"You really are in the dark, aren't you, Uncle Royce?" Annie said, not moving her gaze from Richard. "I was talking to Chief Holman when the line went dead. I'm sure he's on his way here right now."

Somewhere nearby, in the yard, repeated gunshots rang out. Annie cringed as each bullet was fired.

"Jason has probably killed Dane and will be in here shortly to take care of you and Royce," Richard said.

Royce sputtered, then came out of the corner, marched over, picked up the tape on the floor and offered it to Annie. She took the tape from him, all the while keeping her father's gun aimed at Richard.

Royce stood steadfastly at Annie's side. "Should I go see if I can help Dane?"

"I'm sure Dane can handle things," she said, and the ring of truth in her words comforted her, reassuring her that Dane was all right. "But you can let Chief Holman in when he arrives."

"It will be my pleasure." Royce gave Richard a sternly disapproving look.

The French doors flew open. With his Ruger held to the man's head, Dane escorted Jason Webber into the den. Blood oozed from a wound in Webber's shoulder. Annie let out a sigh of relief. In the distance a siren wailed loudly, announcing the approach of Florence's finest, led by Chief Holman.

Richard glowered at Webber. "You assured me that you could handle things!"

"I'd suggest you not turn on your accomplice," Dane suggested. "After all, he was just following your orders when he took care of Martin Edwards and when he hired a guy who was probably a local Mobile thug to murder Halley Robinson."

"Dane, you could make things all right for me," Richard said, a tentative smile teasing his lips. "Do this one last thing for me. For...Lorna."

"For Lorna!" Dane shouted. "God, Richard, you'd actually try to use my relationship with your dead daughter to try to get out of this? You disgust me!"

After the longest seven minutes of Annie's life, Royce Layman opened the door and welcomed Chief Holman and four officers into the house. Outside a SWAT team surrounded the Harden home.

Richard Hughes's downfall was front-page news the following morning and every radio and television station reported nothing else the entire day. Jason Webber turned on his boss, confessed everything and tried to make a deal with the district attorney. During the next few days, the Hughes scandal became a nationwide news frenzy. Four days after Richard's arrest, Rene Edwards called Annie, who assured the frightened woman that it was safe for her to come out of hiding.

Annie eased open the door to the guest room and found

Dane packing his bag. She'd known he wouldn't stay much longer, but he hadn't told her that he was leaving today.

"Where are you going?" she asked from the doorway.

He glanced over his shoulder. "I'm going to pick up a car and head out for Point Clear this morning, then take that long overdue vacation sailing in the Caribbean."

"I don't suppose there's any reason for you to hang around here, is there?" She took a hesitant step over the threshold.

Dane zipped his bag closed, then turned to Annie. "None that I know of. What about you, know any reason I should stay?"

Annie wrapped her arms around herself and rocked back and forth on her heels. What did he want? Did he expect her to ask him to stay? "I want to thank you. For everything. You saved my life more than once and I'll always be grateful." *Don't go*, she wanted to plead with him. *Don't leave me. I love you.* But the last time she'd told him she loved him, he had dismissed her declaration and made her doubt her own sincerity.

But she did love Dane. She had come to realize that he was nothing like Preston. She wondered how she could ever have compared the two men. And she realized that Dane possessed only her father's best qualities and none of the bad ones.

Dane Carmichael was a man she could trust, a man she could count on and a man who accepted her for the woman she was. If he loved her, he would never try to change her. But that was the catch—he didn't love her.

"I'm grateful to you," he said. "You were right all along about Richard. About everything." He lifted his bag off the bed. "I'm glad it turned out that your uncle wasn't involved."

Annie realized how Dane was suffering. He had been forced to accept the loss of all he had held dear. "I'm sorry that…I wish Richard had been the man you thought he was."

"Tell your mother goodbye for me." Dane hesitated as he passed by Annie. He leaned over, kissed her on the cheek and smiled. "Be happy, brown eyes."

He walked out into the hall. Annie turned and watched him go down the stairs. *Run after him,* an inner voice screamed. *Don't let him leave!*

"Dane!" She ran down the stairs and caught up with him at the front door.

He paused, then turned slowly and faced her. "What is it, Annie?"

"I wanted you to know, before you left, that I think you're a fine, good man. A true Southern gentleman. You aren't anything like my ex-husband. I'm sorry that I ever thought you were."

Her words were like a balm to his soul. He hadn't even realized how much he longed to hear them. The last thing Dane wanted to do was leave Annie, but he needed to be sure she could accept him for the man he was instead of the man she'd assumed he was. He couldn't bear the thought of never seeing her again, of never holding her, kissing her, making love to her.

He'd had to face some unpleasant truths lately and perhaps the hardest one to face was admitting that his perfect Lorna had been imperfect.

But Annie isn't Lorna! he reminded himself. She was nothing like his fragile first wife nor was the way he felt about her the same as he'd felt about Lorna. Annie was a strong woman, capable of being a true life-partner. And what he felt for her was far stronger and more powerful than the delicate love he'd known during his marriage.

Real love would be strong enough to weather any storm. With Annie he could have that kind of love.

And now that she had admitted she wanted him—truly him—he could take the next step to his new life.

"Annie?"

"Yes?" She looked up at him with those big brown eyes and the very sight of her robbed him of breath.

"I think we should get married," he said.

"Get married? You and me?"

"Everything we went through together changed both of us. We were forced to face the truth about ourselves and our beliefs and the kinds of lives we had chosen to live."

Annie started to speak, but before she could utter a sound, Dane jerked her up against him. "Ah, Annie, don't you know that all I want is for you to be happy. I'm willing to do whatever it takes to have you in my life. But if you don't want to get married again, we can—"

"I didn't think I'd ever want to remarry," she admitted, standing on tiptoe so she could drape her arms around his neck. "But that was before I fell head over heels in love with you. So, big boy, you're stuck with me for the rest of your life."

He kissed her, all the passion and promises in his heart combining in that one act. When they were both breathless, he ended the kiss. "Let's get married right away. No big wedding. Just you and me and a couple of witnesses. How about asking Sam and Jeannie?"

"Sounds wonderful," she sighed.

"And how about a month's honeymoon cruising the Caribbean on the *Sweet Savannah*?" he asked, nuzzling her neck.

"Sounds like heaven." She licked a trail from the vee of his open shirt, up his neck and to his chin. "And I really think you should get me pregnant on our honeymoon. After all, you're already forty and I'm thirty-five. If we're going to have a couple of kids, we need to get started right away."

Dane tensed. "I thought you didn't want children."

"I've changed my mind. I want *our* children."

"Are you sure?" he asked. "I mean are you really sure? You're not agreeing to have kids just for me are you?"

"I'm sure. And I'm doing it for both of us."

"Annie, I love you."

"It's about time you told me." She smiled. "You know what? I want our son to be the same kind of Southern gentleman his father is."

Dane lifted her high into his arms and swung her around and around, then lowered her to her feet, letting her body drift slowly down his. "My gut instincts tell me that our first child will be a girl and she'll be the same kind of feisty, independent Southern lady her mother is."

Nine months, three weeks and one day later, Dane was proven right when Dana Sophia Carmichael came into the world screaming at the top of her lungs.

* * * * *

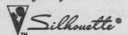

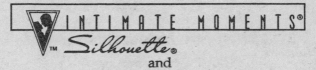

DOREEN ROBERTS

invite you to the wonderful world of

RODEO MEN

A secret father, a passionate protector,
a make-believe groom—these cowboys are
husbands waiting to happen....

HOME IS WHERE THE COWBOY IS
IM #909, February 1999

A FOREVER KIND OF COWBOY
IM #927, May 1999

THE MAVERICK'S BRIDE
IM #945, August 1999

Don't miss a single one!

Available at your favorite retail outlet.

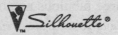

Coming in July 1999

Back by popular demand, the very
first Man of the Month title, plus two
brand-new short stories!

DO YOU
TAKE THIS
MAN?

by
bestselling authors

DIANA PALMER

ANNETTE BROADRICK   ELIZABETH BEVARLY

He is friend, lover, provider and protector.
He's as sexy as sin. And he's all yours!

Celebrate the 10th Anniversary of
Silhouette Desire®'s **Man of the Month** with the
story that started it all and two brand-new stories
featuring sexy, superb heroes, written by
three fabulous authors.

Available at your favorite retail outlet.

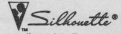

THE MACGREGORS OF OLD...

#1 *New York Times* bestselling author

NORA ROBERTS

has won readers' hearts with her enormously popular
MacGregor family saga. Now read about the MacGregors'
proud and passionate Scottish forebears in this
romantic, tempestuous tale set against the bloody
background of the historic battle of Culloden.

Coming in July 1999

REBELLION

One look at the ravishing red-haired beauty and Brigham
Langston was captivated. But though Serena MacGregor
had the face of an angel, she was a wildcat who spurned
his advances with a rapier-sharp tongue. To hot-tempered
Serena, Brigham was just another Englishman to be
despised. But in the arms of the dashing and dangerous
English lord, the proud Scottish beauty felt her hatred
melting with the heat of their passion.

Available at your favorite retail outlet.

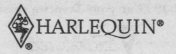

*This August 1999, the legend
continues in Jacobsville*

DIANA PALMER

LOVE WITH A
LONG, TALL TEXAN

A trio of brand-new short stories featuring
three irresistible Long, Tall Texans

GUY FENTON, LUKE CRAIG
and CHRISTOPHER DEVERELL...

This August 1999, Silhouette brings readers an
extra-special collection for Diana Palmer's legions
of fans. Diana spins three unforgettable stories of
love—Texas-style! Featuring the men you can't get
enough of from the wonderful town of Jacobsville,
this collection is a treasure for all fans!

*They grow 'em tall in the saddle in Jacobsville—and
they're the best-looking, sweetest-talking men to be
found in the entire Lone Star state. They are proud,
hardworking men of steel and it will take
the perfect woman to melt their hearts!*

**Don't miss this collection of original
Long, Tall Texans stories...available in
August 1999 at your favorite retail outlet.**

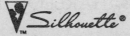